The Daughter of God

SANDRA LABRUCE

RSE Publishing
Laurens, South Carolina

© 2012 Sandra LaBruce. All rights reserved.

Cover design by Marcia Campbell
Cover layout by Dan Fowler

ISBN: 978-0-9837103-8-7

Printed in the United States of America

This book is dedicated to the memory of my grandmother. I hope she is pleased. I also dedicate this work to my niece, Hope Wettach, who has traveled by my side on this journey. Your kindness and generosity has been more than I deserve. I thank God for placing you in my life.

Prologue

This is how it all began.

A homeless, pregnant woman with a near overdose of drugs coursing through her bloodstream staggered down the dark streets of downtown Charleston. The pain was horrendous; she began begging for help from anyone who came near. Her baby was due, and her contractions were coming closer and closer together. She was lost and confused and had no idea where she was headed.

A bystander tried to quicken his step and pass unnoticed, but she was quick to grab his arm and plead for assistance. The man pulled away, brushed at his sleeve, and hurried on. The desperate young woman pounded on a store window and begged for someone to let her in, but the people inside turned their backs as if she were invisible. She stared at her reflection in the glass with despair; her appearance made it useless to expect help from anyone.

Her long blond hair was twisted and matted into an oily knot; it hadn't been touched by a brush for some time. Her clothes hung loosely over her dirt-encrusted body. The faded blue dress was soiled, torn, and falling from her shoulders. Her strong body odor, carried by the wind, was foul and nauseating.

The drugs continued to make her hallucinate. Her mind played tricks, making her wonder what was real and what was imagined. She began to see people who were not there and hear voices in her head. Images faded in and out as she wandered the streets alone. Everything was frightening to her; she wanted to crawl into a hole and die.

People turned and stared as she passed, shaking their heads with disgust. None of that mattered to her right now. She felt the end of her pitiful life was near, and there was no one to help.

A storm had begun to brew, and the wind swept violently through the trees. Pine needles, leaves, and branches tumbled down the street, racing to nowhere, but seemingly everywhere, traveling wherever the darkness led and the eyes could not see—just like the stranger who cried in the night. The essence of life was blowing aimlessly in the lashing wind, and death was in the air. The wind hissed, surfing through, over, and around everything in its path, sucking out all the warmth that the sun had left in the summer air.

The rain began to pour; it was deafening as it bombarded the tops of cars and store roofs throughout the downtown area. The vibration was as loud as a herd of wild horses running free. The earth shook in anger as the lightning lit up the streets of the city in an eerie fireworks display.

The young woman stood alone against the wall of a store trying to seek shelter for herself and the unborn child. The chilled air sent goosebumps down her wet arms. Her body trembled and her teeth chattered as she screamed into the street.

"I hope you all go to hell! You hear me! Go to hell, you worthless sons of bitches!"

Her warm tears spilled down her shivering face and mixed with the water of the cold rain. Her wet, shriveled hands wiped at her eyes as she tried to get her bearings. She searched the now empty streets for somewhere—anywhere she could find shelter and warmth.

The temperature was cool for the month of June and her clothes offered no protection against the elements. Her eyes were straining, squinting in hopes of spotting a refuge. A church appeared in the distance, lighted by strobes of lightning strikes. They sparked down the streets with wild bursts of energy, lining a path like a landing strip at an airport. Lowering her head and using her arm as a shield, she headed down the sidewalk hoping to find a haven in this place filled with unfriendly people. She thought for a second how ironic it was that Charleston was called, "The Holy City," but that gave her an idea: Surely she would not be turned away from the sanctuary of a church.

It was quite dark, and she could identify objects indistinctly at best, but she saw that she was on a broad cobblestone street with large buildings fronted by ornamental shrubs and trees. Slowly, she continued on the course seemingly laid out by the lightning. Perhaps the gods were on her side and leading her to safety. She pushed onward against the brutal storm.

As her foot left the sidewalk to enter the street, an excruciating pain brought her to her knees. Her hand quickly latched on to a street light post to keep her balance. She squeezed the cold iron pole to help ease the pain, and screamed in agony as the spasm surfed through the tense muscles of her frail body. "Dear God, help me! Please help me," she begged.

The rain fed a strong current down the gutter, which encircled her knees and sucked at her unsteady frame as it rushed down to the manhole waiting in the dark. To her, it had the strength of an outgoing tide pulling her out to sea.

Her contractions were getter stronger. The pain ripped around her pelvis, sending spasms through her slender body. Warmth ran down her legs. The trees danced in the shadows of the night, allowing a glimmer of light to reveal a stream of red that trailed off down the gutter. Her baby was near birthing. She knew she had to find safety.

From behind the plate glass, their view distorted by wind-whipped rain, onlookers dissected her with no empathy or thought of giving a helping hand. She screamed in horrific pain and saw their indifference as they ignored her pleas. She doubled over and fell into the street. Gathering her strength, she slowly lifted her head and tossed her wet hair back. She tilted her head in their direction and stared back, not understanding why no one would come to her aid. She cursed all the monstrous people who were shopping in comfort and not caring she was about to give birth among them.

She gritted her teeth and sucked the air as her contractions slightly subsided. Her eyes followed the shadows in the store windows and continued to look around at all those who watched her travail.

"What is wrong with you people?" she screamed. "Can't you see I need help? I hope you all go to hell!" she shouted to them all.

Struggling to her feet, she stumbled on as the rain assaulted her body like stinging ants. Her head bobbed, her knees knocked, and every inch of her being shook from the wind-chilled rain, the insufferable pain, and the fear of having her first baby all alone.

Torrents of water blasted steadily on the car tops, splashing against the windshields, and encircling the tires of the parked cars. Waves of black clouds barricaded the sky with darkness. The thunder rumbled and the lightning flashed; the summer storm had begun to release its rage.

Holding the bottom of her stomach with one hand, she tried to shield her eyes with the other. Scouring the street, she searched for the church through the pouring rain. Again, lightning struck, melting an arrow into the asphalt and exposing a cross that, in her confusion, wavered in the wind out front. She saw a man waving for her to come inside. Finally, there was help. Pressing forward against the rain, the wind, and the cold, she continued toward the church. With her legs straining, taking one step at a time, her feet searched for stability.

"Susan," the buoyancy of a voice echoed through the squall. She became increasingly aware of the strangeness that resonated in the air. She stopped and tried to define the sound, but it was useless. Cupping her hands around her eyes, she desperately searched for the voice that called out to her. Again, there was the man, still motioning, waving for her to come.

She was half tempted to turn back, but she was never one to give up on anything, so she continued. How was it possible that this man knew her name? She knew no one in this city. Was she hallucinating again? She closed her eyes, shook her head, and looked once more. He was still there. Her lips quivered and she shivered as the temperature of her body continued to drop. She was weak and nauseated, and the sacred monument seemed to get further and further away. Every step was painstaking and strenuous, but she could not give up.

She was relentless, and her determination carried her to the front steps of the massive church. Nothing was going to stop her.

Finally her perseverance paid off. She had crawled the last few steps, but she made it; she was finally safe. The rain ran down her face, washing away her warm tears as she gazed up at the two large doors.

"Please help me, God. Please give me strength to get inside."

She looked around for the man who had waved to her, but no one was there. Fastening a tight grip to the wooden handrail, she slowly pulled herself toward the enormous doors. Weak and unsteady, she took one step at a time, her legs heavy and reluctant to work. She stopped midway, her head resting on the rail, and waited for an excruciating contraction to release her. Minutes later, reaching the top, she pounded with what energy she had left on the closed doors.

"Where are you?" she shouted. "I need help!" She saw no one, and no one answered.

Grasping the silver doorknob and sobbing uncontrollably, she pushed with all her might. The left door swung open, and the pregnant woman, holding her stomach, fell in. Lying face down on the floor, she wept.

"Why me, Lord, why did you pick me?"

Sucking in a gulp of air, she turned herself over on her back. Arching up on her elbows, she planted her wet feet on the heavy door and pushed it closed. Sliding her fatigued body back to the floor, she closed her eyes and rested for a brief moment.

She sensed that there was hope; at any minute, the man would return. After lying silently and gulping in deep breaths, she slowly exhaled and rested, absorbing the warmth and rejuvenating the strength that had drained from her soul.

"Bam!" She was startled by a book that fell from the pulpit.

"Hel . . . lo," she weakly cried out. There was silence; no one answered. "Is anyone there?" There was no reply.

On hands and knees, she began to crawl. The blood flowed and trailed behind, blending into the red carpet runner. The aisle was long, but a force overcame her and pushed her, drawing her toward the pulpit.

She screamed for help as another pain drew her into a fetal position. Recovering, she struggled onward, clutching pews for support. From the corner of her eye, she saw the man standing at the altar.

"Please help me," she begged. She gasped for a breath of air and waited for a reply, but none came.

"I need some help, please. Can you come help me, please?"

She slid back to the floor, closed her eyes, and tossed her head back and forth. "Why do you not answer me?" she shouted and sobbed. "Why? Who the hell are you?"

The silent man stood and stared down the aisle. She lifted her head and stared back.

He was dressed in a long white robe and was smiling. He said nothing; he just held up his hand and motioned for her to come to him.

"Oh, I'm in terrible pain, why don't you come to me?" she

cried with a crackling voice. "I need your help," tears streamed down her face. "Please help me. I'm begging you. Help me, please! I can't make it on my own."

Still, there was no response.

She staggered to her feet. Holding on to each pew, gripping and pulling, she found the inner power to continue. Her legs were enervated, bloody, stiffened, and spread wide; her shoulders were tilted back, and her pelvis was pushed forward, but she continued. Her clothes were heavy, saturated with rain and body fluids. It was almost more weight than her weakened body could carry. The young woman's bloody footprints marked each horrific step she struggled to take.

Finally, she stumbled. On her hands and knees, she began to crawl once again. Weak and vulnerable, she knew her quest must end; she couldn't go any further. She fell to the floor and rolled over on her back. She was done.

Above, a stained glass window came into her view. The young woman looked up, crying and sniveling with every breath. She was cold, wet, and in unbearable pain. Extending her hand and weeping loudly, she called out, "Please, Lord, help me." Then, her hand fell back to the floor. Curling up on her side, straining every muscle in her body, she screamed out in pain as her baby pushed for its own life.

Her screams echoed through the church, vaulting from wall to wall. Rocking, rolling back and forth, gritting her teeth, and clenching her fists, she beat on the floor and fought the pain to pure exhaustion. Her body was fading along with her will. She kept looking all the while for the man she had seen, but no one came to her aid.

"Ah," she screamed. "Aaaaaaah!" Her pitch was getting higher and higher though her volume dropped.

"Where did you go? Don't leave me alone. Please, please help me. I'm scared; please come back."

Thrashing back and forth on the floor, she noticed all the

religious sculptures staring down on her. Each had a look of loving sincerity on its face. If only they could help. Their lifeless eyes simply looked down upon her.

The man she had seen evidently had disappeared and left her alone. He had abandoned her just as everyone else had always done. She wondered again if the drugs were causing her to hallucinate. Did she really see this man? Was it a flashback from her addiction? She didn't know, and in her anguish, she didn't care. All she knew was she didn't see him now.

She stretched and strained, moaned and groaned. She inhaled and exhaled, taking short breaths and long breaths as she tried to relieve her pain. Nothing seemed to help; it was just a waste of energy. She gritted her teeth, clenched her fists, and beat on the floor some more. Her baby was coming and she was scared to death.

She turned over on her back and stared back up at the stained glass window. It depicted Jesus holding out His hands. He was there to comfort and ready to help, just as she had been taught as a child. But now, He was just there.

"If only you could reach me," she said to herself, her lips quivering. The tears streamed from her eyes. "If only you would take away the pain," she softly whispered.

With that request, a contraction ripped through her body like a raging bull. Her demeanor quickly reverted to anger. She screamed out to the image, "This is your child inside me. Now, do something. You put this thing inside me; now take it out! I never asked for it, and I never wanted it. You did this to me. Now get it out! I want it out!" She screamed the same words over and over again, but nothing relieved the pain. If anything, it intensified.

The contractions continued throughout the night. The young woman begged, cursed, and screamed until there wasn't one ounce of strength left in her. She was exhausted and giving up. The beginning of a new life now seemed like a time of death for both her and her baby.

She lay with barely enough energy to gasp for air. She whimpered as she saw a bright light come into the room.

"Someone has come to help," she mumbled faintly. "I'm in here," she softly muttered. "I'm in here."

She followed the light with her eyes only to see it coming from the stained glass window.

"A passing car," she whispered as she tried with no success to sit up. "Help," her voice vibrated from exhaustion. Her fatigued body could barely produce enough oxygen for the words to come from her lips. Then she dropped her head back to the floor. She lay weak and almost lifeless as she stared at the light that still glowed through the window. Its bright rays were spectacular, like a rainbow that glimmered straight down onto her weary body. It began to warm and soothe her aching frame. Lying motionless and speechless, her eyes fluttered and gently closed. She prepared for death; she could take no more.

As this unusual light seemed to rejuvenate her body, she tried again to speak. She mumbled, "You have used me for this." She gasped for a breath of air. "This is all for you, isn't it? This is," she gasped again, "what you wanted me to live for. What kind of God are you? I hate you for what you've done to me." She clenched her fists and took a massive gulp of air into her lungs and filled them to capacity. And with all the volume she could produce, she yelled, "If I die, it dies too; you cannot have this baby without me. I welcome death," she shouted sternly. "Do you hear me? I . . . welcome . . . death." Her aching body was racked with terrible spasms. She screamed a horrendous owl-like screech, each muscle throughout her body twisting in pain. Her feet turned under, her hands and fingers curled into deformity, her body commenced to shake uncontrollably. She could bear no more. She knew God was listening and was displeased with her defiance. Death would surely be the fate for her and her innocent child.

She began to crawl again, dragging her blood soaked legs behind her. She slithered like a snake to a statue that she could barely see in a corner behind a red velvet drape. Her blood was still flowing, leaving a crimson trail to the figure that peered from the edge of the altar. A force still pulled her along until she finally reached the sculpture. She lifted her head and recognized it was the Virgin Mary.

The woman's energy was depleted, but she was unwavering, though nearing defeat. She scooted close and wrapped her arms around the feet of the statue. She tried to muster the energy to hoist herself upward, but she could only slide back to the floor.

Again, she searched within for the strength to touch the hand. Again, she reached for the cold plaster statue that held out her hands so freely. Finally, she grasped the fingers of the Virgin Mary and began to lift the weight of her body. Clutching with both hands, she held on to the sacred figure and struggled to get to her feet. She dragged her frail limbs beneath her and fought for the will to stand.

The statue wobbled and swayed back and forth. Susan's weight was too much, and it tipped over. Susan knew it was going to fall. She tried desperately to keep it upright, but she was too weak. Gravity was unforgiving. Waving her hands in the air to protect herself and her unborn baby, Susan closed her eyes tightly and waited for the next disaster that was sure to come.

Holding her breath, she peeped with one eye and watched the statue in slow motion solemnly fall to the altar. It bounced and vibrated on the slats of the hardwood floor.

Then, all in one piece, it quietly settled as if it were placed right beside Susan and her unborn baby.

Opening her eyes, she stared into the tender white face of the woman she believed to be the mother of the Savior. The

Virgin Mary appeared to come to life and gestured a consoling smile. Real or not, it was reassuring.

Susan tilted her head and stared into the most beautiful face she had ever perceived. With the comfort of another being, real or just a figment of her imagination, she returned to fetal position. With one hand holding on to the statue, and the other on her unborn child, she lost the battle she had been fighting. She gave herself to God.

Hours had passed. Susan had been unconscious from the exhaustion she had endured. Somehow her contractions had subdued enough for her to have an opportunity to rest; the strength that was needed for birth was restored. Birth came while she slept in a comatose state.

She was awakened by a soft touch. Slowly opening her eyes, with vision blurred, Susan saw a man kneeling beside her. She blinked and rubbed her eyes. He was still there. He bore a resemblance to Jesus, and he was holding a baby, her baby.

She whispered, "Am I dreaming? Am I dead?"

"No, I'm here."

"Why did you leave me?"

A faint voice replied, "I never left you; I was always here, right beside you."

"Is that my baby? Is it the chosen one?"

"Yes, she is yours. And she is the daughter of our Father."

The exhausted woman looked up at him and asked, "Why was I chosen?"

"Because you believed," he replied. "You never lost faith," he softly said to her.

"But I cursed you, and I wanted to die."

The man smiled, "But I forgave you, and I wanted you to live."

"But I did lose faith. I thought God had abandoned me."

"Only because you were scared did you say those things. You have suffered through many challenges in your life, and you will have many more to come. You must always remember our Father will be here, and trust yourself to do the right thing.

Your baby will lead you in another direction. Listen to your heart. Find the strength in your faith, and always ask what would be best."

"But I don't go to church, and I've lost touch with all of my family." She looked away and whispered, "They disowned me."

"None of that matters right now. Just keep your faith no matter what. Ask for forgiveness, and you will be forgiven. We are always a whisper away. Close your eyes and we are there. Open your heart and we are there."

The young woman exchanged a smile with the man. No longer alone and her baby safe at her side, she lost consciousness once more.

"Get in here with that stretcher and hurry up. She doesn't have much time," a voice echoed through the church. "She's lost a lot of blood here."

"Oh my God," another voice called from behind. "What in the world happened in here? Has she been shot?"

Susan's body lay limp in a pool of fresh blood; she was barely clinging to life. The paramedic began taking her vitals. Her blood pressure was low and her heart rate was falling.

"If we don't get her to the hospital, we may lose her."

She slowly opened her eyes and realized she had been found. The man who resembled Jesus must have gone for help. There were people all around her trying to assist and save her, real people, nice people.

"Where is my baby?" she asked frantically.

"Baby?" someone replied. "You have a baby in here?"

"Yes, she was just born. Did he take her? Oh no," Susan began to panic.

"Calm down, Miss, we'll find your baby."

"He took her! He took her!" she shouted.

"Who took her?"

"Her father, God, He was here when she was born, and then

I passed out. That's when He must have taken her."

The two paramedics glanced at one another. One of them noticed the needle marks on her arms; he motioned with his head for the other to observe. Susan struggled to her elbows and scanned the room, tears flowing down her cheeks.

"Ma'am, you have to calm down and tell us what happened here."

"I told you, I just had my baby and God took her from me. He got me pregnant and used me to deliver His child. I almost died. I wanted to die, but He wouldn't let me. Now, He's taken her somewhere."

"Look Miss, we're going to lift you up and put you on the stretcher. We need to get you to the hospital. Don't worry, someone will stay and look for your baby. What's your name?"

"You think I'm crazy, don't you?"

"No ma'am, we're just trying to help."

"I saw the way you both looked at me. I'm not crazy. Find my baby," she screamed and tried to roll from the gurney. Her arms were swinging, slapping, and fighting the paramedics.

"Calm down," the young man insisted. "Someone bring me something to settle her down."

"No, I don't want anything to calm me, I just want my baby. Please, please find my baby," she wailed.

The two technicians proceeded to hold her down and administer a sedative to quiet her. Her hysteria subsided, and she let out a low whimper. Her lips quivered as her eyes darted from left to right then rolled to the back of her head.

"Man, that woman has been on a wild trip, huh?" the young paramedic whispered.

"Yeah maybe, but look, I think she's right." He lifted her skirt and exposed the blood that ran down her legs. They then realized she was telling the truth about giving birth and had to search for the child. They quickly hoisted her up and carried her to the door.

"We need an officer in here. This girl has given birth and the baby is missing. We need to begin a search right away."

Several officers came rushing up. The paramedic explained the delusional woman's story but acknowledged that there was a missing infant.

Scrambling through the church, officers on each side were checking on and under the pews. Every aisle and every bench was checked thoroughly. The trash cans were emptied onto the floor to make sure the baby was not discarded and left to die. Then, one of the officers noticed a glow of light that radiated from the statue that was lying on the floor at the edge of the altar. He quickened his step to the front of the church. Leaning over, he reached down and gripped the edge of the soft velvet curtain on the floor. He was speechless when it revealed the beautiful baby that awaited his help. Peacefully lying there with a precious smile on its face, the infant was quiet and encircled by a warm, mysterious light.

The police officer knelt down beside the statue as a strong light from a TV camera flooded the area. He quickly turned and noticed a reporter from WCIV.

"So what's the story here?" the young brunette asked.

"The story is a woman gave birth in the church."

"I heard her yelling something about God taking her baby. What was that all about? Is the infant going to be all right? It looks like an angel."

"That's what the mother says too."

"That's what the mother says?"

"She says her baby is an angel from God. She actually said that God is the father of her baby. She was so messed up on drugs, I'm surprised she even remembered giving birth."

"Are you saying she was using drugs while she was pregnant? And let me get this right. She actually said God was the father of her baby."

"Yes, that is what she said."

"God is the father of all of our babies if you want to look at it that way. Is it a boy or girl?"

"It's a girl. And for the record, I only call it as I see it. Her arm had so many tracks, a train could have rolled down them. Hell, a couple of trains could have traveled down the tracks. And just look at that baby. She seems perfect lying there with the mother of Jesus. How miraculous is that?"

The reporter began to snap pictures. "Wow, this is going to make a great story. Got to get some shots for the website too."

Pictures were taken from every angle. The infant flinched a few times as the lights seemed to startle it, but never once did it cry.

The two took a second to ponder the amazing sight of the little baby who was snuggled in the arms of the Virgin Mary. A little girl safe and sound in the arms of the mother of Jesus, nothing could be more perfect.

A bright light emanated from the altar. It was a glow that no one could explain; it was bright and golden, hovering in space as it rested on the newborn infant. There was no plausible explanation. It appeared to be a protective shield engulfing a miracle child. And the reporter captured it all on her camera.

The policeman yelled out to the paramedics, "Tell her we have her baby. We found her near the pulpit, and the infant is fine. She's fine."

The paramedic waved his hand and smiled.

"Everything will be fine. The officers have your baby. You just hold on, little lady."

"My baby," her finger lifted as she muttered words that were not intelligible.

"The officers have her. She is fine," he repeated. "She'll be coming to the hospital with you. You just hold on."

Her body quivered as she strained to lift her head to see who had her child. Her vision was distorted, and she was unable to speak. Her mind wavered in and out. She visualized

Jesus holding her baby, then the officer, then back to Jesus. Closing her eyes, blinking, she tried to decipher what was real and what was not. Visions of her life seemed to flash through her mind.

"Is it you, Jesus?" she mumbled aloud as her exhausted body drifted to sleep.

Shannon, the reporter from WCIV, continued to shoot the scene. The officer reached to cover the infant with the torn velvet curtain.

"No, wait!" she demanded. "I want to capture this just as it is—the halo, the position in the arms, and the radiance around this child. This will be the lead story on the news today: 'Angelic baby born in the arms of the Virgin Mary.'"

"I have to agree with you there, she does look like an angel."

The paramedic gently lifted the infant and carried her to the waiting ambulance.

As promised, the miracle baby was the talk of the entire Charleston area. It was a healthy baby girl who glowed like an angel. The baby nestled in the arms of the Virgin Mary. There were no names, just a mysterious stranger who gave birth in the church.

Two days later, Susan regained consciousness. Her eyes, at half-mast, darted about the strange room. She was delirious and searching for something familiar around the perimeter. She was unaware of her surroundings until a nurse entered her room.

A tall woman with blue eyes and red hair, perhaps in her early forties, the nurse removed the chart from the foot of her bed and was reading the last report.

"Where am I?"

"You are in St. Francis Hospital, honey. I will be your nurse. My name is Donna. You've lost a lot of blood. If the reverend hadn't found you when he did, you wouldn't have lived another hour. It's a good thing you went to the church and got out of that storm. No one even knows who you are. You didn't have any identification on you, and we didn't know who to call. Several people said they tried to help you on the street, but you just screamed at them. Reverend Joshua dropped by a couple of times to check on you, but he didn't have a clue who you were either. There has been a stream of people inquiring about your well being.

"They're liars! They didn't try to help. No one tried to help. I begged them, and they all just turned their backs."

"I'm sorry, just try to stay calm. You've lost a lot of blood."

"My baby, where's my baby?" she said, trying to sit up.

"Your baby is fine. She is so beautiful. The nurses in the nursery just love her. As soon as you get a little stronger, we'll bring her in so you can feed her."

"It's a girl? Is she all right? I mean is she healthy?"

"Yes, she is perfect. The doctor has already checked her out and did not find a thing wrong. She's healthy, twenty inches long, and she's an eight-pound bundle of joy. The paramedics who brought you in have an awesome picture of her. She was lying in the arms of the Virgin Mary."

"The Virgin Mary?"

"Yes, you evidently knocked over the statue. How the baby got into her arms . . . well, it's a mystery. The picture shows her cuddled up, right in her arms. She was warm, quiet, and just as snug as a bug in a rug. It sure was weird, and it has a lot of people talking."

"Talking about what?"

"They're talking about the baby being in the arms of the Virgin Mary. Don't you find that strange? The whole town is flabbergasted. Everyone has been sending flowers, see." The nurse waved her hand around the room to call attention to the vases all around it. "You've gotten so many flowers, we had to start leaving them at the nurses' station. Look around."

The young woman looked around the room then back to

the nurse. "No, I don't find it strange at all that my baby was in the arms of the statue. What I find strange is that people in this Godforsaken city sent me flowers. They can send flowers, but no one would help me when I needed it? What the hell is wrong with these people?"

"What do you mean, no one would help you? Like I said, we had quite a few people come by who said they offered you shelter, but you just wandered out into the street. You were just a stranger to them, but they saw you were pregnant and wanted to help."

"Liars! They all are liars."

"Okay, okay, I'm sorry. You need to keep calm."

"Whatever, I just thank God my baby is all right."

"Yeah, I bet you do. So, does the father need to be notified? Do you have a number to call?" the nurse asked as she checked the young girl's pulse.

"No, He knows."

"Well, he can't know that you have given birth. We don't even know who you are. Let me get this paper out of your chart and you can answer some questions."

The nurse walked over to the table and picked up a clipboard and pen. "Now, what is your name?"

"My name is Susan, Susan Shaw."

"What is your husband's name?"

"I'm not married."

"Oh, I'm sorry. Would you like to put the name of the father on your baby's birth certificate?"

The nurse looked up from her clipboard. Susan turned her head and did not respond.

"Susan, you need to put something down. Do you not know who the father is?"

"Of course I know who it is."

The nurse stood stern, tapping her pen, waiting for an answer. "Well."

"It's God," she whispered.

"Excuse me."

"I said *God*. God is the father."

The nurse raised her eyebrows and sucked in a breath of air, "Ah, how about I just put, *not known*?"

"No, you asked me a question and I answered it. Now write it down: God is the father of my baby."

"Susan, I can't write that down."

"And why not?"

"I just can't."

"You can and you will. God is the father of my child, and I would not have gotten pregnant if it hadn't been for Him. If you don't write it, I won't answer any more questions."

"Oh, I understand, you blame God for you getting pregnant. You didn't think you could have children?"

"No, you don't understand. I don't blame Him; He is the father. And I had no idea if I could get pregnant. I wasn't thinking about having a child. That was the furthest thing from my mind. Look at me. Do I look like I need a child? I'm nineteen years old, homeless, and I have no family. Do you think I need a baby?"

"Okay, that's all right. Let's move on. Have you picked out a name for your baby?"

"No, we are not moving on until you put the name of the father on my chart. I told you that I will not answer any more of your questions."

"Come on, Susan."

"Come on what!" she shouted. "Put the name down, or give me the damn paper and I will."

"Okay, I am writing it down, please, just calm down." Although she thought the answer to the question was ludicrous, she wrote it down to keep peace. She then turned the clipboard for Susan to see. Susan smiled and nodded.

"Her name is Gracen. My baby, you asked for her name.

She was conceived by the grace of God. I will call her Gracen. When can I see her?"

"Okay, you will get to see her soon enough, just a few more questions."

The nurse went over all the questions on the list. She told Susan about the nursery and who her appointed doctor was. Susan couldn't care less about the instructions the nurse was giving her. She witnessed her lips moving, but she never heard any words. The nurse carried on, but Susan's mind stayed focused on Jesus being beside her, talking to her, comforting her as she was in labor in the church, fighting for the birth of her sacred daughter. She could not understand why a person like her would have this child, God's child. And if He was there beside her, why did He let her go through so much pain? And the people in town, could they have really reached out to her and she just shrugged them off?

"Do you have any questions for me, Susan?" the nurse asked, interrupting her thought. "Susan," the nurse called out a second time.

"No, I just want to see my baby."

"She'll be brought up to you real soon. Now you try and get some rest. We'll wake you when we bring her in."

"Okay, I will. Thank you, Donna."

The nurse left the room. Susan was exhausted and confused. Was she hallucinating from all the drugs she had been doing? Was she dreaming, or was it all true? She didn't think it was a dream, but her lifestyle left her unsure of the reality of events in her life. And how did her child manage to get into the Virgin Mary's arms? She didn't recall giving birth.

"Please God, come back to me. Don't leave me alone again. I need you to help me. It is essential for you to help me get off of all these drugs that I have wasted my life on. Please help me with our child; help me get clean; help me be a good mother."

Susan tried to hold her eyes open, but her eyelids fluttered as the calming medication took effect. Her eyebrows were arched, but the lids were locked tight from pure exhaustion.

"Please," she whispered as she escaped to the world of dreams.

Semi-conscious, she heard that voice again. "I will always be beside you. And you must keep your faith, always. Believe in the baby. Never forget who she is. I will walk beside you, carry you in my arms, and fill your heart with love again. Don't give up."

2

"Excuse me, nurse. Can you help me?"

"What's the problem?" the nurse answered, looking over the top of a chart she had been reviewing. Her eyes fixed on a tall, dark-eyed man.

"My wife," the man paused briefly and leaned over to read the nurse's nametag that was fixed to the breast of her shirt.

"Donna, you know the doctor said my wife probably won't make it through the night. She will most likely die before morning."

"I know, sir, and you have my deepest sympathy."

"Thank you; you're too kind. But she is asking for her baby. She knows she's going to die and is begging to hold her baby before she goes."

The nurse set the paperwork on the counter with a confused look on her face. "Mr. Hudson, I think I must have misunderstood you. She does know your baby didn't make it, right? The doctors did everything under the sun to save her, but it didn't happen. Did you not tell your wife that her baby was stillborn?"

His head dropped. "No, I couldn't. That is all that she talked about, Donna. She's so weak, but every sentence she mutters is about our baby. She can't wait to see and hold our baby. She is so weak," a tear bedded into the corner of his eye. "I cannot let her die with that emptiness inside her. She would be heartbroken, and her soul would never rest."

"That may be true, Mr. Hudson, but nevertheless, she has to be told. You don't have a baby for her to hold. You must tell her."

"I know, but I can't."

"Would you like the doctor to come back in and talk with her?"

"No, I . . . I thought, well maybe you get one for me."

"Get one for you! Get one what?"

"A baby."

"A baby, how could I possibly get you a baby?"

"Just talk to the other mothers. Please, just ask one of the other mothers if she would let me borrow her baby. Just for a few minutes, just to let my wife die in peace."

"Borrow a baby?"

He took out his wallet, "I will pay. Look, I have one, two . . . five hundred dollars here. Just ask one of them, please. Just let her hold the baby for a few minutes. That's all I'm asking. I'll do anything, please, please, I'm begging you." He placed his money on the counter.

"Mr. Hudson, it is not about the money," she said pushing it back toward him. "I don't think any of the mothers will go for this. And, you would be lying to your wife."

"So what? What if it is a lie? What if that were you? What would you want to believe? Would you want to die never seeing your baby, knowing that's why you've been fighting, prolonging your battle with death? Realizing you saved all your strength, giving all that you have, to give birth to a dead fetus! Her spirit might not rest if I tell her and her heart . . . damn, Donna, her heart would be torn to pieces. She has been holding on just for this child. What would it hurt to just ask? Just ask."

Donna stared into the eyes of the desperate man. "What happens if she lives?"

"Come on, Donna. You know she has a five percent chance of living through the night, let alone living another day. Her cancer has spread into all her organs, and she can barely lift her head. Giving birth to our baby took all she had. That was all she has been living for, and she gave it all to the baby. She prayed every night just for the strength to give birth. Please don't take that from her. You know she's going to die." The nurse focused intently on the heartbroken man. She watched the tears roll down his cheeks as he pleaded. Pushing the money back toward him, she replied, "I will see what I can do. I'm not going to make any promises, but I'll ask a couple of the new moms."

"Thank you so much. I do appreciate it with all my heart."

He reached out and kissed the nurse's hand. Gratitude was all over his face. "You don't know how much this means to me . . . to us. Thank you, thank you." He turned and walked back to his wife's room.

"Was that Mr. Hudson?" another nurse asked, entering the nurses' station.

"Yes. You are not going to believe what he asked me to do."

"Sure I would. Anyone with all that money thinks he can do anything. They are so egotistical."

"No, he isn't like that at all. He's a very passionate man who loves his wife very much. He wants to pay someone to let his wife hold her baby. His wife was never told that their baby died. She is begging to hold her child before she goes."

"You're kidding?"

"No, I'm not. He has five hundred dollars that he is offering to pay."

"Five hundred dollars just to hold a baby? Wow."

"Yes. He wants me to ask some of the mothers in here."

"What did you tell him? You told him *no*, right?"

"I told him I would ask around."

"What! Are you crazy? You know we can't do that."

"Look, it's not going to hurt anyone to let her hold a baby for a few minutes."

"Just because he is rich, he thinks he can buy a baby? Like I said, narcissistic."

"No, you said *egotistical.*"

"Same damn thing."

"It wasn't like that. He was really genuine."

"Yeah right, well it's your job, Donna. You do what you want. Whatever he is, he's a good looking thing—tall, dark, handsome, and rich."

"I think you're the one who's narcissistic."

"No, honey, I'm realistic."

Donna continued to look through the charts of the new mothers. There were not many to choose from whose babies could pass for the Hudson's. There were three Hispanics, two African Americans, and only three Caucasians—one boy and two little girls. She pulled the three Caucasians' charts and started down the hallway. The first stop was Room 206. She tapped on the door and continued her stride inside. The new mother was holding the baby in her arms.

"Hello, Laura, how is the little one doing?"

"Oh, he is great and perfect in every way. Look at him. He is so beautiful. I'm glad you stopped in, Donna. I have some questions. I just love the way he stares up at me. And his little grin . . . "

Donna interrupted. "What kind of questions do you have?"

"Can I keep my baby in my room full time? I've heard a lot of horror stories about babies getting mixed up in the hospital, and I could not bear to lose him."

"Oh, honey, you don't have to worry about that ever happening here. Your baby is safe. He will be just fine in the nursery."

"I'm sure he would, but I would feel better if I could keep him with me. And all the germs that people bring in too. I'm sure there are a lot more germs in that nursery. Can't I just keep him in here? I know I would be able to sleep better too."

"Okay, that shouldn't be a problem. I'll leave word at the nurses' station. They'll bring you a little bassinet for him to sleep in, but you will be the one hearing him cry in the middle of the night."

"Well, I need to get used to that," she laughed.

"Is there anything else I can do for you?"

"No, ma'am. That's all I can think of."

"All right, I'll check on you later."

Donna walked back into the hallway. "Strike one," she said as she walked to the next room. Stopping at the door, she read the card that was posted in the slot, "Room 210, Mrs. Kathy Wetzel, girl, 6 lbs. and 8 oz."

"Sounds good. Here goes nothing."

"Good morning, Kathy. How are you and your little girl doing this morning? She is just so cute," Donna said, reaching for the infant's hand.

"We are just wonderful, and we can't wait to get out of here and go home."

"Oh, I bet. Everyone knows there is nothing better than your own bed and your own bathroom."

"You got that right. I've been waiting on my doctor to come in. I'm hoping he'll say I can go home today."

"Today? Who is your doctor, sweetie?"

"Dr. Wilson. He said if I was feeling okay, he might release me. I feel great, but I think I would feel much better at home."

"Where are you from, Kathy? I mean, you have a bit of an accent."

"I'm actually from a small town outside of Columbia, but my mom is from Germany, and I think I picked up her accent. Sometimes, it's not where you grow up, it's who you grow up with."

"Yeah, I hear you. Well, you definitely have a different accent than what we're used to around here."

The two women laughed and made small talk. Donna was searching for a way to bring up the request without sounding uncouth.

"I need to ask you a strange question," Donna said, walking around to the other side of the bed.

"Uh-oh, here it comes."

"We have never had this request before, but I need to ask. We have a young mother who gave birth to a little girl yesterday. Unfortunately, the baby didn't make it; she was stillborn. The mother has terminal cancer and probably will not survive too many more days. Actually, the doctors say she won't make it another night, so her clock is ticking, so to speak. She is begging everyone to bring her baby in to see her."

"I thought you said her baby died," Kathy interrupted.

"It did. The problem is that her husband doesn't want her to know. He hasn't told her and doesn't want anyone else to either. He doesn't want her to die with a broken heart. Her baby is what has been keeping her alive. She had been saving her strength to give birth, but I guess it just wasn't meant to be. The family is very wealthy, and he is willing to pay."

"To pay, pay for what?" Kathy snapped.

"Pay to let his wife hold someone's baby. He wants his wife to die happy. He thinks she is hanging on just to see and hold their child. He is willing to pay five hundred dollars, more if you want it. He just wants his wife to hold a happy, healthy baby."

"That is so sweet. I thought you were going to say he wanted to buy my baby. I was beginning to get pissed off."

"Good God, no. I would never go that far."

"Who is this man?"

"His name is Jerry, Jerry Hudson."

"You tell him for me, I would be happy to share my child with his wife. I think that is so wonderful. He must really love this woman."

"Yes, I believe he does. Let me go inform him and bring back the money for you."

"No, I don't want his money. Just surprise him. I'm a little nervous about letting my baby go to strangers. Will you be in there the whole time?"

"Of course. I don't want anything to happen to your little one."

"This woman, she doesn't have anything contagious, does she? I mean, my baby can't get anything from her, can she?"

"No, of course not. She has cancer, melanoma, which is a skin cancer. The majority of the time, it's caused by over exposure to the sun. There is nothing to worry about. There is no way I would put this little one in harm's way," Donna said, lifting the baby from Kathy's arms. "I will bring her back very shortly. Don't worry; she will be in good hands. I know Mr. Hudson will be very grateful to you."

"Please be careful with her," the young mother cried out as the nurse carried her baby away.

Donna was thrilled to have achieved her task of borrowing an infant for the dying woman. She had seen how devastating it is to tell someone her baby was stillborn, and she couldn't imagine telling a woman who had lived only to give birth. She did not blame Jerry Hudson at all.

"Knock, knock, look who's here," Donna said, entering into the room.

"Oh my goodness, wake up honey," Mr. Hudson anxiously replied. "Look who has come to see you. Honey, open your eyes."

The weak, frail, woman opened her eyes. She squinted and blinked, trying to get a good look at the visitor in her room. Her parched lips cracked as an uncontrollable smile came upon her face. Jerry took the baby from the nurse's arms and placed it next to his failing wife. She slowly lifted her head and kissed the newborn's hand.

"She is precious," a faint whisper escaped through her lips. "She is everything I thought she would be. Thank you so much for bringing her to me." Saying these few words was a task for her fragile body.

Jerry looked at Donna. He stood close to the bedside and made sure the baby was safe in his wife's arms. She was enervated and defenseless against her disease; she had to summon all her energy just to hold the tiny child. A glimmer of life sparked into the inertness of her eyes. A smile of contentment glowed across her face as the tiny fingers reached up and brushed over her pale cheek. Tears of joy flowed from her eyes when she snuggled the baby girl to her breast.

"She is beautiful like an angel. Look at her Jerry, isn't she beautiful?" She continued to struggle with her words, taking short breaths between syllables.

"Yes she is, honey, just like her mother."

"Please don't insult this baby. She is perfect."

"So are you. You've never looked more beautiful to me than now. You have the motherhood glow."

"Do I? I feel wonderful, not sick at all, now that my little one is here."

Donna and Jerry looked at one another, their deceitful lie, as bad as it was, had worked. They stood quietly at opposite sides of the bed until the fragile woman drifted back to sleep with the baby snuggled to her chest.

Jerry gently removed the baby from her arms and stood silently staring down at his dying wife. The baby held on to his finger as he walked around the bed to Donna. As a smile crossed her face, she carefully accepted the baby. He slid his hand into his pocket and pulled out his wallet.

"No, that is not necessary. The mother of the child was glad to help and understood perfectly well. She thought you were very honorable for doing this for your wife."

"Please, thank her for me. If I can do anything for her, you tell her to let me know."

"I will. I want you to know I feel the same way. Your wife is very lucky to have you."

"Thank you, but I have been the lucky one."

Donna returned the baby to her mother. She made small talk with her for a few minutes and relayed what Jerry Hudson had said. She expressed the joy her baby had given Mrs. Hudson and thanked her for her kindness.

"I'm glad we could help. See, my little baby is already making people feel better."

"Yep, that she is. I'm sorry to have to take her away again, but it's time to go back to the nursery. So, give kisses and hugs, and she'll back shortly."

Donna walked back down the hallway to return the infant to the nursery. She noticed that there were three babies still in their beds. Two of them were screaming at the top of their lungs. They seemed to be keeping time with one another. She ambled her way over and rocked their bassinets a little to quiet them.

Over in the corner of the room, she saw Gracen, the drug-addicted woman's baby. The infant was very quiet, turning its head from side to side, gazing around the room. Donna walked over and stared down at her.

"Aren't you a sweet little angel," she said, tickling the infant's chin. Gently, she lifted her into her arms and moseyed around the room with her.

"Little Gracen, what a lovely name. I bet your dad will be beating the boys away from the door when you grow up. Well, that is, if your mom tells you who he is." The baby squirmed and began to whimper.

"Oh, I'm sorry, you must have understood me. Of course, you will know who your dad is. Let's just hope your mom gets better real soon. Little girl, you are going to have a rough road ahead of you. You have a mother who lives only to take drugs and a father who is supposed to be God. Now if that's not a hell of a combination. If God was your father, I think he would have picked a better person to have his child—at least a person who wasn't on drugs. You might be better off if she doesn't make it. Oh my God, I can't believe I said that to you. What a terrible thing to say! I'm sorry. Don't listen to me, little one, I'm just babbling. I'm sure your mom is going to be fine."

The nurse waltzed around to the left side of the room where the incubators were located. *Look at the little Gonzalez baby in there*, she thought. *His mother was very healthy and went to her doctor's appointments as scheduled and still had complications. It will be a miracle if he makes it. His lungs did not fully develop. Look at him on those machines.* "It's a shame to have to witness something as tragic as the death of an infant," she mused aloud, "but that's not for you to worry. You have enough on your plate, so to speak. And with that, little Gracen, it's time to put you back to bed and go check on her. You just hang on; we'll get you a jump start on life."

Nurse Donna returned Gracen to her bassinet and went back to the nurses' station. She reclaimed Susan Shaw's chart and walked down the hall, reading as she went.

"It's a wonder either one of them made it with all those drugs in her system," she whispered to herself.

"Knock, knock. How are you doing?"

There was no answer. She pushed the door open and continued into Susan's room.

"Susan, it's time for your medicine. Wake up, wake up," she said lightly shaking her arm.

The nurse rummaged for the string over the bed. The coarse cord slid through her fingers and stopped at the knot, pulling the light on. Susan did not move. Again, the nurse called out to her. She shook her arm more vigorously, but there was no response. "Susan, Susan, can you hear? Wake up, honey. Susan!"

Susan moaned a little. She tried to lick her parched lips. "Something is wrong with me," she groaned.

"You've lost a lot of blood, Susan. You should be feeling

better in a couple of days. We're trying to replenish that now. That's what these bags are supposed to do; they're filled with liquids and meds. All this will make you all better real soon. Can you sit up, honey?"

Susan did not answer. "Susan, honey, come on, you need to try and sit up a little. I know your mouth is dry. How about some water?"

The nurse pushed the button to bring the bed to a sitting position. The motor hummed and resonated with a buzz before it slowly began to rise; Susan lay limp and slid down as the metal frame moved upward. The nurse tried to get her upright, but Susan did not respond. Donna pulled the sheet back and slid her hand beneath Susan's shoulders. She struggled to pull against the dead weight and keep her shoes planted on the slick tile. She glanced down to see what was so slippery only to witness a pool of blood. The sheet slid from the bed to the floor.

"Oh my God!" Donna shouted. There was blood everywhere. She frantically fumbled with the call button. Her hands shaking and voice crackling, she called for assistance. Within moments, two more nurses entered the room.

"What's wrong, Donna?"

"Susan isn't responding. There's blood everywhere. I think she's hemorrhaging."

"Check her vital signs."

"I did. Everything is elevated. She has a temperature of 103.2 and her BP is ninety over forty-nine."

"Have you called her doctor?"

"No. I haven't left the room."

"Well, he needs to be called immediately."

"Okay, what should I tell him?"

"Come on Donna, what's your problem? You know the drill. You're not an amateur."

"I know, I know. I just said something earlier that I shouldn't have. My mind is just cluttered with those thoughts."

"Well, clear your mind, and go call the doctor."

Donna ran down the hall to the nurses' station and looked up the doctor's number. She scurried over, too distraught over the unpleasant things she had said to little Gracie earlier, to think clearly. Surely this was not her fault but even still, the words lingered in her mind.

"Dr. Bolt, this is Donna Valis, Susan Shaw's nurse at St. Francis. When I went into the patient's room to administer her meds, Ms. Shaw mumbled a little and that was it. She is not responding to anything. There is no movement. Her breathing is shallow, and her vital signs are elevated. Her bed is saturated with blood. I believe she is hemorrhaging. Her BP is ninety over forty-nine, and her temperature is 103.2."

"Try to keep her stable, I will be right there."

Donna hung up the phone and ran back to help the other nurses. Before she could reach the room, one of them came running out.

"What's wrong?" Donna asked.

"Code blue. We've lost her! We've got to shock her! Come help me get the machine."

Donna turned and ran with the nurse back to the station. She seized the intercom from the wall and called, "Code Blue."

"Code Blue, Room 213, Code Blue, Room 213, STAT." They broke into a run as they pushed the machine down the hall.

Tamra, an RN on duty, had been performing CPR while she waited for the machine. Another nurse had administrated some drugs to stimulate Susan's heart. Nothing was working.

"Everybody stand clear," an intern said, entering behind them and taking control of the situation. He grabbed the paddles, rubbed them together, and placed them on her chest. Her body jerked and arched up from the bed. Tamra felt for a pulse while the others watched and waited. She shook her head and responded, "Nothing." The intern prepared the paddles again. "Clear," he said. Again, her body jerked. Her limp arms fell from the bed, and then, her small frame relaxed, lifeless on the bed. The nurse checked for a pulse, and they all looked at the monitor. The line was flat. There was no pulse.

"Anyone want to call it?"

"Please, don't stop. Could you try one more time?" Donna asked with tears in her eyes.

The intern stared momentarily and turned back to the lifeless woman. Once more, he yelled, "Clear," and yet again, he placed the paddles down. Everyone waited, but nothing changed. The orderly returned the paddles to the machine and shook his head.

"Let's call it. The time is . . . " Donna pushed him aside and picked up Susan's hand before he could finish his sentence.

"Breathe, damn you, breathe!" she shouted.

She hit Susan's chest and screamed again, "You have a baby to care for, breathe. Don't give up! Come on, you can do it."

The intern tried to stop her. "She's gone, Donna. Let her go."

Donna threw her hands in the air. "No, I can't, she is still here." Donna tried to continue CPR, but the other nurses grabbed her.

"Please don't stop. Please, try one more time," Donna begged.

"No," a voice exclaimed, entering the room.

"Everyone turned around. It was the doctor. Donna wiped the tears from her eyes. She looked up at the doctor, and then turned back to Susan. She seized Susan's arm and began shaking her.

"Don't give up! Don't give up!"

"What is wrong with you?" the doctor yelled. "Have you lost your mind? She is gone. Now let her be. Someone escort this nurse out of here."

"I just thought . . . "

"We're not paying you to think with your emotions, Nurse.

You are to be professional at all times, under all circumstances. Is that understood?"

"Look!" the intern shouted out.

The lifeline on the monitor had a small rise in the line and a faint beep expelled from the speaker. Everyone was quiet and shocked to see Susan take a deep breath. She sat straight up and fell back to her bed.

Doctor Bolt rushed to her side. "Get that nurse out of here," he ordered, pointing to Donna.

Donna was ushered from the room. Head nurse Carmen Bentz accompanied her to the nurses' station.

"What the hell happened to you in there?" Carmen asked.

"I don't know. I just didn't think she was dead. You know that I normally would never lose it like that. I guess after all she's been through, I didn't want her to give up."

"I don't know why you did what you did, but it was a good thing you felt that way, because without that last vicious shake, she probably would have died. You might have saved her life, but now you may be in jeopardy of losing your job. Bolt was not happy."

"I don't care. I'm sure I can find another job."

"What in the world were you doing in there?" a voice shouted.

Both nurses jumped. They were startled as Dr. Bolt lashed out.

"I have never seen such unprofessional work in all my life. You know as a nurse you never get involved. What were you thinking? Were you thinking? Are you related to this person? Where was your head?"

"I'm sorry, sir. I don't know what happened to me. I really don't even know this woman. You're right, that was very unprofessional. I've been a nurse for ten years, and I have never reacted like this. There is something about this patient; I'm not sure what it is. I just felt compelled not to give up on her."

"Well, she is damn lucky you felt that way, because if it hadn't been for you, she would be dead. As far as giving up, she gave up on herself a long time ago. You do realize she's a drug addict?"

"Yes sir, I do. But with all due respect, she is still my patient."

Doctor Bolt stood silent and stared at the nurse. He walked over and picked up Susan's chart. He took his pen and followed each line as he read.

"The father of her baby, God. What the hell is this?" he shouted.

"Well sir, she insisted God was the father," Donna answered.

"And you believed her?"

"No sir, I didn't believe her."

"What do you mean you didn't? Do you now?"

"No sir, I mean she insisted I put it down. She wouldn't answer any questions unless I wrote it down, so I did. I didn't think it would hurt anything."

"Oh no, it doesn't hurt anything; it just makes you look a little . . . How should I put this—stupid? You know this woman is not in her right mind. With all that crack she has stored up inside her, she probably really believes God is the father, and that's fine. That is, as long as the nurses do not comply with her beliefs."

"No sir, I don't believe it. I was just trying to comfort her. Is she going to be all right?"

"Miss Shaw should be fine the rest of the night. I have assigned another nurse to her. She is sedated, and the hemorrhaging is under control. I believe you have put yourself too close to this patient for some unknown reason. You are to switch places with another nurse. Carmen will switch you. If you have any questions about her patients, get with her."

"But sir, I think I'll be fine. I hate to abandon her, especially now that she's so sick, and I have my other patients to think of."

"Donna, I am not going to address this anymore. If you are going to be concerned with anyone, it should be that infant she brought into this world, because that child is going to go home with her. Wherever home is. She is the one that is going to have to struggle to stay alive."

The doctor handed the chart to Carmen and turned to look back at Donna. Without saying a word, he shook his head and walked away.

"I cannot believe he called me stupid," Donna whispered to Carmen as he left the station.

"Donna, honey, he didn't call you stupid. He was merely trying to say that it would not look good if someone else were to read that. You do know your name is on that paper."

"I know it is. If you had been the one asking the question, you would have written it down too. She was so upset when I refused, I had to. What difference does it make who the dad is? She probably doesn't even know who the father is. What better person to pick than God?"

"The sad thing is we know nothing about this woman. No one has come to see her, and no one has called. She has no address, no phone number—she has nothing at all. And the doctor is right. What about her baby? The hospital will not let her take the child if she doesn't have a home. We have a lot of problems ahead of us with Ms. Shaw."

"Well, I think she was starting to trust me a little. She evidently has had a rough life and probably doesn't trust very many people. I hate I can't go into her room now to find out more about her. She'll think I've abandoned her like everybody else."

"No one said you couldn't go visit her. She was just taken off your list of patients. If you would like to visit with her on your time, I don't see anything wrong with that. I'm not going to say a word."

"Thanks, Carmen. After my rounds tonight, I think I will

check in. Right now, I need to go introduce myself to my new patients. I think I'll go check on little Gracie too."

"Little Gracie. Is that Miss Shaw's baby?"

"Yeah, her name is Gracen, but I call her Gracie. Her mother said she was conceived by the grace of God."

"I don't know if I would go that far, but I would say she has survived by the grace of God."

"I agree there. Gotta go."

3

Donna walked down the hall toward the nursery. She saw Jerry Hudson standing in the hallway leaning against the wall, his eyes covered by his hands. Closing the distance between them, Donna believed his wife must have passed away. She was trying to find some comforting words to express as she approached him.

"Mr. Hudson, are you all right? Is your wife . . . ?"

"My wife is better," he interrupted. "Since you brought that baby to see her, her spirit seems to have lifted. I know it won't last long, but it is so wonderful to see her smiling. Do you think the lady who let us borrow her baby would possibly do it again? I really hate to ask, but if you would just look at her. Look at the change in her."

"The man clutched Donna's arm and pulled her toward the doorway. "I can't, Mr. Hudson, I'm sorry, I can't help you."

"I know I shouldn't ask this of you, but I must. If you would just look in on her, you would see. Please?"

"Even if I could do it again, it's not right. You are just delaying her death. She is only hanging on for that child, who isn't hers."

"And that's wrong? If that were your loved one, would you not want her to fight and hang on to every day that she could? Haven't you heard the saying, 'just one more day'? That is what I want: just one more day. Please, just one more time. It won't hurt anyone."

Donna pushed the door slightly and peered inside at Mrs. Hudson. Her husband was right; she did look much better. She was sitting up and sipping some broth from a cup, something she had not been able to do earlier.

Donna eased the door closed. She stared into Mr. Hudson's desperate eyes. He reached for her hand and held it with both of his.

"Please, just one more time. Will you help me?"

There was no way she could deny that look of desperation, even though she knew it was wrong.

"I'll see what I can do. I don't even know if that baby is still here. She was supposed to be released."

"Any baby will do. My wife won't know the difference. I can't thank you enough for doing this for her and for me."

"Don't thank me yet. I might not be able to do it again."

"Thank you for trying."

Donna spun on her heel and continued to the nursery. She entered through the swinging doors and strolled behind the glass windows. She saw a couple wanting to see a particular baby, so she walked over to the glass to help. They pointed to a baby in the corner. Donna moseyed over and read the nametag: it was Kathy Wetzel's baby.

"Good" she said to herself, "she is still here. These must be relatives."

Moving the baby to the front next to the glass, she smiled and turned to walk away. Before she took a step, a tall, dark-haired man knocked on the glass again. Donna turned back around. He motioned for her to come to the other side of the glass. She smiled, nodded, and hurried around.

"What can I help you with?" she asked as she stepped into the hall.

"That baby, the one you pushed next to the glass. You should have seen it. It had a glow around it."

"Excuse me, a glow? What do you mean a glow?"

"We just stopped by to look at the babies. My mom is on the first floor, and we always come up and see the new ones when we're here. We've never seen anything like it. There was a glow in the bassinet. The baby seemed to be smiling at something and just as happy as it could be. We looked for a light that might have been reflecting on it, but there wasn't one. The whole bassinet was glowing."

Donna laughed, "Well I don't know what the glow was, but I'm glad the baby is happy. In fact, it's time for her to go to her mother. I'm surprised she's not crying. You know how feeding time is," Donna smiled and turned back to the infant. She patrolled the room and saw Gracen's empty bassinet. Looking around, she spotted a nurse feeding an infant in the corner. She stooped and stared at the nurse, wanting her to trade babies. There was a closeness she felt to Susan Shaw's baby. Even though she didn't believe Susan's story, she still felt something special about little Gracen. But knowing she couldn't be partial, she went about her business. She picked up Kathy's newborn and waved to the nurse as she exited the room.

Walking down the hall to Kathy's room, she talked to the baby as she went. The adorable infant seemed to be listening, responding to each and every unfamiliar sound. Donna stopped and took a closer look. The baby's eyes seemed to be focusing on her; that was unheard of at this age.

"You're going to be a smart one," she said walking into the room.

"Look who I have," she blurted out as she entered. "I have this very special little girl for you, and she already is showing how smart she is."

Donna looked up only to see an empty room. She took a survey around the room. Everything was gone. All the flowers, cards, and Kathy's clothes were gone. She turned back to the hallway with a puzzled look on her face. She searched for the name card on the door, but it too had been removed. "Your mother must have been moved to another room, but don't you worry, we'll find her. We'll just have to go back to the nursery and ask where she is."

"Hey Carmen, do you know where Kathy Wetzel has been moved to?"

"Mrs. Wetzel has gone home. She was released about two hours ago."

"How come her baby wasn't released?"

"Her baby was released," Carmen said, strolling over to Donna. "Why? What's the problem?"

"I just picked up her baby from the bassinet. It's feeding time."

"Let's see, little one." Carmen lifted the baby's arm, and the infant squirmed. "I'm just looking at your wrist band to see who you are. Aren't you so pretty? And your eyes, they're so bright," she said, turning to Donna.

"Donna, did you look at her band?"

"No, I looked at the name on the baby's bed."

"Well, you should have looked at her arm. This is Susan Shaw's baby."

"It is? She was in the Wetzel bassinet. I never looked at her wristband. Oh my goodness, that would have been a terrible mistake. She was in Mrs. Wetzel's baby's bassinet, and I just assumed. I saw Gracie's bed empty, but I thought one of the other nurses had her."

"Donna, I think you might need to take some time off. You've been putting in a lot of hours lately. Would you like me to request it for you?"

"No, I'll be fine. I just didn't pay attention to what I was doing."

"That is what I'm talking about. You can't afford to make mistakes like that. I insist that you take some time off."

"Okay, Carmen, you're right, but please let me finish this week first. It's just two more days, then I'll have three days off."

"All right, Donna, but you are to work eight hours only, no overtime."

"Thanks. Is it all right if I take Gracie to see her mother?"

"I don't think that's a good idea. Why don't you just give her to me, and I'll take her."

"Oh, come on, Carmen, I already have her, and I'd like to talk to Susan for just a minute. She hasn't held her baby yet."

"I do need to check on my patients. Look, you take the baby in, but do not stay. All we need is for her doctor to come back and catch you. Just take the baby to see her, and make it quick. Do not leave that baby with her. Do you understand?"

"Sure. Thanks," Donna said, leaving the nurses' station.

"Well, Gracie, let's go see your mom. She's going to be so excited to see you."

Donna eased open the door to Susan's room.

"Look who I have here," she said in a soft voice.

Susan fought to open her eyes, and gradually lift her head. A huge smile lit up her face. Using both of her arms, she mustered the energy to push herself up in the bed. She shifted and positioned her body securely. Susan held out her hands. Donna placed the infant in her arms and returned the smile.

"She is beautiful," Susan whispered faintly, looking down at Gracen for the first time. "She is just beautiful. Look at her. She already has a smile on her face."

"She appears to do that a lot. She is a very contented baby," Donna replied. "I am so glad she's normal, given that she came from me. I really hate who I've become. I didn't have a choice, you know. I had nowhere to go. I just got so consumed in the drug world, nothing else mattered. When I found out I was pregnant, I tried to stop doing drugs. I really did, but I had been hooked for so long, I couldn't stop. I tried to get a job, but you saw what I looked like when I came in here. No one would even talk to me. I tried to find healthy food to eat, so my baby would get enough vitamins, but that was hard to do sometimes. I loitered around the churches and prayed a lot. I thought really hard about giving her up for adoption. Actually, to be honest, this really sounds awful, but I thought about selling her. I needed the money. I knew I had nowhere to take her; I had no home. I still have no home."

"What about now? Do you know what you're going to do with her? I mean, do you have somewhere to take her?"

"No, not yet, but I know her father will not let us down," Susan said, smiling at the baby.

"Susan . . . about her father?"

"I know you don't believe me. I didn't believe it either for a while, but it's true. God is the father of my baby."

"Why do you say that?"

"Because it's true."

"How could that be possible? You know no one will ever believe that."

"Yes I know, but I believe it."

"Do you actually believe God himself got you pregnant or is that just a metaphor?"

"It is what I believe."

"Well, explain. How could He have gotten you pregnant?"

"Have you ever seen God?" Susan asked.

"God? No, of course I haven't."

"Do you know anyone who has?"

"Susan, you know I don't."

"Well, I don't either, but Mary got pregnant by him. God has never even existed on earth, but the majority of people believe Jesus was his son. Are you a Christian, Donna?"

"Somewhat, but not as much as I would like to be."

"If you've read the Bible, you know that Mary went through hell to have Jesus. She was degraded by most, because we all know she wasn't married. No one believed her—no one but Joseph. When Jesus came to me and told me this was God's child, I thought I was crazy. I thought all the drugs were making me hallucinate, but the further along I got in my pregnancy, the more I believed Him. At first, I did everything by the book. I cleaned myself up and did all the right things. As months passed by, I got scared of raising a baby by myself. A month before she was born, I slipped off the wagon and started using again. I tried to overdose several times because of my weakness, but He wouldn't allow it. I cut my wrists, really deep, but the cuts closed up and healed. I really believed I was going insane. I cut my wrists over and over again in the same spot, but I lost no blood. "Look," she said, holding her left wrist out, exposing a light scar. "He would not let me die. I'm sure you took blood samples when I came in, so you had to have seen the amount of crack cocaine in my system. Anyone in the medical field should know that neither my baby nor I should be here. I'm telling you the truth. We should not be here, but she is perfectly normal, and look at me, I haven't gone through any withdrawal at all."

Donna looked intently at Susan, studying her for a minute, not saying a word. She was still trying to absorb the ludicrous story that Susan had just told.

"Why do you think He chose you?" Donna asked.

"I haven't a clue. Why did he choose Mary? She was supposed to be a peasant girl, a virgin. She was not some wonderful queen and had done nothing spectacular. She too was someone that no one would have believed, a nobody, just like me. And look at the world now. There are thousands of statues of her, and all Christian people believe the virgin birth to be true."

Donna listened as Susan continued.

"And speaking about her being a virgin, I think that is absurd. Why would God, as we know our God, degrade a woman like that? Think about it. Back then, it was very unusual for a woman to get pregnant out of wedlock. And a woman from the Middle East would've been stoned to death. For Mary to have been pregnant and not married had to humiliating.

Can you imagine what she must have gone through? She had to convince everyone that she was pregnant by a God no one could even see. Would you have believed her? Hell no, just like you don't believe me. And what about Joseph? How could he believe Mary? This was a woman he hadn't touched, and now she was pregnant. He would have been the laughing stock of the town."

"So, you don't think Jesus is the son of God?"

"That's not what I said. I have no idea if He is or isn't. Just as you have no idea if Gracen is or isn't. All I'm asking is why God would degrade a woman like that."

"I'm not sure."

"Of course you're not. Would you like to hear what I think?"

"Yes, I would, I think."

"I think when Jesus grew up, he became a healer, something no one had ever heard of before. Here was an ordinary man who was able to heal people by just a mere touch; come on, how awesome that must have been. A man, an ordinary man, was able to do the things only God should be able to do. I imagine when people started spreading the word, they probably believed that he was God himself, at first. But Jesus probably told them that he spoke for God. Putting two and two together, they came up with a story. A story that was so bizarre, it passed from person to person about a virgin getting pregnant by God. The story caught on and went from there. Or maybe it's all true."

"I've never thought of it like that," Donna sat bewildered.

"A beautiful young, perfect man had to be the Son of God. Who else could he be? As a story gets passed around a room, it changes again and again. Things get added, and things get taken away. Sometimes, by the time the story comes back around, it is totally fabricated, and no one is even sure how it started."

Susan went on with her story. She had plenty to say, and

she wasn't stopping, even to get a breath of air until she got to the end.

"You know how stories are told about someone's life after that person has died. When people are dead, most people normally don't say bad things about them. And after years go by, you forget the bad things, and the good is all that seems to be remembered. I'm not saying Jesus was bad or anything like that. I'm just saying He may not have been as perfect as the Bible depicted."

"Think about it, Donna, who wrote the Bible? Man. What man do you know you can believe? Not a damn one of them. Mary may have been no more than an ordinary woman who happened to give birth to a child that may or may not be God's. I believe that people could not imagine a poor simple peasant woman being worthy of such a miracle. So Mary became a figment of their fantasy, a made up miracle that was passed on century to century. Two thousand years later, their story is still here. Most people don't question it or try to figure it out. It is what it is."

"Go on," Donna said.

"I believe Jesus was a healer. I believe He was as close to God as He could be. I also believe He was a messenger and a source of salvation. I believe God wants people to believe in Him, and I believe that is why I got pregnant with Gracen. Gracen is the new, modern day Jesus. She is the new salvation. She will be the one to convince the world that God does exist. She will be our healer and messenger. She will speak His words and make us believe.

"I am a drug-addict and homeless, a nobody that no one will believe. Mary's baby was born in a manger in a barn, and my baby was born in a church, on an altar, in the arms of Mary. I speak the truth, and I rightly don't give a damn what everyone thinks. This is my baby, and I will find a home. God is the father, and we will make it. He will find a place for me and my baby in this world, I know He will."

Donna stood up, "I've never heard the story being told like that and I have never heard that Mary had been ridiculed before the birth of Jesus, but I guess it's possible."

Donna was confused but had a brand new outlook on Jesus. It was disturbing to think about what she had been taught all her life. As far-fetched as it sounded, it could very well be true.

"Well Susan, all I can say is I've never even thought of the Bible like that. I was brought up a Baptist, and we went strictly by the Bible. It kind of makes sense, but it scares me to think that way. My grandmother always said that you don't question the Bible. I wish you all the best in trying to convince people. If that is what you believe, then so be it. But I can't say I agree with you. And, you're right, it'll be very hard for anyone to accept and believe your story. I will do everything I can to help you find a place for you two to stay, but I'm not sure what to make of your story, though I'm surely not one to call you a liar. Right now, I need to get this little one back to the nursery."

"Can she please just stay with me a little longer?"

"No, I'm sorry I have to take her back, hospital policy. You need to rest so you can regain your strength."

"Okay, my little precious angel, Mommy is going to see you again real soon." Susan kissed her baby and lifted her up to Donna.

Donna wrapped her tightly in her blanket and turned toward the door. Looking down at Gracen, she turned back to Susan.

"Susan, there's a man down the hall who has asked for a favor. His wife had their first child two days ago, and it was stillborn. His wife is dying of cancer, and it took all she had delivering her baby. No one has told her the baby did not make it. Her husband wants to borrow a baby for his wife to hold for a little while. She keeps asking to see her baby, and of course she doesn't have one. We had another patient who let us borrow her new baby, but she's gone home. I was wondering if you would mind if Gracen could help keep this dying mother from grieving. I know it's kind of a lie, but it's all we have to help her hang on."

Susan stared at the nurse, not saying a word. She turned her head toward the window and quickly looked back.

"Wait! She was marked. Jesus said she would have His mark on her. Does she have any unusual birth marks?"

"I don't know."

"Please, bring her back. Let me undress her and see."

"Susan, that is really not a good idea. I really have to get her back, and you need your rest."

"Please, it won't take but a minute. Please, then you can take her to see that lady. Please."

"Okay, but we have to hurry." Donna retreated to the bed with the baby. They carefully began undressing her, examining every inch. They looked all around her neck, back, stomach, legs, and feet but found nothing.

"I don't understand. He said it would bear His mark."

"I'm sorry, Susan," Donna said, pulling the gown back on the baby. "Maybe it was all just a dream."

Susan began to cry. Her tears rolled down her cheeks and dripped off her chin. She stared down at her child and gently touched her face.

"It doesn't matter, I know who your father is, mark or no mark."

Donna lifted the baby from the bed. She looked down at Susan and patted her hand.

"It's okay, Susan, no matter who the father is, you are the mother, and that is all that should matter."

"Thank you," Susan softly replied, sliding back down in her bed. "Hey, Donna."

"Yes."

"There's been another miracle today."

"What's that?"

"Me. Look at me. I have my strength back, and only two hours ago, I was almost dead."

"You're still weak, but I see where you are going with it."

"Gracen made me better, just as she will the other mother. She is a healer just like Jesus. I could feel the warmth spread through my body when I held her. I could feel myself heal from the inside out."

Susan pulled the blankets around her shoulders as Donna exited her room. Tears rolled down her cheeks as she began sobbing in her bed, not understanding what to do. She believed she might be losing her mind. Was she dreaming? Was she on so many drugs she dreamed all this up?

Donna walked down the hall feeling pure empathy for Susan. She knew this young mother really believed God was the father of her child. Donna knew she too was starting to believe Susan, even though it was preposterous. She still tried to examine little Gracen for some kind of mark as she walked toward Mrs. Hudson's room.

Ambling down the hallway, she looked up and saw Mr. Hudson standing outside his wife's room. As soon as Jerry saw Donna coming toward him with a baby, he strode to meet her.

"Oh, thank you, thank you. My wife is very weak again. She constantly asks for the baby. I was worried you would be too late. Please, may I carry her in?"

"Sure you may, just be very careful with her."

Donna handed him the infant and followed close behind to the room, occasionally peeping over her shoulder, hoping not to get caught.

"Honey, wake up, look who has come to see you."

Mrs. Hudson opened her eyes. She shifted slightly and struggled to sit up. Her cancer wracked body trembled as she began to pull herself into position. Donna hurried to assist her, placing a pillow behind her back for support. They lay the baby across her stomach. Both Donna and Jerry gave a helping hand to hold the infant in place. The baby squirmed and nestled to her body. Donna felt a warm sensation in her hand that held the baby. The infant squirmed a little more and Donna's hand became warmer.

She gazed up to Jerry to see if maybe he had noticed the same, but he gave no indication that anything was different.

"Please give her to me. All I want to do is hold her close to my body," Mrs. Hudson whispered in a faint voice.

Warmth from the miracle child seemed to energize the frail woman and make her better. Maybe Susan was right. Mrs. Hudson did find strength from somewhere. Could it have been from this baby?

"Jerry, I am not afraid to die. I have been blessed to have you in my life. Because of you, I am a better woman. You have taught me to hope and pray for a better life, and I have received the blessing. With this baby, our beautiful little angel, and you, I can leave this world happy."

"Don't talk like that, Mary. You're getting better."

"Look at her. There is a holy purpose shining in her eyes. You are so beautiful," she whispered down at the precious little girl.

Little Gracen gave a tiny smile as if she had absolutely understood. Mrs. Hudson's face glowed like a flickering candle.

"She looks like an angel. I believe God gave us an angel," Mrs. Hudson said, kissing the baby's forehead. "Look at her. She is so perfect. I can't say it enough. I want to unclothe her and see how flawless she is. I want to see all of her. I want to count all of her toes and all of her fingers." Her voice was raspy but distinct as she began to unclothe the child.

"Hold on, honey, let the nurse help you," Mr. Hudson said, reaching for the baby. "You are very weak and you may drop the child."

Mrs. Hudson quickly retorted, "The child, the child happens to be your baby. You say it as if it belonged to someone else."

"I didn't mean it like that. You just scare me. She is so fragile, and you are so weak. But then again, watching you with her, it appears you are getting better by the minute."

"Your husband is right, Mrs. Hudson. Let me help. I assure you, she has all her fingers and toes. I have checked her from top to bottom myself."

Mrs. Hudson did not listen; she proceeded to check out what she believed to be her baby. She lifted her gown and pulled out one of her little feet and then the other. She kissed her feet and gently tucked them away.

"I think you are right. They're all here," she said as she wrapped her back in her blanket. "I am convinced she has everything. Just look at her, honey, I can't believe she came from us."

"What are you talking about? She looks just like you," Jerry responded in a worried voice.

"Gosh, you sound like I doubted that she is ours," she struggled with the words of discouragement. "I was simply implying she appears to be perfect. I am thankful she is. I was just so worried, you know, with the cancer and all."

"Don't worry honey, she is fine."

"She smells like a fresh bowl of rose petals," Mrs. Hudson gave a little chuckle as she sniffed the baby's hand.

"I noticed that too, I thought it was my imagination. I wasn't sure what a new baby is supposed to smell like, but I didn't think it would smell like flowers."

"No, it's not your imagination. She does smell like flowers."

Mr. Hudson gave a sigh of relief. Before he could say a word, his wife cried, "Something is wrong with her, look!"

Both Jerry and Donna quickly looked to see what was so upsetting to her.

"Look at her hand. Oh my God, it is in her other one too.

She's bleeding! Both of her hands are bleeding. What did I do? Help her, please do something."

"Honey, calm down. You didn't do anything. Nurse, please do something," Jerry said frantically.

Donna looked at the baby's hands. She gently pulled back the tiny curled fingers, exposing her palms. She looked at the first one, then the other, trying to find the problem and reassure the Hudsons the baby would be fine.

"I think someone probably made a small paper cut when they got her hand prints. I'll take her back to the nursery and put a little something on it. Don't worry, she'll be just fine."

Rapidly wrapping the baby up in her blanket, she scurried from the room. Walking at a fast pace, almost a slow run, she scampered down the hall with the infant. Donna turned toward Susan's door and quickly pushed her way in.

"Look! She has it. I found it. She is marked," Donna shouted to Susan with excitement.

"What?" Susan asked confused and dazed, waking from her nap.

"Your baby, you were right, she has it. She has a mark.

"What, I wasn't dreaming?"

"No, you were not dreaming, look." Susan held out Gracie's hand.

"Oh my God, she's bleeding! What did those people do to her?" she snapped.

"She's fine. They didn't do anything wrong. This is the mark, the mark, just like Jesus. Haven't you ever heard of stigmata? That is what she has. It is the mark of Christ."

"Oh dear God, thank you, I thought I was going crazy. Now I know I'm not totally insane. She is the daughter of God."

"Well, I don't know about the daughter of God, but she may be the daughter of Christ."

"Nurse Valis!" a voice screamed out.

Donna jumped to her feet. She spun around to see Dr. Bolt

standing there. His eyes were filled with rage; his face was red, and the veins in his neck were bulging.

4

"Dr. Bolt, I was just helping the other nurses, sir. They were very busy, so I told them I would help by bringing the babies to their mothers."

Dr. Bolt was angry. Of course he could not say too much in front of the patient, so he said all he could.

"Please excuse yourself, and take the baby with you," he said with a fake smile on his face.

"Dr. Bolt, look at my baby, she has . . ."

Donna cleared her throat and interrupted. Susan looked past the doctor at Donna. Donna shook her head, so Susan did not inform him about what they had found.

"She has what?"

"Oh, she is all right, you know how new mothers are. She has a little rash that concerned Miss Shaw, but I'll take care of it."

Donna left the room in a hurry before the doctor could examine the baby. She wasn't sure what would be said about their conversation about stigmata, not knowing if he had even heard it.

Returning to the nursery and washing the infant's palms, she knew she was holding a miracle in her hands. She tucked Gracie in her bassinet, but before she walked away, she double-checked the name card.

Donna began to think about how Susan and Mrs. Hudson seemed to get better. She moseyed over to the Gonzalez baby and noticed he was still gravely ill. She had an idea. Actually, it was a test of faith.

Reaching over to Gracen's bassinet, she wheeled it close to

the incubator that the Gonzalez baby rested in. "Let's see if you can help this premature infant. I can't let you lie down with him, but you're close enough to spread a miracle to him. Make me a believer," she whispered.

"You had me worried. What took you so long? And why are you putting that bassinet right there?"

Donna looked up: it was Carmen. "I'm sorry, Carmen, I ran into a little trouble."

"Not again, Donna. What happened this time?"

"Dr. Bolt walked in when I was in Miss Shaw's room, and he was not happy.

"Oh no, what did he say?"

"He didn't say a whole lot. He just basically asked me to excuse myself and take Gracen with me."

"What part of our last conversation did you not understand, Nurse Valis?" Doctor Bolt asked, walking into the room. "Did I not tell you to redirect your patients? Did I not say I thought you were too close to this patient? Did you disobey my orders for a reason? Or is it that you just don't really give a damn about what I have to say?"

"No sir, I didn't disobey you. I was just taking the babies to their mothers. The other nurses were busy. I didn't think it would be a problem."

"Well, it is a problem, especially when you were corroborating her far-fetched story. What kind of nonsense were you two talking about when I came in? Did I hear you say something like *stigmata*?"

Carmen looked over to Donna, waiting for her response, but Donna said nothing. She glanced over at Gracie, wondering if she should show them her hands. Under the circumstances, would they believe her, or would they come up with some medical nonsense? Finally, after what seemed forever, Donna spoke.

"Yes sir, you did hear us talking about stigmata. Miss Shaw

had asked if I had ever heard of it, and I told her I had. That was it."

"Stigmata? What did she want to know about stigmata?" Carmen asked.

"I'm not quite sure. We had just begun to talk about it when Dr. Bolt came in."

"Well, I am glad I came in when I did. You cannot be putting any more crazy ideas like that in that woman's head. Next, she'll claim her child has stigmata. It's bad enough she already thinks her child is the daughter of God. Look here, Donna, do I need to have you transferred to another floor, or are you going to follow my instructions and stay away from Miss Shaw?"

"But Dr. Bolt I was only . . ."

"I don't care what you were only doing. I do not want to see you in her room again."

"Dr. Bolt, that was my mistake," Carmen spoke up.

"I don't care whose mistake it was, I don't want it to happen again. Is that understood?"

"Yes sir, completely," Carmen replied.

The doctor stood staring at Donna, waiting for a response. Donna stared at her feet and softly mumbled, "I understand."

"Good, now that we are all on the same page, we will not be having this conversation again."

He picked up a chart and sat down at the nurses' station with it.

Donna motioned for Carmen to step out of the station. She was hesitant but followed Donna to the hallway. Dr. Bolt gazed up and saw the two women talking. Carmen's hands were flying in the air, apparently scolding Donna to no end. Dr. Bolt glared at the two of them but could not hear a word. He watched them for a few minutes and continued to scan the chart. Periodically, he would glance up at the women. He was suspicious of them. They appeared to be arguing about his decision. Carmen seemed furious. Dr. Bolt's curiosity got the best of him. He rolled his chair away from the desk and stomped into the hall.

"What is the problem out here? What are you two arguing about?" he asked.

The two nurses looked at one another. Each waited for the other one to speak up. Carmen took a breath and turned to Dr. Bolt. She swallowed hard, took another deep breath, and began to speak.

"Donna was updating me on the Shaw baby. She thinks she might have something wrong with her hands. She thinks . . ."

Donna interrupted her, "I think she's a little bit jaundiced. Carmen is upset because I thought she should call her pediatrician. I was just agreeing with her when you walked up."

"Is this true, Carmen?"

Carmen eyeballed Donna and cocked her head to the side. Donna raised her eyebrows, begging, pleading with her eyes. Carmen gawked with one eye squinted, never looking at Dr. Bolt, but replied, "No sir, that is not true." Donna's mouth dropped open. She knew she was about to be fired.

"That is not true at all," Carmen said, turning to Dr. Bolt. "Donna is trying to be a good nurse, but she is trying too hard. She listens to her patients and tries to believe what they're telling her. Miss Shaw was concerned about her baby, and she believes that she has sti . . ."

Donna interrupted again, "A stomach virus—Miss Shaw is just worried about her baby, that's all. Her skin color seems to be discolored a little. Carmen was just telling me that it was probably from all the drugs Miss Shaw had taken."

"I agree," Dr. Bolt said. "I agree with what Carmen was saying to you. I think you are putting too much faith in patients and not enough in medicine. If she had jaundice, I'm sure her pediatrician would have known. He would most definitely have checked her for that if it concerned him. I also sense you are too involved with your patients, as I mentioned before. I am going to have you transferred tomorrow. I feel it would be better for you and the patients to have a little distance from this floor."

"But I have to . . . "

"You have to be transferred," Dr. Bolt repeated.

Donna looked up at him and then back at Carmen. She was hoping Carmen would speak up, but she didn't, not at first anyway. When she did speak, she didn't say what Donna was hoping to hear.

"I agree, Dr. Bolt. I would also like to request for Donna to have some time off. She's been pulling a lot of double shifts lately."

"Okay," Dr. Bolt said, looking at Donna. "I will request three days off and a transfer from this floor when you return. Carmen, if this becomes a problem, you make sure you call me, and I will address it."

"Yes sir, I will."

Dr. Bolt turned back to the nurses' station, signed off on the charts, and left the hospital.

"Carmen, I can't believe you did that to me, especially after what I just told you."

"That's why I did it. For you to believe that woman gave birth to the child of Jesus Christ is ridiculous. How could you even imagine something like that?"

"But it's true. Come back to the nursery, and I will prove it to you. She has the mark. She has stigmata in both her hands."

"Donna, get real."

"Please Carmen, just come look. What is it going to hurt for you to just look?"

"I don't have time for nonsense."

"It's not nonsense, I promise. Come on, it won't take more than a minute."

"All right, I need to go to the nursery anyway."

5

The two nurses strolled back into the nursery. They saw little Gracie lying fast asleep in her corner. Donna lifted the baby's tiny hand and opened her fingers. Carmen peered over her shoulders, waiting to see.

"I don't see anything," Carmen replied in a discouraging tone.

Donna looked closer. She turned the hand over, but there was nothing on it. She reached in the bassinet and retrieved the other tiny little hand. Prying open the fingers and examining the small palm, again, she saw nothing.

"I don't understand. It was there. I saw it. I know I didn't imagine it. I swear it was there."

"Maybe you just wanted it to be there. Maybe you just wanted to believe."

"I did want to believe, but that wasn't it. I saw it. So did the Hudsons."

"The Hudsons," Carmen snapped. "What do they have to do with this? What have you done?"

"I . . . I took little Gracie in for Mr. Hudson's wife, and when she was holding her, that's when her hands starting bleeding."

"Oh my God, you didn't say anything, did you? I mean, you didn't say what you thought it was. And why did you have that baby in that room? The Hudsons lost their baby."

"Mr. Hudson asked me if I could bring a baby in for his wife."

"For his wife!"

"His wife doesn't know her baby died. I didn't think it would hurt anything. I asked Susan Shaw and Kathy Wetzel first."

"Mrs. Wetzel, too! Oh my God, Donna, what has gotten into you? Do you want to lose your job? You know you can't do something like that."

"I told him I couldn't, but he begged me. His wife is dying, and he didn't want her to die with a broken heart. His wife kept asking to see their baby. You should have seen her face: it was like she was getting life back. She glows when we bring the baby to see her."

"Does she think this child is hers?"

"Yes, but . . . "

"But nothing. How hard do you think it's going to be now?"

"We aren't planning to tell her."

"I cannot believe you put the hospital in this predicament. We do not have a choice about telling her. She is going to know."

"But Carmen, it will kill her."

"She's going to die anyway, and I am not going to jeopardize my job for this. Wrong is wrong, and that was wrong. What happens if she doesn't die? She wasn't supposed to make it through the other night, and she's improved since then."

"Come on Carmen, you've seen her. All the doctors said she would be lucky if she makes it through this week. She made it through the other night and that was a miracle, but you know she can't last much longer. And if she does make it another week, she should be comatose."

"As awful as it sounds, I hope her doctors are right, for your sake."

"And no, I did not tell anyone else about her hands. Well, no one else but Susan Shaw. I had to tell her."

"Oh my God, Donna, does it never end? Why do you want to fill her head with this nonsense?"

"Carmen, I'm telling you it was not nonsense. We all saw it."

"Well, I guess it must have disappeared, just like magic,

huh."

"I guess it did," Donna answered.

"Well, whatever you all saw, it is gone now. It also left no signs of ever being here," Carmen said, looking down at the baby. "As for you, Miss Donna Valis, it is time for you to leave. I will call you when we get your new schedule. I want you to take the next couple of days off and rest. And when you get back, I don't want to hear any more about this . . . this stigmata stuff. Even if it were true, no one would believe it, so leave it alone."

"Why?"

"Why not! Because we don't live in biblical times. We don't have apostles and disciples walking around here. You don't see angels and God does not talk to us, not out loud anyway. We don't have healers and saints who walk among us. We live in a Godforsaken world filled with rapists and murderers. This is the new world, and it's not a very good one."

"Maybe it is time for a change; it's time for a miracle. It's possible—anything is possible. Think about the baby when they found her. She was lying in the arms of the Virgin Mary. You saw the pictures. The media was going crazy over it at first, but because Susan is a druggie, everyone discarded the story. No one would print anything about her. At first, they were saying it was a miracle child, but now it is a hush-hush child."

Carmen shook her head and replied, "I can't believe her far-fetched stories, and I can't believe you actually believe in them either. It's preposterous, Donna, just plain ridiculous."

"If you had seen what I did, you would be a believer too. Answer me this, did you look at Susan Shaw's chart when she came in? Did you see the drug level in her bloodstream? Neither she nor her baby should be alive. She told me stories about trying to commit suicide and nothing worked. She cut her wrists several times and didn't even bleed."

"Good God, Donna, you have lost it. You know what? I'm

not even going to discuss this anymore. If you want to believe all that stuff, I am not one to stop you. You just go ahead and clock out. I have work to do."

"But Carmen . . . "

"No buts, that is all I have to say. I want you to leave this floor now. Do not say another word. Just leave."

"Before I leave, would you do me a favor? I put Gracen next to the Gonzalez baby for a reason. I want to see if she can help him. Mrs. Hudson and Susan have gotten better, and I believe it's because of Gracen. Keep her close to him for a couple of days. You have nothing to lose. Just for my peace of mind, I would like to know if he gets better. Can you at least do that for me?"

"Donna, please leave."

Carmen never answered the question. She stood and watched as Donna got on the elevator.

6

Donna left the hospital as she had been ordered to do. She was disheartened, but still optimistic she could prove what she saw. Her mind raced in every direction. Where should she start? Whom could she talk with and how would she know where to go?

She scurried to the parking lot, tapped her remote, and unlocked the door of her red Honda. Donna began to drive home, but thoughts of little Gracen plagued her. She could not think of anything but stigmata.

A horn sounded behind her as the traffic light changed from red to green.

Donna threw her hand up and resumed her drive to her quaint little apartment on the outskirts of the city.

As she entered her complex, she retrieved a key from her purse. She slid the brass key with the pink rubber top into the slot and waited to hear the click of the lock. As the door creaked open, a black-and-white cat named Blackbeard was there to greet her. She closed the door and secured the deadbolt. With pure exhaustion, she rested her head on the painted wood of the locked door. The cat weaved back and forth through her legs as she stood quietly.

She reached down and patted his head and made her way to her bedroom. Blackbeard followed close on her heels. She strolled to the far side of the room and retrieved her laptop. As she turned and walked around the room, the feline leaped on the bed and teetered on the edge, begging for attention. It followed her every movement.

Donna was unmindful of her pet, for she was on a mission.

But her cat had been alone all day and was going to claim some attention. He soared from the bed and landed at Donna's feet almost causing her to fall.

Apologetically, Donna lifted the tomcat, snuggled him under her left arm, and held the computer in her right. She entered the kitchen and set the computer on the glass top table. She knelt down and gently placed her feline companion on the floor. After a few strokes to his back, she stood up and retrieved his favorite canned food from the cabinet. Approaching his silver bowl, the tom meowed with contentment. Donna responded with a pat, slipped a chair from the table, and seated herself in front of her computer.

"Where should I start?" she asked herself. "Stigmata, where else?" she said eagerly as she began to type.

There were several sites to study and a lot of information to absorb. Donna was diligent and sat reading page after page.

Surfing the web, making a list of possibilities, she began to read about a saint named Pedro Pio and how he came to receive stigmata. It confirmed the scent of flowers, which Gracen carried. There was no mistaking the aroma in the air; it was roses, just as with Saint Pedro Pio. He too had the unexplained bleeding in the palms of his hands.

Donna was ecstatic to have found this information, but now what could she do with it? She stayed up late reading document after document about stigmata. Everything she was reading led her to the same conclusion that Susan might be right. Gracen was the chosen one. If not before, she now was truly convinced Gracen was a gift from God. Unsure of what kind of gift, she wondered whether she could be His daughter or just a messenger. Just like the explanation Susan gave of Jesus: was He God's son or a brilliant healer?

She wanted to find more proof, but how? She was exhausted, and her mental capacity to hold information had deserted her. Unable to concentrate any longer, she stood up and pushed her chair back toward the table.

She stretched her arms high above her head. With all her muscles taut, she rolled her shoulders and yawned. She reached down and clicked the *off* button and watched as the image on the computer screen slowly faded away.

Donna sluggishly walked to her bedroom and removed her clothes. She gathered her leopard print pajamas and moseyed on to the bathroom. Laying her sleepwear on the dressing table, she stepped into the shower and turned the faucet to *warm* in hopes of rejuvenating her body. Leaning against the cold tile of the wall, she let the water drizzle down her exhausted body. Her mind was cluttered with more information than she could digest. She wondered if the Catholic Church could help her. Surely if anyone would know, they would.

Lathering her body and removing the hospital smell, Donna could not think of anything else. Under the load of what she had learned, her mind traveled a hundred miles an hour. She was trying to reconcile what she had been reading with what she had been taught all her life. It was a whole new concept of religion.

Stepping onto the stone floor, she reached for a towel and began to slowly dry her body. She slipped on her pajamas and studied herself in the mirror. *Not bad for a redhead.* She chuckled. Although it was late, she was too restless to go to sleep. She decided to get a bite to eat first. Going back into the kitchen, she removed some left over chicken from the refrigerator and slid it into the microwave. Then she heated a can of Campbell's soup and sat down to eat.

She nibbled a little at a time, daydreaming about stigmata. *What if the child did have it? Was she the chosen one sent here before the end of time? Would God let a woman like Susan be the mother of a chosen one? Would I be one of her followers? Could she be an apostle with the message? With 2012 supposedly the year of destruction, was she sent to save us and give us hope?* She had so many questions and no answers. There had to be answers at a church.

She finished eating, washed her dishes, and sauntered to bed. She would have a long day tomorrow following her quest; she needed a good night's sleep. She hoped desperately to find some solutions. After a silent prayer, asking God for some guidance, the weary nurse fell asleep.

7

It was 11:00 a.m. on Wednesday. After sleeping in and enjoying a little R&R, Donna relaxed on the sofa with an open phone book in her hand. She searched for a Catholic church that might be able to help her. She found one in West Ashley about thirty minutes away from her home in Summerville.

After her tranquil morning of sipping coffee and making a list, it was time to get some answers. She slipped on some casual clothes, brushed her hair, and slid her feet into some comfy shoes. She took a quick glance in the mirror, gathered her purse and keys, and leisurely walked to her car.

Driving down the familiar route to the Catholic church on Highway 17 South brought back many memories. In one, she was a child, visiting the beautiful church with a friend. There always seem to be a presence of God and tranquility there. It was an imprint of religion that had never wavered and never was forgotten. This is why she easily chose this particular church.

Donna had a list of questions she thought might be significant. She retrieved it from her purse as she sat in the large parking lot planning her strategy.

Sitting in front of the massive building and staring at the beautiful stained glass windows, anxiety began to pry at her nerves. She felt a little ridiculous about the questions, but she had made a fool of herself for a lot less important things before. This would be no different.

Stepping from her car, she adjusted her shirt, smoothed the seat of her pants, and walked up to the large doors. Closing her eyes for a quick prayer, she turned the large knob, and pushed the door open.

The inside was very quiet and dimly lit. The sanctuary was large with a twenty-foot ceiling. Standing erect, she peeped around the corner. Seeing no one, she called out, "Hello." There was no answer. "Hello, is anyone in here?" she called out again.

"Yes," a voice returned.

Donna turned on her heel toward the sound. A short, bald man with a friendly smile on his face quickly came into view. He wore a white shirt with a black collar around his neckline; surely he must be the priest.

"May I help you?" he asked.

"I'm not sure, but I hope so. Are you the priest here?"

"I am one of them," he replied. "What is it that you need?"

"Are you busy? I have a few questions, and I'm afraid it might take a while. I was wondering if you could spare a little bit of your time."

"I can make some time for you. Come, sit down, and let me see if I can help you." He gestured for her to have a seat at the front of the church.

She followed, took a seat, and gazed around. She saw Jesus everywhere. He was on the stained glass windows and in pictures throughout the building—and He was the subject of many statues.

"You have a beautiful church."

"Thank you, but the church is not mine. It is God's house and it belongs to all the people who come here to worship and learn of our Father."

"Good, that is why I'm here. I have some questions about stigmata. Are you familiar with it?"

"Stigmata," he responded with a questionable demeanor. "Stigmata is not a subject that comes up every day, but of course I am aware of it. What do you need to know?"

"I want to know how to get it."

The priest laughed, "You can't just get it. It's a gift, a gift from God."

"Oh, I don't mean for me, and I didn't mean 'get it.' I meant to ask how you would know if someone has it."

"There are many different marks of stigmata. There are marks of the passion of Christ. It's the same embellishment that Christ endured on His last days. It may be the marks of the nails in His hands or feet, or it could be the band of thorns around His head. It could even be the whipped whelps around the rib cage. There are many different marks of stigmata. Why do you ask?"

"How old do you have to be to get it?"

"I don't know if there is an age limit," he laughed again. "I think if God decides that you are a chosen one, it will be His will to decide the age."

"Could it happen to a baby? Are there any babies that have been documented with stigmata?"

"Babies? No, I don't believe so. A baby cannot give a message. God chooses someone to relay his message."

"Do you believe in stigmata?"

"Yes, I do. Tell me, dear, why all the questions on stigmata?"

"I know this is going to sound crazy. I really don't even know where to start."

"Start at the beginning. Do you think you know someone who thinks he or she has stigmata?"

"Yes, I do, but it's a baby. I'm a nurse at St. Francis Hospital. I work on the maternity ward. I see a lot of mothers and babies come and go. The other day, a homeless woman came in. She had just given birth to a beautiful little girl. She told me this far-fetched story that no one would believe."

"And you do?" the priest asked.

"Not at first, but the more I talked to her, the more I was convinced she was telling the truth."

"What did she tell you?"

Donna twisted in her seat to see if anyone else had seated

themselves in the room. She turned back to him, leaned forward, and whispered in a very soft voice, "She says that God is the father of her baby."

The priest jerked back and glared at her as if she were insane. He inhaled sharply and grabbed at his chin.

With hesitation, he replied, "God is the father of us all."

"Yes, I know that."

"Why?" he asked.

"Why what?"

"Why would this young woman ponder such a thing, and why do you believe her?"

"Several things have brought me to this conclusion. She was a drug addict with a serious problem. She had tried to commit suicide more than once, but injuries that would kill anyone else didn't do it for her. Then, there's the fact that she was homeless the whole time she was pregnant, but the baby is perfect, Father. Not a flaw anywhere on her."

"That is not so unusual. I have spoken with many young women who have gone down the same road and had perfect children, but that doesn't mean they are physically of God. I mean we are all God's children, but He is not our physical father. Jesus is the only descendent of God. It is not written that there is any other descendant."

"It is not written," Donna said sarcastically. "You mean the Bible does say that."

"Yes, that is what I mean."

"So what? Does that mean it can't be so?"

The priest shot her a displeased stare. He shook his head and raised his eyebrows. He squinted, puzzling, searching to find words to reply to her comment. "What is your name, dear?"

"Donna Valis."

"Well, Donna, I have been asked a lot of questions in my time as a priest, but I think this is the first of this kind. I'm not sure how to answer it. I presume anything is possible, but why do you believe this is so?"

"I was brought up in church. We went to church every Sunday, and I've always believed in God and miracles. We weren't Catholic, but I even believed in saints and all that. I never even thought about there being any other children of God, but this baby is different. She is illuminated with a soothing glow around her, like a halo. She is always happy and she smells different—she has an aroma of flowers."

The priest laughed. "I think I need to go see this baby."

"Would you really?" Donna started babbling. "That would be great! Her name is Gracen. Her mother said she was conceived by the grace of God, so she named her Gracen. We call her Gracie. I also need to tell you about her hands."

"What's wrong with her hands?"

"Oh, nothing is wrong with them now. But, yesterday, her hands were bleeding. Both of them were bleeding. There is a couple who had a stillborn baby at the hospital. The mother of the baby is dying of cancer. She is unaware that her baby was born dead; you see, her husband couldn't tell her. She had been asking to hold her baby before she died. He asked me if there was a baby he could borrow for his wife before she passed away. He did not want her to die with a broken heart. I ask Susan Shaw if I could take Gracie to her and she agreed. When the dying woman held that infant in her arms, her face started to shine with life. She seemed to get better instantly. And while she was holding the infant, the room filled with the scent of roses. Then, Gracie's hands starting bleeding."

"They were bleeding?"

"Yes, Father. Of course, the woman holding the infant was hysterical, but I knew right away what it was. I rushed out of the room and took her to Susan, who is the real mother. She had told me that God said the baby would be marked. I couldn't wait to show her."

The priest began to get very interested. "So, what happened then?"

"Well, the doctor came in and ordered me to leave the room. I almost got fired for encouraging Susan and talking to her about her baby having stigmata. After everything settled down, I told the head nurse what had happened. She wasn't happy either, but we walked down to the nursery so I could show her what I had seen, and it was gone. All the marks had disappeared."

"What do you mean, *gone*?"

"It was gone, disappeared. There wasn't a sign of any kind. Her hands didn't even have a scratch on them, and several other people saw it besides me, so I know I'm not going crazy, even though it sounds like I am. Have you ever seen stigmata on anyone?"

"No, I have not witnessed such a miracle. It is extremely rare, you know."

"Yes, I know. I read all about it on the computer last night. I was up very late learning all I could learn on the subject."

"So you know the odds are not in your favor, although I wish it to be true. Do you think the mother of this baby would allow me to visit her? I would love to meet Gracie and her mother."

"I'm sure she would love for you to come see her. I can give you her room number. Do you think you will be able to tell?"

"To tell what?"

"To tell if Gracie has stigmata?"

"I don't know, Donna, like I said, I have never witnessed it for myself. It would be wonderful if you are right, but I wouldn't get my hopes up."

"But it is possible, right?"

The priest leaned back on the pew. He took a deep breath and craned his head back. Cupping his hands together and sitting up straight, he replied.

"Well, life is all about miracles. We look for marvels in the world every day and receive plenty that are overlooked or dismissed as something else. If what you say is true, I will make a promise to pursue it. I will not let it be swept under the table."

"So it could happen? A baby can have it?"

"Yes, I guess it is possible. I've never heard of a baby having stigmata, but I guess miracles come in all shapes and sizes."

"I am so glad I came here, Father. No one else would believe her. I had to. You've made me feel a lot better. Let me write down the name and room number for you. I have a very busy day today, as I am sure you do as well, so I should be going."

Donna stood and retrieved a pen and paper from her purse and jotted down the information. She shook his hand and thanked him again and again before retreating.

"By the way, my name is Father Wilkins," the priest called out as she got close to the front door.

"Excuse me?" she twirled around.

"My name, you never asked my name."

She laughed, threw her hand up and continued out the door.

8

The following morning, Father Wilkins was up bright and early. The conversation he had with Donna and the mental picture she painted had captured his attention. He had to go to the hospital to see Gracen. He had to satisfy his curiosity. If he did not, he would always wonder if this had been a miracle or not. And he did give his word.

He showered, shaved, got dressed, and sat down at an old oak table to eat his breakfast. Swallowing the last bite and placing the plate in the sink, he gathered his Bible, keys, and wallet—and out the door he went. He was eager to see the baby and anxious to meet the mother.

It was mid-morning. The brightness of the sun was blinding. The glare ricocheted off a car bumper and struck a direct line to the priest, momentarily blinding him. Shielding his eyes, he pulled to the front of the hospital and parked at the curb. With one leg out of the car, he stopped, looked in the mirror, straightened his collar, and scooted across the leather seat of his blue Volvo.

Scampering toward the hospital, he greeted many pedestrians in need. Finally, after a half hour, he entered the elevator and headed to the nursery. He stood in front of the big glass window and looked carefully at each baby. He didn't know what he might be looking for, but he didn't want to overlook a thing. He studied each and every infant from head to toe.

"Can I help you, sir?" a voice asked from behind.

He spun around. Head Nurse Carmen was waiting for an answer. "Yes ma'am, I came to see Gracie. Which one is she?"

"Just look for the one that's quiet. She very rarely cries. She's over in the corner," Carmen pointed. As she turned, she noticed she was not there. Carmen walked to the other side and brought a baby from behind the incubator. "Sorry, my mistake. Somehow, she always seems to be hiding by the sick ones. I think she may be comforting them. See, doesn't she look like an angel?"

Father Wilkins craned his neck. He saw a glowing light just as Donna had said.

"Why is there a light on the child? Is she sick?"

"There are no lights on her. It's just the reflection from the overhead lights. Several people have said that, but it's just all the overhead lighting."

"Oh, I see, may I have a closer look? I know I'm not family, but I would like to take a closer look."

"Sure you may. Let me push her to the front for you. Carmen walked around and pushed Gracen closer to the window.

Through the smudged glass, she seemed to be just an ordinary child. He peered through the viewing window, dissecting what was visible. He wasn't seeing anything that told him what he needed to know. He tapped on the glass for a second time to get the nurse's attention.

"May I hold her?" he asked.

"No, I'm sorry, you can't. If you were family, or if the mother says that it's all right, I can allow it, but that's our policy. I'm truly sorry.

"That's all right. I understand. I'll go in to visit the mother now, if that's okay."

"Sure, are you a friend of hers? She hasn't had anyone come visit since she has been here."

"No, I'm not actually a friend; I haven't even met her. Someone told me about her being all alone, about her being homeless. I thought maybe I could help in some way."

"I'm sure she will appreciate that. Her room number is 213.

She should be delighted to have a visitor."

Father Wilkins smiled and excused himself. He strolled down the long hall glancing at the numbers on each door as he passed. Halfway down the corridor, a man approached him.

"Excuse me, Father," the man said. "Is it possible for you to have a moment to come into my wife's room for a prayer?"

"Is something wrong, sir?"

"My wife has cancer and is dying," the man explained, looking away. "I was wondering if you could come in and pray with us."

"Why is your wife on the maternity ward?" Father Wilkins asked, knowing he must be the man Donna had spoken about.

"We had a baby, but we lost her. She was stillborn."

"I am very sorry to hear that. Of course I will pray with you."

Father Wilkins extended his hand and introduced himself. Jerry Hudson did the same and the two men entered the room. Father Wilkins was very surprised when he saw Mrs. Hudson sitting up. She had been described to him as near death. She looked weak, but far from gravely ill.

"My wife has been feeling a lot better today," Jerry said, walking over to her side. "We hope you will pray for her to keep getting stronger."

"Of course I will. I am very happy to see you feeling better."

"Thank you, Father, but it is because of our little baby that I got better."

"Because of your baby?" the surprised priest asked.

"Yes, as soon as I held her in my arms, I felt better. I knew I had to fight with all of my might to live for her, so I am. I want to live. I have to live. With her and God by my side, I will. Jerry calls her Gracen. I think that name fits her perfectly."

Father Wilkins looked over at Jerry. They both knew there was no baby, but Jerry was unaware that the priest knew. The two men gathered around the bed and began to pray. Standing on either side, holding Mrs. Hudson's hands, they began their blessing. They asked God repeatedly to heal her, to remove the disease that had plagued her body and give her life instead of death.

The prayer lasted for about fifteen minutes. Afterward, Mrs. Hudson thanked Father Wilkins, and he and Jerry walked into the hallway.

"You have to tell her, Mr. Hudson," Father Wilkins said.

"How do you know?"

"A nurse—I believe her name was Donna—came to me and told me the story."

"Yes, that would be Donna. She has been an angel to us."

"You still have to tell your wife the truth."

"I know, but how? It will surely kill her. You heard her. She is better because of the baby."

"Yes, but it is a baby that is not hers. The longer you wait, the more difficult it is going to become."

"I know, I know."

"Just ask God to help you. He will guide you." Father Wilkins reached out and lifted Jerry's hand. "Ask Him. He'll be there for you. He'll tell you what to do."

"Your faith is evidently a lot stronger than mine. I do believe in Him, but I don't think He can help me out of this predicament that I've created for myself."

"Just pray. Let Him lead you in the right direction. You'll feel so much better to get rid of this deceit. Deceit can be a terrible thing. The guilt that some people carry from it destroys their lives. Don't let that happen to you. If you need me for anything at all, don't hesitate to call." The priest reached into his pocket and retrieved a business card. "Here is my phone number. Any time you or your wife need me, call."

"Thanks, Father, I appreciate your kindness."

Father Wilkins patted Jerry on the back and walked away. He followed the hallway until he found Susan Shaw's room,

213.

"Hello," he said, tapping the door and pushing it open slightly. "May I come in? Are you up to a visitor?"

Susan sat up in her bed and observed the man peeping around the door. She seemed very surprised to have a visitor.

"Sure," she answered. "What brings you to see me? Are you a priest?"

"Yes, I am. Your friend, the nurse, asked me to."

"You must mean Donna."

"Yes, that was her name."

"What did she say? What part of her story did you not believe?"

"Nothing, I mean, not nothing. Okay, let me start over. It's not that I don't believe her; I just need to find out what you believe and what is actually happening here. I want you to tell me everything you can."

"Everything I can about what?"

Father Wilkins was puzzled. The expression on his face was a dead giveaway that he really already knew her answer. He got a little fidgety and began to pick at his fingers, not knowing how to word his questions. "Well, she told me you didn't have a home for you and your baby when you are released. I just thought maybe the church could help you," he replied with a smile on his face.

"That would be great, but does the church normally do stuff like that?"

"Yes, it does. We have helped quite a few young mothers get on their feet."

"That's great," Susan said, groping her sheet. She looked up at Father Wilkins and softly whispered, "It's true you know."

"What's true?"

"What you came here to find out. It is true whether you believe it or not."

"What are you talking about, Susan?"

"God," she answered.

"What about God?"

Susan hesitated. She took a deep breath, glared into Father Wilkins's eyes, raised her eyebrows, and said, " He is the father of my baby."

Father Wilkins leaned toward her and reached for her hand. She jerked away from him and crossed her arms. She scowled at him for a brief moment, and in an angry voice she said, "So, you don't believe me either."

"Yes, I believe you."

"I didn't think priests were supposed to lie. If you are going to lie to me about what you believe, how could I ever give you my trust, Father?"

"I do believe that you believe God is the father of your child, but God is the father of us all."

"Really, Father? I know what I'm talking about. I didn't just pull this story out of my ass. God is the father of my baby. He got me pregnant. He told me no one would believe me, just as no one believed Mary. He also told me my baby would be marked, and she is. She has stigmata."

"Susan, I want to believe you, I really do, but there has to be some kind of proof."

"I told you she has stigmata."

"I heard what you said. Donna said the same thing. That is one of the reasons that I came here. I wanted to see for myself."

"Well, did you? Did you go see my baby?"

"Yes, I did."

"And."

"And there was nothing there. I'm sorry, but she had no marks that I could see."

"That's crazy," Susan shouted. "I saw the marks. Her hands, her hands were bleeding. Donna saw them. So did those other people. Did you ask them?"

"Calm down Susan, it'll be all right."

"Don't tell me to calm down, damn it. I didn't ask for all this to happen to me! I didn't even want to be pregnant. I can't even take care of my own self, let alone a baby. To hell with all this. I know what I was told whether you believe me or not."

Father Wilkins stood in disbelief. He could not believe this woman was talking to him with such language. He was at a loss for words. Before he could respond in any kind of way, Susan was ordering him from her room. He backed toward the door as she continued to curse and shout at him. He never said another word; he just backed away and left the room.

"So you didn't believe her either," a voice said from the hall.

Father Wilkins turned around only to see Carmen standing behind him, holding Gracie in her arms.

"I don't know what I believe, but it really isn't my beliefs that matter. It is not I who needs to be convinced."

"If it's not you, then who?"

He peered into Carmen's arms and avoided the question.

"So this is the little angel," he reached for the baby's finger.

"Yes, here she is. Now you may get a little closer glimpse of our miracle child, but she doesn't look much different than she did from behind the glass."

"She is very precious," he replied smiling down upon her.

"That she is, but now you have to excuse me. It is time to go see Mommy."

"Okay, thank you very much for your help."

"Oh, you are quite welcome, but I didn't do much," Carmen replied, pushing the door open a little wider.

Father Wilkins excused himself and walked down the hallway. When he reached the end, he stopped and looked down at the floor. Slowly turning around, he stared down the corridor. Carmen was leaving Susan Shaw's room and continued on to the next room. He slowly began retracing his steps until he reached Susan Shaw's room for a second time. Standing outside the door, he listened to Susan talk to her baby.

"I know who your father is and so will you," she alleged to her baby. "People will believe me one day, even if it takes all of my life to convince them."

The priest eased the door open. "May I come in Miss Shaw?"

Susan looked up at the priest standing in her doorway. Hatred encircled her face. "Hell no," she answered, "hell no. You already came in here one time and called me a liar. Was that not enough for you?"

"I'm really sorry, Susan. I didn't mean to imply that at all."

"No? Then tell me, what did you mean?"

"Please, may I enter and explain? I want to understand, I really do."

Susan stared with steam coming from her eyes. Father Wilkins took her silence as a *yes* and slowly entered the room. He pulled a straight back chair beside her bed and sat down.

"Miss Shaw, I want to know why you believe God is the father of your child. It is not my place to say whether you are right or not."

"What is your place?"

"What do you mean?"

"I mean what is your place? If you don't care whether it is true or not, what do you want? Why are you here? All you priests walk around masquerading in robes and acting like saints, but you can't believe in a simple miracle. What a shame. I am suspicious of everyone that I meet because of all this, and that is a shame."

"I want to know. I hunger to believe it is true. I've waited my whole life to see a miracle that God created for the world to see. We witness miracles every day, but only a few people know about them. If this child were to be God's, if you have proof of any kind, I will stand by your side to spread the word."

"Excuse me, I am not accountable to you. But if you want proof, what kind of proof do you need?" Her voice grew louder and louder. "Do you want to know if He actually made love to me? Or did I see Him . . . did I touch Him? Is that what you want to know? Proof, how could I prove any of that even if it is true? Everyone thinks I'm crazy. They believe I just hallucinated from all the drugs I was on."

"I don't think you are crazy. I just want to know what happened to you."

Susan glared at Father Wilkins. She shook her head and glanced down at her baby. With her forefinger, she stroked Gracie on the top of her head. In a soft, low voice she began to talk.

She began to reveal her life prior to that night. "A few years ago, I got in the wrong crowd. I started drinking, doing drugs, and defying my parents. All my friends did it, so I did too. I got to a point where I didn't like myself very much. I hated who I had become." She looked up at the priest. "I was always a good girl. My mom made sure we grew up in church. Every time the church had a service, we seemed to be there."

She peered back down at Gracie. "Anyway, like I said, I didn't like where my life was going. I wanted to do the right thing. One night, I was all messed up, I mean I was totally wiped out. I was scared and all alone. I had done some crack and it was bad. I thought I was going to die, so I went where I knew I could get some help, the church.

"It was really late, and I didn't know if I could even get in. When I got there, the door was unlocked. I opened it and went inside. I remember it being very dark in there. That was the first time I had ever gone into a church with the lights out. It was kind of eerie. Anyway, I went up to the front. You know, to the altar. There was a dim light on up there. I was crying and calling for help, but no one came. I lay in the front, up near the altar. There was a statue of Jesus up there, and I lay down at his feet. I thought if I was going to die, I wanted to be near Him."

"When I was lying there, I remember praying, asking God

to let me live. If He let me live, I wouldn't do any more drugs. Man, I had it bad. I shook like a leaf on a tree. I started vomiting and sweating and had cramps that were unreal. During all this time, I kept seeing someone off and on. They were there, and then they weren't. I kept feeling someone brush my face and hold my hand. I felt someone hold me in their arms and kiss my head. Then, lights were flashing, a cool breeze came from nowhere; I got scared and closed my eyes. I felt someone get on top of me, and quickly, I opened my eyes. I started crying, but it was not because I was scared, it was because when I opened my eyes, I saw God."

"How do you know it was God?" Father Wilkins asked.

"Because the light I kept seeing was just that, a light. The someone who seemed to have gotten on top of me was no more than a light with a faint image. When he lay on top of me, it was not in a sexual manner. He was holding me as if to provide comfort. Every time I looked up at the statue, I kept seeing Him come out of it. He stayed with me all night. The next morning, I was awakened by the reverend. When I saw him, I got scared and ran."

"How do you know it wasn't the drugs you were doing? You said you were pretty much out of it. You could have been just hallucinating."

"After I left the church, I started thinking about what had happened. I did believe it was the drugs." Susan laughed, "I thought wow! What a damn dream."

Susan lifted Gracie up and put her on her shoulder. She patted her back and continued. "Like I said, I didn't believe it either, but it didn't matter. God did what I asked Him to: He let me live. So a deal was a deal. I got clean after that night. I started back to church, cleaned up my act, and even got a job. Life was great. It was great until six weeks later when everything changed.

"I got sick. Man, I was sick as crap. I threw up every time I moved. When my eyes opened in the morning, so did my mouth. I made a doctor's appointment. I thought I had caught a virus or the flu or something."

"The flu, what did the flu have to do with it?"

"It wasn't the flu." She looked over to the priest. "It wasn't the flu at all. I was pregnant. I got pregnant that night at the church."

"I don't mean to be crude, but how do you know it wasn't some drugged up night from before?"

"How do I know? I just know. Listen, I was a drug addict, not a whore. I needed drugs, not sex. I can't believe that you still don't believe me."

"It's not so much that I don't believe you, I just wish there was some proof."

"There is proof right here in my arms," she smiled down at Gracen. "Look at her. She is perfect. There is not a blemish anywhere on her body. Observe her face. Is that not a face of an angel? And her smell—do you smell the flowers of God?"

"Yes, she does look like an angel and she does smell like flowers, but that is not proof."

"Well, I don't need proof; I know who the father is. When I get out of here, I will read more about stigmata, but I know what I saw. God told me she would be marked and she was. I don't know what happened to it, why it went away."

"What went away?"

"The stigmata, are you not listening? The marks on her hands just disappeared, but they didn't go unnoticed. If I had been the only one to see it, I would have thought I was having flashbacks, but several people saw it besides me."

"Knock, knock," a voice interrupted from the door. The priest and Susan turned to look. It was Jerry Hudson.

"I hate to bother you, Miss Shaw. My name is Jerry Hudson. My wife and I are the ones who borrowed your baby the other day. Or should I say I was the one who borrowed her?"

"Borrowed? You say it like she's a cup of sugar."

"I'm sorry. Poor choice of words, may I come in?"

"Sure, come on in, we're having a party. I've gone from no visitors to a room full. Pull up a damn chair and kick your feet up. What can I help you with?" she asked sarcastically.

"Did I come at a bad time?" he asked, looking at Father Wilkins.

"Hell no, there are no bad times in here. Look, I have a priest on one side and a millionaire on the other. How could it possibly be a bad time? This is the first time I have ever been in such highfalutin company, especially when you all chose me and not the other way around."

"I should be going," Father Wilkins said as he stood up.

"Did I interrupt something? I could come back some other time," Jerry said, stepping from the door.

"No, I had nothing important to say. I just wanted to see if Miss Shaw might need some help from the church."

"And I was quick to let him know the church has helped out enough."

"Well, that is one of the reasons I came here. I wanted to see if I could help out."

"What!" she snapped. You want to help too! What's up with you people? I give birth to a baby and now everybody wants to help. Get out! Both of you get the hell out!"

"But you didn't even let me tell you what I want."

"I don't give a damn what you want. Get out!"

Startled and confused, the two men scurried to the door. Jerry placed his hand on the priest's back to hurry him along and out of the room. Susan threw her pillow at the door as it closed. Tears rolled from her eyes and dropped onto Gracen.

"I'm sorry, Gracie, Mommy didn't mean to scream like that. I hope I didn't scare you," Susan reassured Gracie, rocking and holding her close to her body. "I will stay here and rest until I get stronger and then I'll get a job and make a home for us somehow. Don't worry, I can do it."

The door to her room slowly opened once more. She looked up and was surprised to see Jerry.

"Please, Susan, let me tell you what I want. It won't take more than a moment."

"Mr. Hudson, I really don't think you have anything to say that I want to hear."

"Please, call me Jerry," he began talking as he pulled the chair beside the bed and sat down. "Your baby is beautiful, and she is defiantly one of a kind."

"Meaning what?"

"Oh, I just think she is wonderful."

"And why is that?"

"Well, as you know, your baby certainly made my wife better."

"No, I didn't know. How is that? I thought she was dying."

"She is, but since she held your little Gracie, she seems to be better. That is why I'm here. I was told by one of the nurses that you do not have a home to go to. I have several homes. If you would just let my wife hold this little one," he said, reaching for Gracie's finger, "If you could just let her believe this angel is hers, I will be indebted to you. I will set you up in one of my houses and help you get back on your feet."

Susan stared at Jerry for a moment and looked down at her baby. She looked back up at him and asked, "Then what?"

"What do you mean?"

"How long will you help me before you throw me and my baby out?"

"Throw you out? I would never just throw you out. I'm not that kind of a person."

"Well what kind of person are you?"

"I don't know what you mean," he said, squirming a little in his chair.

"I mean just what I said, what kind of man are you? You

borrow my baby, you lie to your wife, and you offer me a house. What kind of a man are you?"

Jerry sat quietly. He was searching for words to describe himself. "I guess you can't understand why I'm doing what I'm doing. I am lying to my wife because I love her, and I want her to live. I will do whatever it takes for just one more day with her. She is my life. If I have to pay you, beg you, or give you a house, it's worth it to me. Material things mean nothing if you can't share them with the one you love. I don't know how to live without her. She is my life, and she is my soul mate. Your baby is her life, and she wants to live for her. She used to cry at night because she wouldn't see her grow up. I could not let her die knowing our baby never even took a breath of air. She is thirty-one years old and barely hanging onto life. So, the answer to your question, I am a very selfish man who wants more time with the woman he loves."

Susan lowered her head. She noticed Gracie looking up at her. Gracie had an expression on her face as if to say it was all right. Susan slowly wrapped Gracie's blanket around her tiny body and lifted her from her shoulder. She lifted her up and handed her to Jerry and replied, "Please be careful with her. If anyone can make your wife better, it's my baby."

Jerry, not understanding what she meant, reached out and took the baby from her. Whatever she meant didn't matter as long as he had Gracen to take to his wife.

"Thank you so much, Susan. I will take care of her just like she was my own."

"Just remember, she is not your own."

"Oh, just a figure of speech, I didn't mean it like that."

9

Days passed, and Jerry Hudson continued to get Gracie for his wife on a regular basis, and his wife's health continued to improve. She now was able to sit up in bed, feed herself, and feed the baby she believed to be hers without any assistance.

As she continued to make progress, Jerry was concerned about the deception and wondered what to tell his ailing wife. What was he to do now? He didn't know how to tell her the truth. He knew Susan would be released soon and the baby would be gone.

He ambled down the hall to Susan's room. He paced back and forth in front of her door, trying to think of a solution. Tapping on the door, he entered her room. He was surprised by Susan's appearance. Her face was pale and chalky. She was weak and incoherent, and she couldn't speak above a whisper.

"Good God, Susan, what happened to you?"

"I don't know. Late last night, I started feeling bad, and this morning, I was worse. I really feel sick."

"Do you want me to get the nurse?"

"No, they've already been in here; they said the doctor will be here soon. How's your wife?"

"She is so much better, thank you for asking. The doctors can't explain her remission. Her cancer seems to be gone for the moment. They say they have never seen anything like it. No one has ever come back when they have gone as far as my wife went. It's mind-boggling. The doctors are totally baffled."

"I can tell you why your wife is better. Can you come a little closer? It's hard for me to speak."

Jerry leaned over the bed rail and listened to her speak.

"It's Gracie. She's your healer. She is the daughter of God. No one believes me—no one except Donna. Have you seen Donna?"

"No, not yet. She's scheduled to be back in today."

Susan swallowed hard and clutched her throat. It was evident that the pain was unbearable as she continued to whisper. "Later, I'm supposed to go downstairs for some kind of test. When she gets here, will you tell her to come see me?"

"Of course, but the other nurses will probably let her know where you are. What you just said, what did you mean, Gracie is the daughter of God? What kind of medicine do they have you on?"

"It is not the meds, you'll find out. Tell Donna about your wife when you see her. Tell her about Gracie."

"About Gracie, what about Gracie and my wife? I don't understand."

She murmured in a weakened voice, "Gracie has been making your wife better. She is your healer."

Jerry looked at her with an astonished expression on his face. He didn't know how to respond to her. Did Susan really believe Gracie was a healer? He wasn't sure how to reply to such nonsense. All he wanted was to ask to borrow her baby again, but now he was fearful it might distress her.

He walked over to the sink and picked up a washcloth. He wet the cloth and returned to Susan's bedside. Wiping her face and brushing the hair away from her eyes, he dampened her cracked lips.

He perceived the features of her face for the first time; she was really a pretty young woman. Her heart was tender and full of compassion, but her eyes were dull, hazy, and lifeless. He wondered how she could have gotten herself into this mess. She had a perimeter around her made of stone, an encasement of armor certainly meant for protection. In his worst hour, he could not imagine ever walking in her shoes. The road she must have traveled was unimaginable.

A voice called from the hall. "Susan, it's time for your test." A nurse rolled a wheelchair through the door.

"She has gotten extremely weak since yesterday. Do you have any idea what is wrong with her?"

"Are you her husband?"

"Husband? No, no," he said backing away.

Susan opened her eyes and faintly laughed but thought what a great catch he would be. "I have no husband. I am a single mom."

"Oh, I'm sorry. Single mom, huh? That's cool," the young nurse replied, helping Susan into the wheelchair.

Jerry scurried over to the door and opened it for them. Susan reached out and grabbed his hand as they passed. The nurse abruptly stopped.

"What's your wife's name?" Susan asked.

"Mary. My wife's name is Mary."

Susan said no more. The nurse continued to push her from the room. Jerry watched as the nurse rolled Susan's weak body down the hallway. She was frail and could barely sit upright in the chair. He watched as they stop at the nurses' station and Susan pointed to him. Jerry turned around and glanced behind him, thinking someone else must be there, but there was no one. The nurse continued to push the wheelchair to the awaiting elevator, and they disappeared.

With his head lowered, Jerry somberly headed toward his wife's room. He searched for words to undo his wrong, but he didn't find any. What would his wife do? Would she get sick again? Would she be mad at him for deceiving her? His stomach got weak and ached. He felt nauseated as anxiety overtook him.

"Hey, Mr. Hudson," Carmen called out as he passed the nurses' station.

"Yes," he answered.

"I don't agree with what you and Miss Shaw are doing. I think it is utterly wrong, but it's not up to me to criticize you or her."

"I know," Jerry responded in a disheartened voice.

"Miss Shaw asked me to take her baby in to see your wife."

"She did?" he replied excitedly.

"You say that like you didn't know."

"I didn't know. She was so sick, I didn't want to ask her."

"Evidently, she knew what you wanted because she had the nurse stop here to relay her wishes to me. I have agreed to do this, but I think it is morally wrong. When she was sick and not expected to live, I could understand why you did it, but she's better now. What do you think this is going to do to your wife when you do tell her the truth?"

"I don't know. I want to tell her, but I'm afraid. I fear she might get worse again."

"Are you scared she might get worse or she might leave you for lying to her?"

Rage raced across his face. "Who do you think you are to talk to me like that? What I do with my wife is my business and doesn't concern you. I will lie, and I will pay any amount of money that I have to in order to keep my wife alive, and that is my business, not yours. If you don't like it, you can remove yourself from her care!"

"Of course you should do what it takes to keep your wife alive."

"If you have a problem with anything that I do Nurse Carmen, I suggest you keep it to yourself."

"I'm very sorry, Mr. Hudson. I was out of line. I'll go get the baby and bring her to your room."

Carmen hurried away toward the nursery. Jerry leaned on the counter at the nurses' station with his head in his palms and sweat beading across his forehead.

"Are you okay?"

He turned to see Donna standing behind him.

"Donna, how are you?"

"I'm fine, but how are you?"

"I'm good."

"And your wife? How is she? She's not . . . "

"No, no. She's much better. Her cancer is in remission. She is sitting up and eating by herself. You should come by and see her."

"You are kidding! That's great. I never thought she would make it through the other night."

"Nor did anyone else, but she looks so much better. Please come by and sit with her."

"I will, but I can't stay but a minute. I am no longer on this floor. I just wanted to stop in and check on Susan Shaw and a few of my other patients. I am so happy to hear she is better. I know you must be ecstatic."

"There are no words to tell you how I feel. All I can say is, *thank God*. He has to be watching over us, and listen, speaking of which, I'm not sure what happened, but Susan Shaw told me to make sure I tell you that her baby did it. I think it must have been all the drugs they have her on."

Jerry looked down the hall and saw Carmen coming with the baby. "Look, I'll talk with you later. They're bringing Gracie in for my wife. I want to be in the room." He glanced around, and then whispered, "She said God was the father of her baby."

"Who said it?"

"Susan. I'll talk with you later."

Donna grabbed his arm as he started to walk away. "It's not the drugs. She really believes God is the father of Gracie."

"What? That's ludicrous."

"Please, will you have dinner with me in the cafeteria? There's something I need to tell you."

There was desperation in her eyes. Without thinking, he

abruptly answered, "Yes, I'll have dinner with you, but I really have to go."

He pulled away and hustled down to his wife's room.

10

Hours had passed and dinnertime arrived. Donna was impatiently waiting for Jerry in the cafeteria. Thirty minutes past the time of their meeting, he still had not shown up. She presumed he wasn't coming, so she ordered her food and sat solemnly at a corner table, nibbling her fries. She sipped her soda, thinking how she could convince Jerry of what she believed.

"Donna, I am so sorry I'm late. I had to wait for Mary to fall asleep."

Donna jumped with excitement. "How is she?"

"She is great! It's unbelievable how much she has improved. The doctors are baffled. They say it could only be a miracle."

"Do you believe that?"

"Believe it's a miracle? Yes, of course I do. That's the only explanation. She was on her deathbed."

Donna slammed both her hands on the table and leaned forward. She stared deeply into his eyes and paused for a few seconds. "I know this is going to be hard for you to believe, but I think Susan is right."

"Right about what?"

"Right about Gracie. I believe she is the daughter of God."

"The daughter of God!" he shouted. "What in the hell are you talking about? Is everyone on drugs around here?"

"Listen. Remember when Gracie's hands were bleeding?"

"Yes."

"Susan had told me earlier that God had told her that her child would be marked. We examined her from top to bottom, and there was nothing on her at all. I thought Susan might just

101

be having some kind of flashback from all the drugs. I didn't believe her either. Then, when your wife was holding Gracie and her hands began to bleed, I knew."

"You knew what?"

"I knew Susan was right. Gracie has stigmata."

"Stigmata," Jerry rubbed his hand across his hair and shifted back into his chair.

"Yes, stigmata, you saw it. Her hands were bleeding, both of them. In a couple of hours, there were no signs at all. There were no marks on her. Then, your wife got better right after that. Think about it."

"Think about it? I think you are crazy as hell. That's what I think. Stigmata? Daughter of God? Have you been taking drugs too? Tell me, what is going on in this hospital?"

"No, I do not do drugs. And this has nothing to do with the hospital. I know it's hard to believe. I didn't believe it either at first. And I'm still not sure she is the daughter of God, but I think she was put here by God."

"And so were we," he said sarcastically.

"Yes we were, but not for the same reason. Little Gracie, I think, was put here to spread the word, to make us believe in something again. To make miracles happen, to heal the sick. She has a purpose here. Think about what I'm telling you. Think about your wife. Gracie healed her. She is the reason I have no doubts about who she is. I wasn't sure whether to believe or not, but now I do."

Jerry shook his head. "I don't know. That's just so far out there. My wife got better because of Gracie, that is true, but it is only true because she wants to be a mother so badly."

"Being a mother has nothing to do with it. She hung on so she could give birth before she died, and she did that. Right after she gave birth, she was ready to die. It has nothing to do with her wanting to be a mother. It is because Gracie wanted her to live."

"Gracie wanted her to live? Gracie is a newborn. Babies don't know anything about living."

"You are right, she doesn't, but God does. God must have a purpose for your wife; somehow, she is connected to Gracie."

"She is connected because I asked for Gracie, remember?"

"No, you asked for a baby. When I brought the first baby to her, there was no change. Even when I brought Gracie the first time, there was no change. But when Gracie's hands starting bleeding, that is when it happened. I'm sure of that now."

"You're sure of that, but I'm not. That's preposterous. I'm not going to put this out of my mind completely, but I'm not going to believe it either. I need more proof, and I still don't know if I would believe it or not. The daughter of God? I just can't buy it—a healer of some sort, maybe," he said, shaking his head in disbelief.

"The next time you hold the baby, look at her. I mean really look at her. She is so alert for a newborn. And her smell—have you smelled the floral aroma she has? That is another sign of stigmata. She has stigmata, I'm sure of it."

"Come on, Donna, look at her mother. She's a drug addict for God's sake, and she's homeless. Don't you think God would have chosen a better person for the mother of his child? You know, someone like the Virgin Mary."

"Do we really know who Mary was? We only know what we've read. Maybe she really wasn't a virgin. Maybe she was a woman of the night, a poor peasant girl with nowhere to go. Do you think man would write that about her?"

"That's your point? Man wrote the Bible."

"No, that is not my point . . . not all of it. I don't think she was a virgin. And I do believe, just maybe, she was already married to Joseph. But because Jesus was a wonderful healer, something no one had ever seen before, a story had to evolve. A story of a magnificent woman who gave birth to a healer, a story that would never be believed in our day and time—just like a story of a drug addicted woman having a baby by God. No one is going to believe a woman like Susan could have such a baby, but think how wonderful that would be if it is so. To me, God says no matter what kind of person you are, you are still worthy. He does not judge you on what you own or what you can buy. He judges you on your faith. Susan says she never lost faith. Even when she cursed God, she still believed in Him. Susan told me these things, and I must say it does make sense. And by the way, your wife's name is Mary."

Jerry sat quietly and listened to Donna talk. She continued to tell him some of the stories Susan had revealed to her. She told him about her cutting her wrists and trying to overdose. She told the story of how Susan thought Gracie was conceived.

"I just can't understand why God would allow her to go through so much hell and still carry His child."

"Think about it, Jerry, she should have died and surely she should have lost the baby. Gracie should have been addicted to drugs, too, but she isn't. God has a plan for her. There is a reason for all of this. I don't understand it, but I am not turning my back on it either. I want to help find the answer. I would love to be a follower and help spread the message, whatever it turns out to be."

"Well, you got a good start. You sure overloaded my mind."

"So you believe me?"

"Oh, I didn't say that. I don't know what to believe. I just meant I have a lot to think about. Look, I know your lunch has to be over. I appreciate what you've told me, I think. I'll keep an open mind, and I'll sit some more with Susan and talk to her about all this."

"Be sure you don't let her know that you don't believe her. She will flip out if you do. If you get a chance, get on the Internet and look up *stigmata*. You'll be surprised."

"I'll try. Thanks."

Donna and Jerry walked and talked as they left the cafeteria and entered the elevator. Jerry pushed the button to the second floor, where he was to get off and he pushed the fifth button for Donna's floor. They retreated to opposite corners and silently watched the elevator doors close tightly. There was a jolt as the gray metal box began to move upward. Their conversation had grown deeply strange and they were both relieved it had ended.

"I will talk to you later," Jerry said as the bell sounded and the doors slid open.

Donna nodded and watched as Jerry stepped from the elevator and the doors slid closed behind him. She continued to the fifth floor where new patients awaited. Her mind was cluttered with hopes that she had gotten through to Jerry. She was fretful he would never believe her.

11

Jerry took the dreaded walk to his wife's room. Before he could enter, he heard screams coming from down the hallway.

"Ahhh," the voice echoed through the air.

Shards of shattered glass impelled the atmosphere. Banging and clashing noises came from the end of the corridor. Nurses scurried in frenzy toward the destructive sounds.

Just as the white uniformed men and women reached the end of the corridor and pushed open a door, a flash of pastel flowers bombarded the hallway, smashing against the opposite wall, barely missing an elderly hospital worker. Pink carnations, yellow roses, and white daisies lay scattered on the white marble floor, along with black soil and torn leaves. Water trickled into the crevices of the wall and slid down to flow across the slippery floor.

An intern's voice echoed over the intercom, "We need a sedative in here." And a nurse quickly ran down the hall with syringe in hand.

From the doorway of Mary's room, Jerry stood and watched curiously, but he had no idea what was going on and who was making all the noise. There was a lot of screaming, yelling, and commotion as things were being broken. The door was swiftly pulled tight to muffle the sound. Intrigued bystanders began to gather and talk among themselves. Patients and visitors congregated in the hallway, but no one had a clue.

After a few minutes, everything seemed to get quiet, and most of the observers started returning to their rooms. But a few who could not resist continued to be nosy. Jerry shrugged his shoulders. He had enough on his plate and was not about to add any more. He slowly eased open the wooden door to his wife's room and stepped inside.

"What was all that commotion out there?" she asked.

"I'm not sure. I waited outside the door for a nurse to come by, but no one ever did. Don't worry about it. How are you feeling, honey?"

"I feel great. I'm getting stronger."

Jerry slid a chair away from the wall and sat beside his wife and Gracie. His wife's face was remarkable. She had the glowing complexion of a new mother as blood vessels transferred color back into her frail body. The grayish tint that had appeared on the skin over her cheekbones had disappeared. Her heart was flowing with joy and ticking a perfect rhythm. Her health had changed suddenly—physically and spiritually. She was alive.

"Jerry, she looks so perfect, but have they checked her blood yet? Do they know if she has melanoma? I didn't pass it on to her, did I?" Mary's voice filled with concern.

"Calm down, honey."

Jerry stood up and pushed the blanket away from her shoulders. "She is perfect. Nothing at all is wrong with her, honey. Please don't worry. She's fine."

Mary kissed Gracie's face. She held her lips tightly against her forehead, and then, slowly, she pulled her away.

"Every time I hold her, I feel warmth go through me. It feels almost like she has a heater inside her warming me from the inside out. I think she is healing me."

"A heater that is healing you, honey? Really? We might have to get your medication changed."

"Yes. Strange, I know, but she is so special. There's something about her. Here, you hold her." Mary lifted Gracie up and stretched out her arms.

"I believe you. That's all right, I don't need to hold her."

"Come on, hold her," she repeated, still holding Gracen out

in her arms.

Hesitantly, he took Gracen from the comfort of Mary's arms. He sauntered to the window and held her in the bright light of the sun. As he looked intently into her eyes, Gracie stared back and gave a slight smile Jerry could not help but return.

"Well, I don't feel the heat, but she does make you feel warm and cozy inside. I assume it is warmth from the heart. You know, love. You can't help but love her."

"That I do," Mary said, reaching out for her.

"Hi folks, it's time for Gracie to go back to the nursery," a nurse said, entering the room. "Baby needs to get her rest."

"Can't she stay just a little longer?"

"I'm sorry, hospital rules. We need to let you get some rest too. You don't want to overdo it."

"But I feel fine," Mary replied, retrieving Gracie from Jerry.

"We have to keep you healthy. You don't want to get sick again, do you?"

"She's right, my love. Gracie can come back later, can't she, nurse?"

"What do you mean, can't she? Of course she can," Mary replied.

The nurse glanced up at Jerry and without saying a word, she gently lifted Gracie from Mary's arms.

"Tell everyone *bye*," the nurse raised Gracie's tiny little hand and waved.

"Bye, precious angel," Mary whispered. "Mommy will see you later."

"Excuse me nurse," Mary called out.

"Yes ma'am, what can I help you with?"

"What was all the noise down the hallway? Is everything all right?"

"Oh, yes ma'am. One of our patients is having a little trouble. But I'm sure she'll be all right."

"Which patient?" Jerry quickly asked.

"I'm not quite sure. I think it may have been Miss Shaw."

"Miss Shaw! Is she all right?"

"She's not my patient, sir."

"Who is that, Jerry?" Mary asked. "Do you know her?"

"I met her at the nursery the other day. She's a new single mother in here."

"Ah, that's a shame."

"Well I need to get this little one back. You need to get some rest, Mary."

The door closed behind the young nurse. Jerry wanted to run out behind her, but he had no reason. He wondered what had happened to Susan. He had to come up with an excuse to go see for himself, but there was none.

After an hour had passed, he had run out of things to say and told Mary she needed to sleep. He dimmed the lights and watched quietly for her eyelids to slowly close. He pulled the blanket around her shoulders, tiptoed to the door, and slipped into the hallway.

The first nurse to come in view was Carmen. He sped across the corridor to her side.

"Can you please tell me how Susan is?"

Carmen was filling out a chart and never looked up. "I'm sorry, Mr. Hudson, but you are not family, and I cannot discuss her condition with you."

"Come on, Carmen, you know I have a relationship, so to speak, with this young woman."

"You are still not family, sir. You know we can only give out information to people whose names are on the list." She looked up from the chart and raised her eyebrows. "And you are not on the list."

"What about Gracie?"

"Oh, I'm glad you brought that up. Susan said you are no longer allowed to see her."

"Please Carmen, don't do this. It will kill my wife. What

will I tell her?"

"The truth would be a good idea. This deception that you all created was bound to end this way. I told you and Donna this was not right, and you did it anyway. Now you'll have to figure out a way to fix it."

"This will kill my wife, and you know it will. I must go see Susan for myself. I have to go talk with her."

"I'm sorry, Mr. Hudson, I really am, but you can't see her either. Her condition is not good, and she has been moved to the intensive care unit. Only immediate family members can see her."

"What's happened to her? Is she going to be okay? Do you know how long she'll be in intensive care?"

"I can't address any of those questions. I'm really sorry."

"Who can?"

"Who can what?"

"Who can grant me permission to see her?"

"No one can. There are no family members on the list. And she specifically said you were not to see her baby. You can surely talk with the hospital administration, but I don't believe it will matter any."

"As much money as I've donated to this hospital, it had better matter. We'll see about it right now."

"You know, Mr. Hudson, it's not always about money."

"That's where you are wrong, my dear. It's always about money."

Jerry stomped away toward the elevator and disappeared. Carmen stood shaking her head as she watched him fade from sight. She slipped the chart into a clear plastic slot on the wall, lifted her stethoscope from the counter, and began to make her rounds.

12

Jerry was quick to tap on the window of the administrator's office, which was on the first floor. The lights appeared to be off and no one inside.

Jerry cupped his hands around his eyes and surveyed the room. There was no movement. He sucked at his lip and gave a loud sigh.

A hospital staffer noticed him from across the hall. He watched with curiosity for a brief moment, and then slid his chair away from his desk and came over.

"Excuse me, sir, is there a problem?"

Jerry quickly turned about only to see a staff person at his side. "Yes, there is. Where is everyone in this office?" he asked, pointing to the empty room.

"I'm sorry, sir, but it's after hours. This office closed for the weekend at five o'clock. Is there something I can help you with?"

"When will it reopen?"

"At nine Monday morning."

"Monday! I can't wait until Monday."

"What is the problem, sir? Maybe I can help you."

"The problem is I need to see a dear friend in the intensive care unit, and I am not family. There is no family, and I'm all she has."

"You said *she*. Is she your fiancée?"

"Good God, no! She's just someone in need. I've been visiting with her on the maternity ward. Something has happened to her, and no one will tell me what."

"So you just met this woman?"

"Yes, a few days ago. But it's more than just that. I really need to talk to her. My wife's health may depend on it."

"Your wife? This story is getting a little bizarre. Maybe you should return on Monday."

"I can't wait until Monday. Look here, my name is Jerry Hudson. I have donated quite a large sum of money to many charitable functions of this hospital. I know rules are rules, but all rules are meant to be broken. I have paid my dues, and now I'm requesting a payback."

"I'm sorry you feel that way, sir, but charity has nothing to do with the law and hospital policy. I have to ask you to wait until Monday."

"Look here, you get on the damn phone and call somebody down here, or I'll have your job. I don't mean to be disrespectful, but like I said, this is about my wife."

"No need to get rude, sir. What is this young woman's name?"

"Her name is Susan Shaw. Call the head nurse on the maternity floor. Her name is Carmen Bentz, and she can bring you up to date on the whole story."

"If you want to have a seat in the waiting room down the hall on the left, I'll see what I can do."

"I'll just wait right here."

"But sir, I don't know how long this may take."

"That's all right, I'll wait here."

"Suit yourself," the worker replied throwing his hands in the air.

Jerry paced the floor from one side to the next, east to west, north to south. He began to count the square tiles as he walked. He incessantly glanced at his watch, questioning the time that it was taking for the staffer to return. He tapped on the glass of the timepiece and put it to his ear to make sure it was still working. He looked down the corridor for a clock to make sure the time was the same. He then pinned his body to the wall, with knee bent and one leg resting against the cold plaster. He tilted his head back and closed his eyes. He visualized Mary getting better and the strength that Gracen seemed to give her. A small grin surfaced on his lips as he reminisced about all he had endured over the last few days.

"Oh what a story this will be," he said.

"Excuse me, sir."

Jerry opened his eyes and collected himself. The man had returned with the answer, one Jerry was confident to be in his favor.

"I am sorry to say we cannot help you."

"What? What do you mean you can't help me?"

"I tried my best, sir, but Miss Shaw left instructions that you were not to come near her. If we allowed this to happen, we could be looking at a lawsuit."

"Look here, you don't understand. This could be life and death here. If my wife does not get to see that baby, it will kill her."

Nurse Bentz told me the story and I passed it on. The truth is, sir, Donna should have never let this happen. Maybe over the weekend, things will be better, and Miss Shaw will change her mind."

"Oh my God! You people don't get it. My wife will die. She will die! I can't take this. I can't believe this is happening. I've got to get out of here and get some fresh air. I need to go think this out and clear my head. There has to be a solution."

"I'm really sorry I couldn't help you, sir."

13

Back on the maternity floor, Mary was hysterical. No one would bring the baby in to see her. Why wouldn't they let her see her baby girl?

And to make matters worse, Jerry had been gone for hours, and no one knew his whereabouts. He did not respond to any calls or messages that were left on his cell phone. Everyone was beginning to think the worst.

Mary begged for her baby and could not comprehend why she was not allowed to see her own child. But time after time her request was denied. Her mind raced with concern about what could be wrong. She continued to ask, and every time, she got the same answer. The doctor would be in shortly to speak with her. Nothing more.

Her blood pressure spiked and her anxiety was hard to contain. She began to convince herself her baby was ill and might not make it. She begged to hold her one last time, but the hospital could not take the chance of a lawsuit. Her body was seized by a fierce fever and began to convulse. Her mind was plagued by irrational fears, and to protect her from sheer madness, it began to shut down. There was no medical reason for the change other than heartbreak.

After the third hour had passed, the doctor and nurses agreed it would be in the best interest of Mary's health to tell her the truth. They had no excuse for keeping Gracen from her, none that would make sense. Gracen was not hers, and the time had come to tell her.

A mild sedative was given to quiet her, and the medical staff gathered around the bed.

"Is my baby all right? Please tell me what is wrong with her. Please, just tell me the truth. All I'm asking for is the truth."

Tears rolled from her eyes, and her lips quivered as she spoke.

Dr. Bolt grasped her hand and sat in the chair next to the bed.

"Oh no, oh God, no," she cried out.

"Mary there has been a great mistake, and I am sincerely sorry that you have to go through this. Your husband was supposed to have corrected this and told you the truth, but we cannot locate him. All of the doctors thought that you would not have survived this long; your recovery has been remarkable. Your husband, although he did something terribly wrong, did it for you, because he loves you. I'm sure he had your best interests in mind."

"What did he do?"

"Mary, your baby was stillborn. She did not survive the birth. The baby that has been coming to you was not yours; she was borrowed from another mother."

"Borrowed? No, no. God, please no. I don't want to hear anymore. You are lying." Mary cupped her hands over her ears. "She looks just like me. She has my eyes and Jerry's smile. She is mine. She is mine. You all are crazy," Mary squalled. "Please don't take her from me. I can't live without my baby." Tears flooded her face. She could barely catch her breath. "Get out. Get out of my room. I want all of you out of here."

"Mary, we can't leave you alone in this state of mind. It could be dangerous. You're trembling. We need to get your vital signs. Nurse, come over here and give me her reading," he ordered one of the floor nurses.

"Don't touch me. Let me die. I can't live without my baby. She's all I have. She gave me life again, and now you want to take her from me."

Mary grabbed the doctor's arm and pleaded with him.

"Please don't take her from me, please. I want to see her, please get her for me," Mary begged. "I want to see my baby," she shouted loudly around the room.

The room grew silent. Everyone felt her pain and sadness. She was desperate, heartbroken, and now weary of life. She wanted to indulge her suffering in silence as she had suffered for so long. She had now been violated and betrayed by all whom she had trusted. The day was drawing to a close with the battle fought and no victory at the end. She lay sobbing, weak, and weary with grief. Her happiness was gone in a flash, and now her life held no meaning.

She sat up in bed and began to hyperventilate. Her breath was short and quick. She clutched her throat and began to grasp for air. Her eyes darted back and forth, and her body lurched backward and convulsed.

Everyone began to work on her immediately. Her blood pressure was dangerously high. Her temperature had spiked to 104, and her body was beginning to go into shock.

"Give her two milligrams of Ativan. We've got to get her stable."

"Her pulse is failing, sir. I think we're losing her."

"We are not going to lose her."

After two hours of constant medical procedures, Mary was finally stabilized. She had a massive heart attack and appeared to have had a stroke. There was swelling in the brain, and the doctor made the decision to put her in an induced coma to protect her from any more serious side effects.

The doctor went over the orders with Carmen. "She is to have around-the-clock care, and she is not to be left alone under any circumstances," he said.

"I'll make sure someone is always here," Carmen, replied.

"Good. If there are any changes, I want to know immediately. And keep trying to contact her husband. If he pops in here, we might have our hands full."

"I'll get right on it. I can't believe he hasn't been here. He is never too far away. He must have needed to get some air."

"You make sure that nurse is gone too."

"Yes sir."

Carmen paged Donna to come to the nurses' station, and as much as she liked working with Donna, she had to comply with the doctor's orders. Donna had made a very foolish mistake that might cause this woman to lose her life and generate a lawsuit against the hospital. She had allowed her personal feelings to interfere with her professional duty.

Donna breezed in unaware of the consequences that lay ahead. The two nurses stepped out of sight into the office that was situated at the left corner behind the counter. The other nurses who ventured in and out of the station heard bits and pieces as the voices behind the closed door grew louder and carried through the wall.

"I told you it was wrong," Carmen shouted.

"I stand by what I did. It helped her at the time. If it weren't for that baby, she would have died days ago. Gracen gave her life. Ten days ago, she was on her deathbed. If this is how you all feel, so be it."

Donna ran from the office and slammed the door behind her. She had been seriously reprimanded for her role in the deceit and was fired. She stormed through the station, lifted a box from the storage unit, and began to gather her belongings. She said her goodbyes and solemnly entered the elevator.

As the heavy doors slowly opened, she stepped into the corridor. She glanced around her surroundings and left the building.

She took the long walk across the dimly lit parking lot carrying the box. Carefully holding it with one hand, she reached into her black purse and began rummaging for her car keys.

As she approached her little red Honda, she recognized Jerry slumped over the steering wheel in his car, two spaces over.

"Are you all right, Jerry?" she yelled out.

There was no answer. He didn't even acknowledge her.

She shifted the box from her hip and slid it into the trunk of her car. Quietly, she walked to Jerry's Cadillac and peered inside.

"Jerry, can you hear me?" She tapped on the driver's side window and called his name for a second time, but still there was no response. She jiggled the door handle, but of course, it was locked.

"Jerry, Jerry, can you hear me? Open the door," she shouted. He didn't move.

Frantically, she pounded the window and moved to the windshield, then the hood. She jerked at the door handle once more. Slowly, Jerry raised his head. He was wobbly and incoherent.

"Unlock the door and let me in," Donna thumped at the window and pointed to the lock.

"Wha . . . t's wrong?" Jerry slurred his words.

"I need you to open the door, Jerry."

He closed his eyes back and slumped back over the steering wheel.

"No, no, Jerry, open the door. Hit the button and unlock the damn car." She tapped on the window a little harder.

Jerry rocked back in his seat and clenched his eyes tightly. He then fumbled around the door slapping at the lock until it clicked. Donna immediately clutched the handle and jerked open the door.

"Are you hurt or sick? Why are you out here? Oh, wow!" Donna took a step back and gasped air, waving her hand in front of her face.

"How much have you had to drink tonight?"

"Don't know and don't care," he murmured. "I'm a grown man, by God, and I can drink if I want to. Want some?" He reached across to the passenger's seat and pulled out a bottle of vodka.

"Good ole vodka, huh," Donna replied laughing. Well, Jerry, what are you going to do tonight? Where are you going to stay?"

"Gonna stay right here."

"You can't stay here in this parking lot and you can't go into the hospital like this either."

"The hospital, are you sick? Why are we at the hospital?"

"No, I'm not sick, I work here, remember? Well that is I used to work here. I got fired tonight."

"Fired, somebody fired you? I'm sorry you got fired. You wanna come work for me?"

"No, Jerry. Right now, I just want to find a place for you to go. You look like hell."

"Take me home, baby," he shouted waving his hand up to her.

Donna laughed, "I don't know where you live."

"I don't either; take me to your house. I'll sleep with you tonight," he slurred, trying to get out of his car.

"I don't think so; you need to hold on a minute."

He leaned toward Donna and whispered, "I have money, and I can pay you for your . . . whatever."

"Jerry, you're drunk. Just keep your pants on, and let me think."

"Okay, if you don't want to make some extra money, I understand."

"Come on. Let me help you to my car."

"Now you are talking, sweetie."

"Don't get excited, I'm just going to give you a place to sleep this off. You can sleep on my sofa until the morning."

"Okey-dokey."

Jerry plopped one leg from the car and began to slide across the seat. Donna reached in and grabbed his other leg and helped him to his feet. He staggered, swaying back and forth. Donna put her arm around his waist and steadied him toward her car. He wobbled with rubbery legs leaning against her body and making it difficult for her to guide him.

Finally, after several attempts, he slumped to the seat. Donna fastened his seat belt and made her way to the driver's side. She stood quietly for a moment, with her hands resting on the top of her car, wondering if this was going to be another costly decision. She had already lost her job, so what else could it possibly hurt? She opened her door and scooted in beneath the steering wheel. She had not a clue that the hospital had been looking for him. No one had ever revealed that to her.

"Okay, Jerry, it's late and I'm tired. We are going to get you to my house, drink a few cups of coffee, and let you sleep this off. Does that sound like a good plan to you?"

"Sounds like a plan," he slurred.

With that being said, they drove away together, leaving St. Francis Hospital and the bright lights of the city of Charleston.

All the traffic lights seemed to be green at the same time, and Donna sailed right through them without hesitation. Making her way over the Ashley River Bridge, she fought with herself about the right thing to do with Jerry.

Donna glanced over at Jerry only to witness a passed out drunk. His uncombed, beautiful salt-and-pepper hair was dull and drooped over his collar. He certainly didn't look like a rich man. Jerry's head bobbed up and down with his chin slapping his chest as the car traveled across the bumpy bridge. Donna grinned, watching this millionaire travel without a care in the world.

A Holiday Inn was situated between the east and westbound spans of the bridge. When it came into sight as she neared the bottom of the first span, she began to think of another plan. It was one that seemed to be more appropriate for the circumstances that both she and Jerry had fallen prey to.

She quickly swerved between the palmetto trees that sat at the entrance welcoming the newcomers to the hotel. Slowly bringing the car to a stop, she began to wake Jerry.

"Hey buddy, I think it would be better for you to sleep it off at the hotel."

Jerry wobbled his head with his eyes tightly squinted. "You're taking me to a hotel?"

"Yep, as soon as I put this car in park, I will come around and help you to your room."

"I have a room?"

"You will in just a few minutes."

Donna parked her car and helped Jerry stagger to the front desk. She reached into her purse and retrieved her red patent leather wallet. She displayed her American Express card and began to fill out the necessary paper work.

"How much is a room just for tonight?"

"It will be $175.00 plus tax."

"Jerry, ole boy, you owe me."

The clerk finished the transaction and handed Donna a key card. She put her arm around Jerry to steady him and continued to the elevator.

As the doors opened, Jerry stumbled to the back corner while Donna pressed the button to the sixth floor. The elevator moved with a jolt, leaving their stomachs on the floor. Jerry cupped his hand to his mouth.

"I think I'm going to be sick."

"Breathe, Jerry. You'll be fine. We're almost there. Come on, come on, come on," Donna repeated to the elevator.

Finally, the metal box shuddered to a halt and the doors opened. Luckily, the room was directly across from the elevator and they made it inside just in time for Jerry to empty the contents of his stomach into the toilet.

"Can't hold your alcohol, huh, Jerry?"

"Sorry, Donna, it's been a long time since I've been drunk."

"So, what's the occasion?"

"Occasion?" Jerry repeated with disgust, "Like you don't know."

"I don't know if I know or not. What's going on?"

"You didn't know that Susan took the baby from me."

"You're kidding."

Jerry ran some cold water in the sink and splashed it on his face. Donna began to fill the coffee pot to help him sober up.

"I thought you knew. I'm not sure what has happened. All I know is Susan said I couldn't get Gracen anymore. She is really sick and no one will tell me what's wrong."

"Gracen is sick?"

"No, Susan."

"I didn't know anything about Susan. I was told your wife was in a coma because she was told the truth, but no one told me Susan was sick."

"My wife is in a coma? What are you talking about? My wife is not in a coma. Susan is in a coma. You were fired?" Jerry asked, dazed and confused.

"Yes, I told you that earlier."

"Donna, I'm drunk. I'm just now coming to my senses. I don't remember too much of anything other than getting sick and now feeling better."

"Here, come sit down. The coffee is finished; let me get us a cup so you'll feel even better. Maybe then we can make some sense out of what's happening."

Donna walked over to the coffee pot near the window. As she poured the hot liquid into the cup, she surveyed the Charleston harbor. What a magnificent sight it was. She filled two cups and turned slightly toward Jerry.

"Do you think you can sit out on the balcony in the cool breeze? That might make you feel a little better."

"Sure, Donna, I feel more weak than drunk. The fresh air probably will do me good."

Donna walked over and unlocked the sliding glass door. She returned for the two cups of coffee and stepped out from the room. Jerry followed.

They both sat down at the small round table and sipped at their hot brew. The night was beautiful. The moon was full, the stars were bright, and a cool breeze blew across the veranda.

"What a night."

"Yep," Donna replied.

"So what happened to you tonight? What's with the drinking?" she asked, sipping on her hot coffee.

"I don't know, Donna. You know I really love my wife. She's always been my backbone. Without her, life just doesn't seem worth living."

"I understand, Jerry, but life does go on. If your wife passes, she would want you to continue. Mary knows that you are a wonderful person and it would not be fair for this world not to have the love and affection you carry in your heart. Don't become bitter. You'll always have your memories."

"Easier said . . . I just wanted to make her happy. This baby brought her such joy. I can't understand what happened with Susan. It makes no sense to me. Everything seemed to be going just fine, then, all of a sudden, when she got sick, she went crazy."

"What do you mean when she got sick?"

"Something happened to her. She was throwing vases of flowers into the hallway at the hospital. She was screaming hysterically and cursing every breath. No one would tell me what had happened to her. I asked Carmen, and she said I wasn't family or on the list, so she couldn't tell me a thing."

"I was unaware anything had happened."

"I tried to go over her head, but I got nowhere."

"Huh, it's strange that Carmen didn't mention it to me. She just said your wife was gravely ill and in a coma."

"What? Are you sure?"

"Yes, I told you that earlier."

"I know, but I thought you had gotten the two confused."

"No, I thought that was why you were drinking. I assumed after you told your wife the truth, you couldn't handle the outcome and started to drink."

"She doesn't know the truth. I couldn't tell her."

"Jerry, she knows. The hospital staff had to tell her."

"What!" He snapped into a rage. "They had no right. How could they have done that? You must have misunderstood."

"Earlier, you said Susan was in a coma. I thought that you were the one who was confused and that was the alcohol talking. The reason they gave was because Mary wanted to see her baby and the staff couldn't let her. She began to get hysterical and believed something was wrong with the infant. The hospital had no other choice. I presumed you were there."

"Hell no, I wasn't there. Where are my keys? I need to go."

"Your car is still at the hospital. I'll have to drive you."

"Oh my God. I can't believe this is happening. What's next?"

Jerry jumped to his feet and raced into the room. He paced around in turmoil. He was confused and chaotic. Donna followed close behind trying to calm him.

"Donna, if anything happens to her, it will be my fault. I've really screwed things up."

"I'm sorry, Jerry. Come on, let's go."

With the adrenaline rush, Jerry was now sober and perfectly coherent.

14

Jerry and Donna hurried to the elevator and swiftly left the building. After the vomiting, the hot coffee, and the shock of his wife's condition, Jerry had quickly sobered up. His mind-boggling confusion about his wife and Susan's illness was disturbing. Could it be possible for them both to be lying in a coma? What a bizarre coincidence.

The short distance back to the hospital was driven in silence. While traveling back across the Ashley River Bridge, Donna glanced out the window and felt the peace that hovered over the black water. It mirrored the image of the gigantic moon and rippled with the wake of a passing ship.

Jerry also watched through the window. He wondered how such a serene night could be hiding all this mayhem. If only the ocean could wash away the pain and sorrow, he would leap from the edge of the bridge and be swept away in the depths of the calming sea.

"Donna, what do you think will happen?" Jerry asked but never took his eyes from the water.

"Happen to what, Jerry?"

"To Mary. Was I wrong for what I did?"

"No Jerry, you were not wrong. I admire you for your determination to help your wife make it through her final moments with a smile on her face. Maybe we should have approached it in a different manner, but who would have thought she would survive?"

"She wouldn't have, if it weren't for that baby. She would have died last week."

"I agree. So is it wrong that you were given an extra week

and a couple of days to be with the woman you love? I don't think so."

"But if she knows her baby died in childbirth, she'll die of a broken heart. How can I live with myself?"

"You did what you felt was right, Jerry. Quit beating yourself up. You are a very good person."

"Thanks, Donna. You're a good person too. Here you are consoling me, taking me to a hotel, taxiing me around, and you don't even really know me. Why are you doing this?"

"I'm not sure. It just feels right. But let's put a lid on all that because we are here and we need to stay focused. Try to keep calm in the hospital, no matter what has happened. You do not want to give them any reason to have you escorted out."

"Yeah, yeah, I know," Jerry retorted, stepping from the car. "Hey Donna, how did you know I was staying at the Holiday Inn?"

"Staying there? I didn't. You mean you already had a room there?"

"Yes."

"What a coincidence. The more we do together, the weirder things get."

"Yep, I agree."

"By the way, you owe me $175.00."

"Not a problem," Jerry said reaching for his wallet.

"That can wait for later. You go see your wife, and I'll go check on Susan. Maybe the other floor doesn't know I've been fired. I'll pull her chart when I get inside the nurses' station and see what I can find out."

"Sounds like a plan. Thanks, Donna."

"No problem, catch you later."

The two separated in the lobby.

Jerry's blood pressure seemed to be rising as he rushed closer to the door of his wife's room. His face was flushed and sweat beaded along his forehead and trickled down his cheeks. His hands were clammy as he placed them on the door handle. He withdrew them for a moment and wiped them on his trousers. The fear of the unknown pried against his strength. He was terrified of what he was going to witness on the other side of the heavy door. Slowly he pushed the wooden door open and slipped inside.

The room was still and dimly lit. The sucking sounds of the machines echoed from wall to wall. "Sshhhhhk. Sshhhhhk." He covered his mouth with his left hand as the image of his wife came into view. Her long dark hair had been tucked neatly into a ball and placed into blue hospital cap. Her beautiful face was a chalky gray. Its natural color once again was depleted. Her facial skin was wrinkled from white tape that was wrapped to secure tubes that were running from her mouth to a breathing machine located at the left side of the bed. An IV, a blood pressure cup, and a heart rate monitor were also connected to her delicate body. She lay disembodied, with her eyes closed and her head falling limp to one side.

A nurse sat quietly on the right side of the room and stood upon Jerry's entrance.

"Are you Mr. Hudson?" she asked.

He paused, and then answered somberly, "Yes I am."

"Everyone has been searching for you. I was told to have you report to the nurses' station if you arrived here."

"What for?"

"I'm not sure, sir."

"Look at my wife. Look what you all have done to her." His voice deepened to a growl and seemed to vibrate with each word. He turned his back coldly to the young nurse and tried to compose himself.

"Please calm down, Mr. Hudson."

He quickly turned around. "How can I calm down looking at my wife's lifeless body? It's my fault she is like this. It's all my fault."

"Please sir, come with me."

The nurse placed her hand on his back and gently guided him toward the door. He stopped and stood steadfast without movement. She eased around him and opened the door. Sluggishly, he turned and shadowed close behind her.

"So, what do they need to see me for this time?"

"I'm not sure, Mr. Hudson."

Making their way down the corridor, he saw Carmen working at the nurses' station. She caught sight of him striding her way.

She returned the chart she had been working on and leaned down and told the nurse on duty not to let anyone disturb her unless there was an emergency. The nurse nodded and Carmen rounded the counter and walked toward Jerry.

"Hello Mr. Hudson, we've been worried about you."

"It's not me that you should concern yourself with."

"Let's not get hasty with any words. Please walk with me to my office. There are some things that need to be discussed."

"You've got that right."

The two continued on, side by side without another word. The hallway was quiet and a chill hovered in the air. The patients were quietly sleeping as the night was disappearing and morning was approaching unannounced.

Carmen abruptly stopped and began to fumble with a key that hung around her neck. She wiggled it back and forth until a loud click was heard. Pushing the door open, she stepped inside, holding the door for Jerry. He swerved around her and continued on to a chair that sat near a window on the south side of the hospital.

"As you know, I was not in favor of the decision to deceive your wife. But it is none of my business what you do in your private life."

"I meant no harm. I did what I did for her benefit. And I will never forgive this hospital for what you have done to her."

"When we couldn't find you, we had no choice but to tell

your wife the truth. Unfortunately, it was not a wise decision. This whole mess only seems to get deeper."

"How is that?"

"Susan regained consciousness for a short period last night. She asked for Father Wilkins."

"What does that have to do with me?"

"Please, let me finish. Because it was late, we couldn't reach the priest. So she asked for me."

Carmen adjusted herself nervously in the desk chair. "She wanted to know what I thought of you."

"Me. Why?"

"Because she requested for us to give you her baby until she was better."

"WHAT!"

"She had us call a notary to draw up papers to assign temporary custody of Gracen to you."

"To me?"

"Yes, to you."

"But why? What am I going to do with a baby?"

"The same thing you would have done with yours, had she survived."

Jerry swiftly stood up. "But that was different, that was my baby."

"So are you saying you could not love this one like that . . . like your own? Maybe I was wrong about your integrity."

"I don't know what I am capable of. And why did she ask for you? Like you said earlier, you've always been against this."

"You are right. I was against it. Susan wanted to know what I thought about you, as a person—good, bad, or indifferent. And I told her the truth. Even though I did not agree with what you did, it did help your wife get better. I do believe your heart is in the right place. Look here, Jerry," Carmen slid the chair back with her legs and walked to his side. "This baby helped your wife one time. Who knows? Maybe she can do it again."

"But my wife is incoherent now. She's in a coma, for God's sake. She won't even know the baby is there."

"You don't know that. Your wife has a strong constitution and with good care and you and the baby by her side, it may soon put her on the road to recovery. Take the baby in to see her. Place it beside her for a while. Just let her feel its warmth, its heart. Miraculous things happen all the time. What do you have to lose?"

Jerry sighed then remorsefully replied, "What I have to lose is my wife. There is a lot more at stake here now."

"Like what?"

"I am afraid she will no longer love me. I'm afraid she won't be able to forgive me."

"There's nothing to forgive here, Jerry, and your wife will realize that if she gets better. This was merely a gesture of love."

"Okay, let's say I do this. What happens if she gets better?" Aren't I doing the same thing all over again? The same thing you didn't approve of last week."

"It is not the same thing now; she knows her baby did not survive."

"So what is the point here?"

"The point is the baby helped her before and may do it again."

"So what? Do you think this baby has magical powers or something?"

"She seems to have something special."

"Okay, so then what happens when Susan is better? Is she going to take it from me again?"

"Look Jerry, I don't know what the outcome may be. I don't have all the answers for you. I just know it might be worth a shot to save your wife."

"So, do I take this baby home with me? I don't want to stay at home with an infant. I want to be here."

"Don't you have family or friends that could help out?"

"No, I'm a very private person. We haven't been in the Charleston area that long."

"What about family?"

"Nope, no family."

Jerry seemed to become a little edgy when Carmen began to question him about relatives.

"Look Carmen, our families are—let's say—not very successful, and I am. When I began to make my money, they began to come out of the woodwork. Both of our parents passed away years ago, and we both have no siblings. So it is pretty much just the two of us. We have cousins and aunts and uncles, but no one else."

"I understand, and I am sure we can find a reason to keep her for another week or so."

Jerry sighed, "I feel like this is some kind of nightmare. I keep thinking I'll wake up."

"Yes I know. I'm right there with you. So, let's just take it one day at a time."

"How is Susan? Is she going to make it?"

"I still can't discuss her condition with you. You understand that, right?"

"No. I don't understand at all. You can give me her baby, but you can't tell me how she is."

"I can tell you she is not well. She is gravely ill, and we don't know if she'll pull through this or not. I cannot give you any medical terms, diagnosis, or conditions."

Jerry shook his head, "Policies."

"Got to love 'em. So, are you ready to go get that beautiful baby?"

"Not quite, Carmen, I smell like a brewery. It's ten o'clock," Jerry said, glancing at his watch. "I need to get cleaned up and maybe grab a quick nap. I haven't been to sleep."

"When you're ready, I have some papers you'll have to sign

taking responsibility of Gracen while she is in your care. Don't be discouraged, Jerry. Everything will work out for the best. You'll see."

"I hope you're right. I can stop back by in a couple of hours."

"Take all the time you need."

"Thanks, Carmen, thanks a lot."

"Just doing my job, sir."

He smiled and walked away.

Jerry left the hospital and took the short drive back to the Holiday Inn. He returned to his original suite that held his personal belongings. The stress was becoming too much for him to endure. He was at the end of his rope.

He took a in a deep breath then exhaled, "What am I going to do with a baby?" he said to himself as he entered the hotel.

He exited the elevator and made his way to his room. As he opened the door, he stood in the doorway and peered at the coldness of the room. Although it was a comfortable space, there was no one there to welcome him. He continued inside, shook his head, and began to undress.

He made his way to the bathroom and got into the shower. He positioned his hands against the wall, stretched his body outward, and lowered his head. The water splashed against the back of his neck as he stood with his eyes closed, rummaging through the disasters that had bombarded his life. The warm water continued to pour down over his physique and began to loosen and comfort his taut muscles. His eyes stayed closed as he began to relax and let the tension dwindle away from his core.

"A baby," he said out loud, shaking his head.

It was apparent he was having a hard time accepting the responsibility of little Gracen.

After a long shower, Jerry felt a little better. He pulled the drapes closed, put on some soothing music, and fell across the bed. The anxiety of the past few days had depleted his energy. Exhaustion was an understatement; he was out like a light.

15

Four hours had passed before Jerry awoke. Although he did not have ample time to rest, his strength was restored and he felt refreshed and prepared to face what lay ahead. He had not heard from Donna and was troubled about Susan's condition. He expected Donna to call him soon. But putting all that aside, it was time for him to get his new addition and reunite her with his wife; so he was off to the hospital again.

Jerry left the quietness of his room and entered the elevator. As the doors opened to the first floor and he stepped out into the lobby, the desk attendant gave a nod of his head. Jerry nodded back and continued to the door.

"How's your wife, Mr. Hudson?" the attendant called out.

"Not so good."

"I'm sorry to hear that, sir. I hope she improves soon."

"Thank you, that is very kind of you to say."

At the hospital, he rode the elevator to his wife's floor and desperately prayed for a miracle. The doors opened and he strode out.

"Hello Mr. Hudson," Tamra greeted him as he entered the hallway.

"Good morning. How's my wife? Has there been any change?"

"No sir, I'm sorry there hasn't."

"Thank you." Jerry turned away and headed for Mary's room. Abruptly, he stopped and turned around. "Miss Tamra, would you please bring little Gracen to my wife's room for me?"

"Certainly," Tamra replied with a smile.

Jerry nodded and continued on.

Again, he stood at the stained, wooden door, took a deep breath, and entered.

"Good morning, sunshine." He sashayed over to Mary's side and kissed her forehead. "Okay, my wife, I am not having you look like this. You look like some old lady ready to give up, and I know that is not for you. So let's remove this cap from your head and do something with your hair." Jerry gently lifted her head and removed the blue cap. "How about a long braid, honey? Well, I think that will be perfect, Jerry," he said, answering himself.

"Here we are," Tamra said, walking into the room.

Jerry was quick to step up and accept Gracen in his arms. "Let's do this," he said trying to convince himself that it was right.

"Mary, little Gracen has come to visit with you. Her mother is very sick, and she needs you to help her." He carefully positioned Gracen in the crease of Mary's arm. Tamra stood nearby and watched.

"Okay Gracen, turn on the magic and help Mary get better."

Jerry held his hands to one side of Gracen to secure her safety. She snuggled into Mary's arm and fell back to sleep.

"Come on miracle baby, do something," Jerry pleaded.

The baby never budged. She lay perfectly still and slept.

"Please little one, do something," he begged, nudging Gracen with a gentle pat.

The little infant squirmed and slowly kicked her feet, giving the impression of finding a comfortable position. She blinked her small eyelids then raised her eyebrows, stretched her tiny body, and began to stare, as if she were looking at something. She gave a crooked grin and nestled against Mary.

"Whoa," Jerry exclaimed and slightly leaned back.

"What's wrong?" Tamra asked.

"Quick, come here."

Tamra promptly complied and approached his side. "What is it?"

"Put your hand on the baby." Jerry grasped Tamra's hand and placed it on Gracen's back. "Do you feel that? Is that normal?"

Tamra shrugged her shoulders and shook her head with confusion. "What am I feeling?" she asked.

"All that heat, what is it?"

"I don't feel anything out of the norm."

"Well I do. Look at the monitor. Her heart rate is faster. And look at her blood pressure: it's rising."

Tamra teetered around the bed and began to check each machine. Jerry stood with anticipation, waiting for the results. He too had a rapid heartbeat. His anxiety was peaking as he waited.

"Now don't get your hopes up, Mr. Hudson. Sometimes these things happen with comatose patients. They may even appear to open their eyes from time to time."

"Yes, so I have been told, but she's responding. I also would like a bassinet brought into the room for this baby. I want her here as long as I am."

"I'm not sure that will be allowed, sir."

"Oh, I'm sure it will be. You ask Carmen when she comes on duty. All the other mothers have their babies in their rooms, and I want this one in mine."

"With all due respect, sir, this is not your baby, and you are not a mother."

The wrath of an Irish temper swept across his face. The rich blood in a crimson tide rushed over his cheeks, neck, and brow. "It's my baby until it is otherwise noted, and you need to respect me not as a man, but as a father. And if mothers may have their babies, fathers should too. You may need to freshen up on your etiquette because yours really sucks. So, if you don't mind, and even if you do mind, just excuse yourself and leave us alone for a while."

"Yes sir, but if you need anything . . . "

"I will ring the bell," Jerry interrupted.

"Please forgive me for my lack of empathy. I was terribly out of line," she replied, blushing with embarrassment. "We nurses have to make our hearts hard just to cope with all the tragedy we deal with."

"I understand, but if you will excuse yourself, I would like some private time with my wife."

"Certainly sir."

Tamra did as she was told and left the room. She pulled the door securely shut behind her.

"Do that again, little one," Jerry whispered. "Please make my Mary better."

Jerry brushed Mary's hair back from her face and crouched down beside her. "Mary," he whispered, "you need to get better. I love you, babe, with all my heart. I can't make it without you. I know I was wrong for what I did, but I was just trying to help you. I wanted you to be able to hold your baby, to grant you your wish, and I am dreadfully sorry if I was wrong. I do have custody of Gracen right now. Her mother is really sick, just like you are. The baby is not able to be with her. I don't know why. She may have a contagious disease or something. I don't know, but she wanted me, us, to keep her baby safe for her. She needs you to do that for her. You are such a loving woman, and I know you'll be a great mom, just wake up, honey, just wake up."

Jerry sat at the edge of her bed and wept. He had often wondered where her strength originated. She always pretended to be perfectly well. Although she was weak and weary, she never complained about her sickness. She was gentle, considerate, and always responded with hopeful words.

Even when her cancer brought the tide of dismay, she had a smile of hope and joy and continued to sacrifice herself to breathe life into this cruel world.

He stared down at her hollow cheeks, her sunken eyes, and thin arms. He implored her not to leave him. His wild moans echoed though the room. He took her hand in his and kissed it gently. He could feel her pulse that bounded like a racehorse. Jerry wondered, if she survived, would she ever be able to forgive him.

"Knock, knock," a voice called from the hallway as the door was pushed open.

"Come in," Jerry replied, trying to recognize the voice.

"How's she doing?"

"Oh Donna, thank God it's you. I don't know what to do."

"What do you mean? What's wrong?"

"Did you see Susan? Do you know what's wrong with her? Is she going to be all right?"

"No, no, and I don't know. They wouldn't let me in and would not tell me a thing."

"Me either. But she regained consciousness long enough to sign Gracen over to me."

"You mean you're adopting her?"

"No, just temporary custody."

"Oh, wow."

"Yeah, I know. But anyway, I began to think about what you had said before, about the stigmata and all that weird stuff. I was thinking that if it were true then maybe she could heal Mary. I've done everything that I know how to do, but it hasn't worked. I don't know what to do to make it work."

"She's not a machine Jerry; Gracen's a baby. She doesn't have an *on and off* switch. You have to believe in her. You have to believe that she is a healer and she has been put here for all of us. You must believe."

"I do believe."

"No, Jerry, you really have to believe. You just want to use her. You don't believe. You want to believe, but you don't."

"I've been doing everything I can to believe in this."

"Take my hand and let's pray."

"Pray?"

"Yes, pray."

Donna grasped Jerry's hand, and she placed her other hand on Gracen. She began to ask God to give the infant the strength to heal Mary, to take away the pain and the disease that inundated her soul, and to rejuvenate and bless her once more. She thanked the Lord for sending Gracen to them and she promised that they would protect and follow her throughout her life. They would help her spread the message.

With his head bowed, Jerry listened to her voice. He commenced to believe the words as she continuously repeated the message. His heart opened, tranquility spilled over his body, and tears flowed from his eyes. He began to pray. He asked God for a miracle for his wife.

Donna never looked up. She was persistent with her prayers. She praised God for sending this angel to help heal the sick, to bring peace, and to convey miracles to our land. She was relentless with her proclamation of faith. She repeated the words softly, over and over again. "We believe. We believe, our dear Lord. We believe."

Little Gracen opened her eyes, stretched a little, and raised her small arm from the blanket. Jerry abruptly stood and grasped her tiny hand. In return, she tightened the grip of her fingers and smiled. An unexplainable glow encircled her frame. The golden circle filled the room. The heat radiated and ascended across Mary's body, leaving a physical change in the atmosphere. The aroma of fresh roses filled the room. A calming sensation overwhelmed all three of them. They knew the healing had begun.

Jerry watched with belief, not making a sound that might interrupt whatever was taking place. Mary's monitors were fluctuating in an inconsistent pattern. Her heart rate was faster and gradually getting stronger. The mysterious phenomenon was a spectacular miracle, and Jerry and Donna were the only witnesses. He was utterly paralyzed with overpowering emotion. His body shuddered with the anticipation as he watched the miracle transport his gravely ill wife back to health. Mary's body began to move, and she slowly stretched her arms. Tranquility arrived without warning as she ever so slowly moved her head from side to side. Jerry wailed with jubilation as he watched his wife open her eyes and look directly at him. The daughter of God was vindicated, and she had executed her first miracle perfectly.

"Oh my God," Jerry praised the Creator. "Oh my God," he repeated with an elated smile. "Mary, you've come back to me." He fell to his knees and wept.

The buzzers began to beep erratically on all the machines. In response, nurses rushed down the hall. Tamra was the first to enter.

"How is everything in here?"

Before anyone could answer, she moved around the bed. "I really hate to disturb you, but these darn monitors will not quit beeping by themselves. Sometimes they go off randomly. It will not take me but a moment, and I'll be out of your hair."

"Nurse, can you take a moment to look at my wife?"

"Sure, Mr. Hudson, just give me a sec. I just need to press this, redo this, and now, we're all done. Let's make sure everything is connected correctly."

Tamra turned and viewed Mary for the first time since entering. She jerked back and stared for a moment. Mary smiled back.

"Like I told you earlier, Mr. Hudson, they may appear to be awake. Please don't let this get your hopes up."

"She's awake," he tearfully responded. "She's awake."

Tamra reached down and clutched Mary's hand. "Mary, if you can hear me, squeeze my hand."

They both waited, but there was no response. Tamra repeated herself two more times, but there was still no reaction.

"I'm sorry, Mr. Hudson, there is no change."

"You are wrong, Tamra," Donna said, stepping from the bathroom.

"Donna, what are you doing here?"

"I'm here with Jerry. I am a visitor, not a nurse."

"I'm truly sorry for what happened to you."

"Thank you, Tamra, but Mary is our concern now. Check her again. She is awake."

"Honey, if you can hear me, blink," Donna stepped around and took control.

Nothing happened.

"Come on, baby, blink. I know you can hear me now, blink."

"Oh wow, that's great," Tamra exclaimed.

"Great, what's great? She didn't blink."

"No, she didn't, but she squeezed my hand," Tamra replied with a smile. "Sometimes their brains are a little slow. It may take a while for her to fully come back. This is absolutely a miracle. I have got to go give her doctor a call."

"Thank you, Tamra," Jerry said with feeling.

"Don't thank me, I didn't do anything. I think the credit should go to you and that beautiful baby."

"Yes, I agree. This lovely little girl deserves all the credit. She's the one who brought life back to Mary."

"How about I take her back to the nursery for a while and let you two talk? I'm sure it is about feeding time too."

"No thanks, Gracen is staying right here. If you'll bring me her bottle, I will gladly feed her."

"If you're sure, I'll be right on it."

"I could not be surer of anything else in my whole entire life right now. Donna is here, and she would be glad to help me with her, huh Donna?" Jerry smiled, turning to Donna.

"Sure, of course I'll help you. Go ahead, Tamra, we've got it in here."

Tamra smiled and left the room. Donna tiptoed over to the door and pushed it shut. She smiled at Jerry and replied, "I told you, I told you that she was special. I told you she was the one. I told you."

"Yes you did, and you were one hundred percent correct."

"Mary, I know you can't talk right now, but Gracen is here lying next to you, and she is going to help you get well. She is our miracle child. God has sent us an angel, my darling, a perfect angel."

A tear drizzled from the corner of Mary's eye and dropped to the pillow where her head rested. She blinked her eyes in acknowledgment as her mind drifted away, still drugged and barely out of its zombie-like state.

Donna gave a salutary grin. She grasped Jerry's hand and squeezed it tightly. He returned the gesture as they both stared down at Mary.

Donna gently slid her hands underneath Gracen and lifted her to her arms. With a gentle kiss to the forehead, she placed the sleeping infant into the bassinet.

Jerry tapped Donna's arm and motioned her to the hall. Donna nodded and they quietly left the room.

"Oh my gosh!" Donna whispered ecstatically. "Did you see what that child just did? We just witnessed a miracle."

"Shhhh, someone might hear you."

"So what? For God's sake, man, didn't you see what she did?"

"I did . . . I know, but we can't tell anyone."

"What! Are you crazy? This is the message God wants us to spread. We have a healer, a saint, a . . . "

"A child," Jerry interrupted and finished her sentence. "This is a baby, Donna, a tiny, innocent little baby. We can't expose her to skepticism and cruelty from the media and all the religious freaks who will come out of the woodwork to see her. Do you know how many people would flock here just to get a glimpse of the miracle child? I'll tell you: millions. What kind of life would that be for her?"

"So we do nothing?"

"Yes."

"I can't do anything about this. This is a miracle, Jerry. We can restore faith to the world. People will believe again. This was a gift from God. Can't you see that?"

Jerry stood with a blank expression. "What I see is a disrupted life."

"Oh, so here we go again. It's all about you."

"All about me . . . really, is that what you actually believe? I have been here day and night, only leaving to shower and eat. I have fed, changed, and comforted Gracen each and every hour that I have been allowed to. I have rocked her, sung to her, and told her about our life, and you are going to stand there and criticize me. I love that baby, and she is dear to my heart. I will do whatever I need to do to protect her. And exposing her to the world, to the maniacs that roam this earth, is not part of the plan," Jerry said through gritted teeth.

Donna was startled by Jerry's demeanor. Never had she seen him so upset. It was clear he was very devoted to Gracen's well being.

"I'm sorry, you're probably right. How are we going to spread the word?"

"What word?"

"God's word, she surely was sent here for a reason, don't you think?"

"Yes, I do. The word will come, just not now. We must protect her."

"I agree, but she is not ours to protect."

"Let's not think about that right now."

"Mary hasn't said a word about what happened. Do you think she remembers?"

"I'm not sure. I am really scared that she doesn't."

"And if she doesn't?"

"And if she doesn't, she doesn't."

"What exactly does that mean? You are going to tell her, right?"

"I don't know."

"Come on, Jerry, you can't go through this again."

"I can go through whatever it takes if it keeps her alive. You saw what happened last time. It nearly destroyed her."

"Yeah, well it nearly destroyed you too."

"It doesn't matter right now. We'll cross that bridge when we have to; right now we need to keep both of them safe. What are your plans for your future?"

"My plans are to beg for my job back."

"Good, I already talked to Carmen, and she's trying to get you reinstated."

"Really, you talked to Carmen? When and why?"

"Two, maybe three days ago, and because I felt as if a lot of this was my fault; I needed to make it right for you. I've watched the care that you have given to Mary and Gracen—matter of fact, all of us. You are a great nurse and your place is helping others."

"Get out of here, Jerry, you are just too kind," Donna smiled and gave him a little push. "I think I need to get my head out of the clouds and go find Carmen." She smiled with gratitude and gave a wink as she turned and sauntered away.

He returned the gesture and went back to Mary's bedside.

Donna was ecstatic to know that Jerry had spoken up on her behalf, although in some ways, she did feel this was his fault.

She walked down the hall to the nurses' station and did indeed find Carmen. She sat alone scouring a patient's chart. Donna was nervous but continued to the counter. She placed her elbows on the counter top and peered down to Carmen.

"Busy?" she asked.

With her head tilted down and eyebrows raised, Carmen scrutinized Donna over the rim of her glasses. She was surprised to see Donna with one of those cat swallowed a canary looks on her face.

"Always busy, Donna, what can I help you with?"

"You got a minute to spare?"

Carmen sighed, closed the file, and placed her hands on top of the manila folder.

"And if I said *no*, would it matter?"

"Come on, Carmen we've been friends for a long time. You know how I am."

"Meaning what?"

"Meaning I let things get a little out of hand here. I am truly sorry. Please put me back on duty. I'm lost without working. You know I'm a good nurse," she pleaded.

"I know you have been a good nurse, but the things that you did and said were irresponsible and foolish. You seem to have changed since Miss Shaw was brought into this hospital. Can you admit that you were wrong with all that stigmata stuff?"

"Look, I should have handled things differently, I admit it."

"Not the question, Donna," she added.

"I don't know what to say, Carmen, because I can't agree with you. I still believe Gracen has a gift for all of us to learn from, and I can't or won't refute that. She is special."

"So what is it that you want?"

"What I want is my job, a transfer to another floor, to the E.R. I really don't care. I am a nurse. I was born to help others, and I am damn good at what I do. I feel good when I go home at night knowing that I may have helped save a life. Not everyone can be a nurse; it has to be in your blood. And it flows through every vein I have."

Carmen snickered, "Every vein, huh?"

"Yep, every one."

"Look, it's already been discussed with the director and the staff committee. Only because of Mr. Hudson's large donation to the west wing was it considered. I was told that you would have to stay away from the maternity ward and Susan Shaw if we were to put you back on the schedule. Is that something you think you can commit to?"

"I have already obligated myself to help Mr. Hudson with Gracen. I can't stay away from her."

"What you do on your time is not my concern. Can you commit to these terms while you are on duty?"

With a giant smile she answered, "Absolutely."

"So be it, the new schedule will come out with your name on it. I'm not sure of the hours as of right now, but I'll let you know."

"Carmen, you're the best. Thanks!"

"Don't thank me, thank Mr. Hudson."

"I already did. You do know that Jerry has requested for Gracen to stay in the nursery as long as his wife is here."

"Yes, I heard that from the director. I guess it is nice to have money."

"Thanks again for your help, Carmen, but I need to scoot. I have things to catch up on before my shift begins."

"Not a problem. Run along."

Days had passed and Gracie continued to stay with Jerry and his wife. Mary's health continued to slowly improve with each day. She became stronger. Her voice was returning. It was soft and not much above a whisper, but that didn't matter because Jerry was thankful just to have his charming wife back in his world.

She seldom spoke and then only a few words. Her main focus was Gracen. If Mary was awake, she wanted Gracen by her side. With one hand clutching her throat, she repeated the words while shaking her head, "Terrible nightmare." No one was sure what she was talking about, but surely, it had to be about the loss of her child.

During the two weeks that followed, there were many anxious days and sleepless nights. Mary was regaining her strength with the passing of each moon.

Mary had traveled to the depths of darkness; she had touched the valley of death but rallied through it all and was on the road to recovery.

Her faithful husband would not give up on her. He stood by her bedside day and night. He would spoon feed Mary every meal, slightly blowing on the hot food, and then placing the spoon through her pallid lips.

As the nights continued to pass, Jerry sat in the chair burying his face in his hands. He was weary and wholly exhausted. One evening, two hours into his usual mini-sleep, he heard a deep quivering sigh break the silence of the room.

Jerry was jolted upward and recognized the moan of his wife. She moved her head on her pillow and stared into her beloved's eyes. With a little cough and gurgle, she cleared her throat.

"You're still here."

She spoke for the first time in a natural tone.

"I wouldn't be anywhere else, my love. I love you so much, I couldn't bear to leave you."

"Thank you. And I love you too."

With those words, Jerry felt relief sweep over his being. Although he knew their trials were far from over, at the moment he had his wife, his soul mate for eternity. She had been resurrected from the dead once again.

With the warmth and tranquility that Gracen transferred to Mary, she continued to improve as the days followed. She was able to sit up by herself, feed herself, and do all the tasks of a normal person except walk steadily. The muscles in her legs were too weak and unable to hold her upright on her own.

All of the hospital staff was aware of the donation from Mr. Hudson, and his wife was treated like royalty. A daily physical therapy regimen was initiated, and the results were remarkable.

Donna came every evening to give support and help any way she could. Her main focus was Gracen. She would do anything to be near her.

No one ever said anything about who Gracen was or who had given birth to her. Mary never acknowledged she knew the truth, and Jerry would not ask.

16

"Jerry, I think we have a miracle," Mary blurted out of the blue.

"I know we have a miracle here, honey. Look at how radiant you are. Your face is glowing with beauty."

"Oh, get out of here! I wasn't talking about me. I was talking about Gracie."

"About Gracie?"

"Yes, Gracie. She is our miracle baby that I never thought would survive the birth. I never imagined I would have the strength to deliver her. Actually, I thought she had died."

"What do you mean, you thought she had died?"

"When I gave birth, I was so weak, and I was in and out of consciousness. I wasn't sure if I was dreaming or not, but I thought I heard someone say she didn't make it. I was so exhausted, I couldn't even open my eyes. I wanted to see her so badly, but I couldn't. I kept waiting, listening for the cry, the whimper, but I never heard it. When I woke up and asked if she had made it, I thought for sure you would tell me *no*. I had already prepared myself for the devastating news, but when you said *yes*, I was ecstatic. Now to find out all of this was a dream, or should I say a nightmare. You just don't know how I feel. There are not enough words to define the euphoria that has filled my soul. My heart is bursting with elation, warmth, and pure happiness. With all these drugs in my system, making me hallucinate and hear things that were not real, I was going crazy. One minute I thought my baby was stillborn, and then came the nightmare where I thought the nurses had told me that she isn't mine. Now I wake up and she is here. It was all a bad dream that was driving me insane. I will be so happy to be drug free again."

Jerry began to fidget. He rubbed his hands together tightly then began to pick at his fingernails. He ran his fingers through his salt-and-pepper hair. He stood up and ironed his pants legs with the palms of his hands and then sat back in the chair.

He cringed and fretfully replied, "I don't know what to say."

"What do you mean you don't know what to say? I'm not asking you to say anything. I just want you to know, and believe as I do, that we have a miracle baby."

"Oh, I believe she is a miracle baby. In fact, I know it. I just don't want you to put too much into all of this . . . stuff."

"All of what stuff?"

"You know, this entire baby thing."

"This baby thing," she said in confounded voice. "What kind of a remark is that? What do you mean? Is something wrong with her?"

"No, nothing is wrong with her. You just have to remember to live for all of us, not just for the baby."

"There you go again, calling her the baby. The baby has a name."

"I'm sorry, honey, I know she has a name. I just have a lot going on, and you're still very sick."

"I feel much better, and I'm getting stronger every day. If there's anything I can do to help you, please ask. I know you are way behind on your work schedule. Do you want to talk about it?"

"No, work is fine. I'm just concerned about your health."

"My health is fine. Jerry, are you sure there's nothing wrong with Gracen?"

Jerry paced over to the window. He grasped the string on the blind and winched it up and down. He ran his finger along the windowsill, looking for some way to tell his wife about the lie, a confession that would surely destroy them both. He needed to let her know that it wasn't a nightmare, it was a fact; Gracen was not theirs. He fought through the chaos in his mind for the right words, words that could ease the pain of devastation, words that would make things right, and not destroy their lives. He found none. He lowered his head and began to softly whisper.

"Mary, there is something I need to tell you. I've done a terrible thing." Jerry lowered his head down on his fist. "I don't know where to begin. I just can't find the words to make things right again."

"The right words for what? What's wrong? Are you sure it's not about Gracie? Please, tell me. I can handle it."

"No, honey, there is nothing wrong with Gracie, but it is about her."

"What is it, Jerry?"

He turned slightly and glanced at Mary lying patiently, waiting for an answer. Jerry went to her bedside. He lifted her hand and held it to his face.

"You know I love you, and I would do anything in this world, for you. I love you more than life itself."

"Of course I know that. What have you done? If it's not Gracie, what is it? Did you have an affair?"

"Good God, no! I wouldn't do anything like that to you."

"Then, what, what can be so terrible that you can't find words?"

Jerry focused on Mary's eyes. He squeezed her hand a little tighter in his. His eyes glazed over and filled with tears. He cleared his throat and began to speak tenderly.

"Every day, I have sat here beside you and watched, day by day, as your life slipped away. I watched you grow weaker and weaker with each passing hour. I begged and pleaded with God to show you mercy and not take you away from me. I offered my life for yours, and I would have gladly given it. I would have given my soul to Satan to save your life. Nothing seemed to help. When you gave birth to our baby, I didn't know what to expect. I didn't know whether to stand by you or her. But when she came out and you slipped away, I . . ."

"Mrs. Hudson?" Carmen entered the room. "Excuse me, Mr. Hudson, could you step out into the hall for a moment?"

"Is something wrong?" Mary exclaimed.

"No, nothing is wrong. I just need to go over some papers with Mr. Hudson. It won't take long."

Jerry sniffed and stroked the tears from his face. Trying to regain his composure, he turned his back to the door with manly embarrassment. He could not think of any papers that had not been taken care of.

"Can this wait?" My wife and I are having an important conversation."

"No, this is something that needs to be addressed right away. My shift changes in about an hour and I need this taken care of before I leave."

Mary noticed the urgency on the nurse's face. "Are you sure Gracen is all right?"

"Yes, Miss Mary, she's perfectly fine, I promise."

"Go ahead, Jerry. We can talk when you get back. Whatever it is, I'm sure it can wait a little bit longer."

"I really hate to interrupt, but it's imperative that I have this taken care of."

Jerry leaned over and kissed Mary on the head. "I'll be right back, honey."

He and the nurse left the room and closed the door tightly behind them.

"What's this about, Carmen? What kind of papers do I need to fill out? I thought I had taken care of everything already. I pretty much signed my life away when I came in here."

"There are no papers, Mr. Hudson. It's Susan Shaw. She wants to see you. I didn't know what else to say. She's awake and sedated, but she asked for you."

"Susan Shaw wants me? Why?"

"I'm not sure, but she asked me to get you right away. She's very ill."

"I don't care what she has. I just want to know what she wants. This roller coaster ride is driving me insane. First, I can have Gracen, then I can't, then I can. Is she pulling rank again and taking her away?"

"I don't think so. There are complications with her health that will not improve. Just prepare yourself."

"Prepare myself for what?" he growled.

Before she could answer, he spun around and headed down the hallway. He babbled to himself as they went on their way.

"Finally, I had mustered the courage to talk to my wife, and I get interrupted; I'll have to start all over if I want to resolve this. Do you have any idea how much I dread this?"

"I'm certain it has to be difficult, sir."

"*Difficult* it an understatement."

Carmen scurried behind him trying to explain something, but Jerry didn't slow down long enough to listen. He knocked twice and continued into Susan's room.

"Jerry, Jerry," Carmen called out, but Jerry continued without looking back.

"Susan, is something wrong? The nurse said it was urgent for you to speak with me," a perturbed Jerry exclaimed, walking toward the bed.

He stopped abruptly at her bedside and raised himself upward. The young mother was almost unrecognizable. Her complexion was dull and ashen. Her eyes were swollen like two large golf balls. He bent down and gazed into her still, white face. She had the appearance of death. For a brief moment, he felt sheer terror.

"Oh my God, what's wrong? What happened to you?"

Susan smiled and gasped, "I look rough, huh?"

"Oh, I'm sorry, I just didn't know how bad your condition

was."

Carmen interrupted, "That's what I was trying to tell you."

"It's all right, Carmen, please leave us alone, and thank you for your kindness," said Susan.

"Are you sure there's nothing else I can do for you?" Carmen asked as she fluffed the pillow beneath her head.

"Yes, I am sure," she whispered hoarsely.

"Okay, if you need anything, just ring." Carmen turned away and closed the door behind her. Jerry dragged a chair next to the bed. He sat down beside Susan and his heart filled with pure empathy.

"Hey, Jerry, can you hold on to my hand?" she asked waving it in the air.

Jerry watched as Susan waved her arm freely above her chest. He, in return, moved his hand in front of her face. There was no reaction to the fingers that wiggled two inches from her eyes; she did not blink.

"Susan are you . . . I mean, can you . . . ?"

"See? No, I can't. Something went wrong."

"Went wrong? Where, how?"

"I had an aneurysm and I lost my sight. I'm completely blind. I went crazy to begin with, but I'm adapting now. I also have a brain tumor, and to top it off . . . you'll never guess, I have cancer. Ironic, huh? You have two women who share the same baby. Both of us look like shit, and both of us have cancer. We both have shared in a miracle. I gave birth to the daughter of God, and your wife is being healed by her."

"I'm so sorry, I don't know what to say."

"There's no need for you to be sorry or to have pity. You didn't do it."

"I know, but I . . . "

"Don't fret over it. I'm used to coping with unexpected disaster. This is Satan's way of paying me back for not giving him my soul. God has a plan for me; I'm sure of that. I'm not sure about the details, but time will tell. Speaking of which, how is your wife? Is she still improving?"

"Yes, she's much better, thank you for asking. Gracen has made a world of difference in her, but I really don't think you brought me here to ask about my wife. When did you find out you had cancer?"

"Today, I found out today. When I was young, I had a mole removed from my leg. Somehow, after all these years, the damn thing or the cells that were underneath it are no longer dormant. Giving birth to Gracie was too much for my body. My immune system was broken down, and because of my lifestyle, it created too much stress and the cancer took over. The brain tumor has been there for a while, too, so they say, I just didn't know it. When everything went haywire, I got very resentful about my misfortune, and that is why I would not let you have Gracen for a while. I'm really sorry for putting you through all of that."

"I'm so sorry. I'm truly sorry. I had no idea this had happened to you. What can I do to help?"

"I want to know what your wife's prognosis is and what are the chances of the cancer coming back?"

"No one really knows. She shouldn't even be here. She should have died. Just as your cancer showed up, hers could too. Nothing is forever. We just pray it won't return. Why do you ask?"

"They have my cancer under control for right now, but I will never see the light of day again. I will always be blind; there is no cure. I guess I should count my lucky stars for whatever you can call a blessing. It could have been the alternative, and I could have lost my life. That's enough about all of that. Last week, you said if you could do anything to help me, you would. Does that offer still stand?"

"Of course it does, but what can I do?"

"What you can do is take Gracie."

"Take Gracie, take Gracie where?"

"As in adoption. Would you like to adopt my daughter?"

"You're kidding, right?"

"Please, I'm not kidding; this is nothing to kid about. Look at me. I am definitely no good for her now. Not only am I a drug addict, an alcoholic, homeless, and crazy, but now I'm blind and have cancer that may reappear one day. What a life."

"I guess it's been hell for you."

"Yep, hell. Have you told your wife? Have you told her that Gracie isn't hers?"

"No, I haven't, not yet anyway. I was just searching for words when the nurse walked in."

"So, does she know or not?"

"Not. She does not know. Why?"

"Don't tell her. I'll sign the papers, and she doesn't have to know a thing."

Jerry slumped back in the chair. He ran his fingers through his hair and rested his hand on his crown. He didn't know what to say.

"I don't know, Susan, all these lies are killing me. This deceit is agonizing to live with it."

"If you don't want her . . . "

"No, no, no, it's nothing like that. Of course I want her; I already love her just as if she were my own. I just don't know about this lie that will be a burden for the rest of my life. I don't want my wife to suffer again."

"But if you tell her, the stress may be too much of an ordeal. It may even bring the cancer back in full force. If that happens, Gracie still won't have a mother."

"I don't know what to do, Susan. Of course I want Gracie, without a doubt. I just don't know what to say, and I don't know how to answer you. I have to tell my wife. I can't keep lying to her."

"If you decide you want her, there are other stipulations that go along with it."

"Stipulations? What kind of stipulations?"

"I want you to hire Donna to take care of your wife and Gracie—full time. I trust her. She believes in Gracie. And of course, I don't want your wife to ever know that Gracie is not her baby by birth. All you have to say is *yes*."

"That's easier said than done. I don't know about this. You'll have to let me think about it."

"Look, I don't know how much time I have here. I need to know my baby will be taken care of if I should die or get worse."

"What other stipulations do you have? Is that all, or are there more?"

"You said that you have many houses. I want to move to California—Santa Cruz, specifically, oceanside. Do you have any houses there?"

"California! I don't have any houses in California. Why do you want to be in California?"

"I want a fresh start, and you said you'd help me. Does the offer still stand?"

"Of course the offer still stands, but I don't know about California."

"Why not?"

"I don't own anything in California."

"But if you wanted to own something there you could, right? I mean, you do have the money."

"Yes, I have the money. In other words, you want to sell your baby to me. That is what you're really asking, right? You want me to buy you a house in exchange for your baby."

"No," she scolded in a deep tone, "that is not right. I want you to buy me a house because you can. And to think that you can buy my baby is ludicrous. You don't have enough money to buy my baby. There is not enough money on this earth to buy my baby. But you are rich. You said that. Even though you don't have enough money to buy my baby, you do have enough money to buy me a house. You want, need, and almost have to have my child for your wife to survive. And I need someone to take care of her, to love her, and to treat her as her own. I think you and your wife are the chosen ones, so to speak. There is some reason your baby did not make it and mine did. There is some reason we ended up in the same hospital, and there is some reason I got sick and your wife got better. There are too many coincidences for this not to be fate. And for God's sake, man, your wife's named Mary. That's a sacred name to be the mother of a sacred child—just a different Mary, the mother of Gracen. My baby needs someone to help her succeed in life, and I know you can provide that for her, but in return, I also need someone to help me. You have plenty of money. You're not going to miss it."

"It's not about the money."

"It sounds to me like you are trying to make it all about the money. Look, I love to paint. I want to sit by the ocean and paint pictures. Even if I can't see, I still have the memories in my mind. I could not bear to live here in the same town with my child and not get to see her. Well, I guess that's a bad choice of words; we know that will never happen. But you know what I mean. I need to be all the way across the United States. I have to be somewhere where I can't interfere. If I were not sick, you would never get my child. I would find some way to raise her myself. Even though I'm homeless, I would find a way to take care of Gracen. But that is not in the cards for me. I am sick and I'm blind. I could never be a good mother, no matter how hard I tried."

"Let's say I buy you a house, then what? How do I know you won't reappear one day and try to get Gracen back from me? How do I know you won't try to come back into her life years from now? How do I know you won't show up on my doorstep one day, and how can I keep this from Mary, knowing that you know the truth, and you may come back and tell her? How do I know?"

"Well Jerry, you don't know, and there are no words to convince you of that. You just have to trust me. Everyone takes chances in life, and this is your chance. You can take it or leave it, which one do you want to do? It really makes no difference to me. I'm sure Donna will be glad to take care of Gracie, and if I have to live on state income, that's what I will do, although I wish a better life than that for her. Whatever the decision is, it's yours. I'm not going to argue with you and debate about what you should or shouldn't do. If you want to think about it, that's fine. Just remember, no one knows when things could get worse."

Jerry stood up and began to pace about the room. He did not know what to do or say. Should he continue lying to his wife and adopt Gracie, or should he just tell his wife the truth? He was scared the truth would kill his wife and the deceit would bring him to disaster.

He hastily returned to the chair at her bedside and sat down. He seized Susan by the arm and held it tightly. He stared into Susan's blank face.

"If you were my wife, would you want to know the truth? Would you want to know, would you?" he repeated.

Susan was hesitant, her eyes fixed to the ceiling, as her head shuddered from side to side. "I think . . . I believe, if I were your wife, it would not make a difference to me as long as I had the child. She would be my child, and no matter who gave birth, I would appreciate the fact that she would always be my child. If I were your wife, I would recognize this might be the only chance of getting a newborn baby. You said your wife already believed Gracie was hers, so let her continue believing it. I know you don't regard Gracie as your daughter or the daughter of God, but she is. Gracie is a healer. She healed your wife; I know she did. There is not a doubt in my mind that she was the one who restored your wife's health. And if you believe in God, He will make things better for us all."

"If you believe she is a healer, then why are you so sick? Why has she not healed you? You're her birth mother."

"I was only chosen to give birth. You know why she didn't heal me. I'm not worthy to be healed. Look at all that I've done. Your wife needs to be the mother of my child. She is the one that God has chosen to raise Gracie. I accept that, and so should you."

"Everyone is worthy to be healed, Susan. We all make mistakes."

"Look here, Jerry. We all see things differently, and I accept how things are. Gracie has healed me. It's just a different kind of healing."

"I hate this because I just don't know what to do. I am so confused."

"I tell you what, go talk to Donna. See what Donna says. She may not even want the job. I'm just asking you to do what I think is best."

"Best for whom?"

"Best for everyone."

"I guess you can believe that from your side, but I'm not sure I do. I just need to think about everything. This is a lot for me to take on. It's a lot that I have to deal with for the rest of my life. I'm not sure I can do it."

Susan raised her head in Jerry's direction with her bulging eyes staring vacantly above his head. In a soft voice, she replied, "She did heal me, Jerry."

"What?"

"She did heal me, in her own way. Think about it. If I did not get sick, if I had not gone blind, there is no way you would be getting my baby. My trying to raise a child with no money, no job, and nowhere to live would have ended in one place: drugs. I probably would have turned back to my old ways. With my getting sick, it's kind of like being healed at the same time. You will be providing me with a new life, one without drugs, and one with a great beginning for my child. The worst part of it is Gracen. I won't have my baby to share it with me. I won't get to watch her take her first steps or hear her say her first words. I won't get to see her off to her first day at school or her first day of college. And I will not be there to give her advice when she needs it most. You shall have that joy and you must make sure you never take it for granted," Susan sniffled as a tear rolled from her swollen eyes down to her cheek.

"Susan, I'm sorry, but I have to go. I'll see what I can do, and I'll stop by tomorrow."

"That will be fine, Jerry. I will let the nurse know that Gracen is to stay with you and your wife for now."

"Thanks."

17

Jerry wandered back to his wife's room still rummaging for the right words. Minutes later, he pushed the door and took that dreaded step. One foot inside the door, again, a nurse called out from behind.

"Look who I have. It's time for Gracie's feeding, and I think she is very, very hungry."

"Thank God," he said to himself. He was safe again.

He watched as the nurse bounced past him and handed his wife the infant. Mary smiled down at Gracie and stroked the side of her face with her fingers. Jerry observed from the doorway how much joy this child was bringing to his recuperating wife. Her recovery was remarkable. Mary's face was radiant and her energy was rising. It was hard to believe just several days earlier she was expected to die. Everyone had given up—everyone but God; He had a plan.

Jerry knew at this moment he would have to give Susan what she wanted. He would live a lie the rest of his life to keep his wife alive. Without a doubt, this baby had to be theirs at any cost.

He sucked in a deep breath of air, expanding his chest, and repeated the words that Susan had said earlier. "If you believe, God will make it better for everyone."

He walked over and sat on the edge of the bed beside his wife. He brushed the hair back from Mary's face and kissed her forehead. He lifted little Gracie's hand with his finger, and she held on tightly.

"Jerry, what was it that you were going to ask me earlier?"

"It was nothing important," Jerry answered.

"Well, it seemed very important to you before you left the room."

"I really don't even know what I wanted. Has the doctor said when they're going to release you from the hospital?"

"Are you trying to change the subject, Jerry?"

"No not at all. Why would I do that?"

"Well, I don't know. It just seemed earlier something was very important to you, and now it's not. What kind of papers did they want you to sign?"

"You know, insurance stuff. You have to sign your whole damn life away when you come in here."

"Watch your mouth; the baby can hear you."

"What do you mean the baby can hear me? She can't understand anything yet."

"Sure she can. You need to watch what you say. I don't want you to be cursing in front of her."

"Yes, dear, I will watch my mouth. So what about the doctor, has he been here? Did he say when we could go home?"

"He did come by to see me, but he didn't say when I will be released. He did say he wanted to run a couple more tests, and I think after that, he may let me leave this house of horrors. That is, if all the tests come out good."

"Of course the tests will come out good—you look terrific!"

"I feel a lot better. I can't wait for the three of us to get home and start our new life as a family."

Jerry smiled and leaped from the bed. He moseyed over to the window and stared into the distance as Mary continued to talk to the infant. Could he trust Susan? He really did not know her at all. On the other hand, what choice did he have?

He watched and listened to Mary cooing at little Gracie. There was no way that he could take that joy from her.

The next morning, Jerry went to the nurses' station to find out what floor Donna was on. If Donna knew the secret, she would be another person he had to be able to trust. He must sit down with her and talk.

"Excuse me, Nurse. Can you tell me what floor Donna is on?"

"Donna who?" the nurse asked.

"You know, Donna the nurse with the red hair. She's tall, she has red hair, and she's very loud."

The nurse laughed, "Oh, that Donna."

"Yes, that Donna. You know her, right?"

"Sure, I know her. Everyone knows Donna. I believe they moved her to the fourth floor. Hold on a minute, and I'll check."

The nurse walked over and picked up a schedule. She scrolled down the chart until she found Donna's name. "Yep, she's on the fourth floor this week. Is there something I can help you with?"

"No, I really need to see Donna. Do you know what her hours are?"

"No, I don't have any idea what shift she's on today."

"Thanks anyway, I'll just go to the fourth floor and see for myself."

Jerry strolled down the hall to the elevator. As the metal doors opened, he stepped in and pushed the fourth floor button. He was scared to death he might make the wrong decision. When the elevator doors opened, he just stood there against the wall, not knowing whether to get off or stay on. The clunking noise as the doors began to slide closed reminded him to throw his arm out to trigger the motion detector. Slowly, he got off and quietly walked to the nurses' station. As he approached, he took notice of two ladies huddled together, hugging and crying hysterically. Three nurses were gathered around, trying to take charge and control the situation. It was evident something terrible had happened to someone they cared for. Jerry stood patiently waiting for assistance, but everyone's attention was riveted on these ladies. Jerry's impatience got the better of him, but just as he turned to leave,

Donna showed up. He hurried in her direction.

"Donna, I was looking for you. I am so glad to see you. Do you have a few minutes to talk?"

Donna continued to the station as he talked.

"Of course I can take a few minutes for you. Is anything wrong with Gracen? Is she all right?"

"No, Gracie is fine, but I think you might need to go see Susan. She's not doing well at all."

"Oh no, what's wrong?"

"No one has told you? You really don't know."

"Know what? No one has told me anything."

"She has cancer. So much has happened in the last few days that none of us was aware of."

"Oh my God, cancer? We are talking about Susan, right, not your wife?"

"Yes, we're talking about Susan. Mary is doing fine. She is really doing very well. Matter of fact, the doctors are thinking about releasing her from the hospital. Her cancer is in total remission. It's like Susan and my wife changed places. And that's not all."

"There's more?"

"Susan is completely blind. She had an aneurysm the other day, and it took her sight. She's a courageous woman."

"Oh no, poor Susan," Donna rolled a chair out from the counter and sat down.

Jerry sat down in a chair beside Donna. With a bewildered look on his face, he stammered, "I cannot believe what just entered my mind."

"What's wrong Jerry?" Donna asked.

"I never even thought of it before."

"Thought of what?"

"Susan and my wife: think about it; they have changed places. My wife is cured. It is like she's never even had cancer. She was on her deathbed, and now she's full of life. Now look at Susan. She was full of life, but now, she lies on her deathbed. At best, she's facing cancer and blindness. I just can't believe it. I can't believe it."

Jerry shook his head. He clasped his hands together and worked his fingers back and forth.

"Believe what? What are you talking about?"

"I just told you. The two women switched places. For some reason, God had the two women switch places. Susan had said the same thing earlier, but I didn't digest what she was talking about. Maybe Gracie is the daughter of God. He has to have something to do with this. It makes perfect sense. I just cannot believe this. Me with the daughter of God—why, why would He choose me and my wife? Why would He give us His child? It makes no sense to me. I can't even believe I'm saying this. I must be losing my mind."

"Calm down, Jerry it will be all right. I think I had the exact same reaction, and it floored me too. To think that there is a child born from the blood of God in today's world is astounding. To think that we even get a part in this child's life is a shock to me. For what reason, who knows? It's crazy, but it's true. Now I guess the question is, 'What do we do?'"

"That's why I'm here. Susan sent me up here to talk to you. She wants me to adopt Gracie, and she wants you to be Gracie's nanny."

"Gracie's nanny. Adopt Gracie? What are you talking about?"

"Just what I said. We adopt Gracie, and you are to be her nanny. She doesn't want Mary to know that Gracen is not her birth child. I'm not sure that's the right thing to do. I hate lying to my wife, but I don't know what else to do. Susan also wants to move to California, away from all of us. Those are her terms, and that is the only way that we get Gracen."

"California? Why California? Does she have relatives there? Is she going to give up all rights to Gracie? What about Mary's friends? What if Mary finds out?"

"That's what I'm afraid of. What if she does find out? What will it do to her? I don't know if I should tell her first or just adopt her and pay the lawyer to keep it a secret."

"No one can decide that but you. I just want you to know I wholeheartedly support your decision, whatever it is. I will never breathe a word. You can trust me."

"I trust no one."

"Well, Mister, you are in a hell of a predicament to say that. You don't have much of a choice, now do you? If you can't trust people, especially in a situation like this, you will spend the rest of your life in misery. If you want me to sign something, I will."

"Sign something. Like what? You want me to write up a contract saying you cannot disclose any information about the adoption, not even to my wife?"

Donna stood up and stared at Jerry. They stood eye to eye not saying a word for a moment.

"Actually, yes, that is what I was talking about. You kind of said it a little better than I would, but we're on the same page."

"I don't know, Donna. This all seems like too much."

"Like you have never lied to your wife before?"

"Not like this. Not something that is so . . . so damn . . . I can't even think of the word."

"It doesn't matter. I know what you're trying to say. But what is the final answer? Or should I say, what is the final decision?"

Jerry paced the floor trying to make up his mind. He rubbed his hands together, ran his fingers through his hair, and then sat back down. He tapped at his lips and shook his head.

"I'll have the papers drawn up tomorrow."

Without another word, he spun around and walked from the room. Donna was left with nothing to say.

18

After a sleepless night, Jerry went to see his good friend, attorney Jim Bello. On a note pad, he had jotted down some stipulations of his own to be added to the adoption contract. He also wrote what he thought to be fair in the contract for Donna. She would be giving up her nursing career to be a full time nanny.

"Good morning Jerry," Jim Bello said, extending his hand for a friendly shake. "What brings you here?"

"Good morning, Jim," Jerry replied, vigorously shaking his hand.

Jerry seated himself in a brown leather chair close to the desk. "I need . . . " he stopped in the middle of his sentence and stood back up. He strolled back to the door and eased it shut.

"What's wrong, Jerry? Is Mary worse?"

"No, Jim, not at all. Mary is fine. She's being released from the hospital tomorrow."

"Released? The last I spoke with you, she wasn't doing well at all. Did they find some kind of miracle drug?"

"Yeah, they did: a baby. A baby made all the difference in the world. Every time Mary held the infant, she got stronger and stronger. If it wasn't for that little girl, Mary would have died."

"Baby? I thought your baby was stillborn."

"It was, Jim."

Jerry took a deep breath, crossed his arms and began his story. "This is going to be a bizarre story, so listen carefully." He began to elaborate. He told all about Susan and how she had allowed him to borrow her baby, and how her illness and Mary's seemed to get reversed. He outlined the stipulations that Susan wanted and the stipulations that he wanted, which was for Mary to never know.

"Jerry, I know we're friends, but I can't do that. They would take my license if I did this and it ever got out. I would lose the firm . . . everything. Mary has to know. You have to tell her. Both of you would have to sign the adoption papers."

"I can't tell her," Jerry groaned. "Susan won't let us have the baby if I tell her. I don't care what it costs. I don't care if I go broke. You have to find a way."

Jim saw the desperation in Jerry's face. He knew Jerry very well, and he knew there was nothing that he would not do, no law he would not break to make this happen.

"All right, Jerry. Let's talk about it. Tell me, who else knows?" Jim asked, getting pen and paper ready.

"What do you mean? Knows what? What in the hell are we talking about—the adoption or the baby?"

"Is that not one and the same? This secret that you're trying to hide: who knows about it?"

"Just Susan, Donna, and myself."

"Who is Donna?"

"She's the nurse at the hospital that Susan wants to be the nanny."

"The nanny."

"Yes, the nanny."

"Does anyone else know?"

"I don't believe so."

"You have to know for sure."

"No, no one else knows. I'm positive."

"Okay, who is the doctor that delivered your wife's baby, and who is the doctor that delivered Susan's?"

"I am not sure which doctors are which. Mary has so many doctors. I don't know which one delivered the baby. Some are cancer doctors. Another delivered the baby, and others look after the baby. I don't know the doctors' names. I just don't know. What difference does it make?"

"Jail time difference, and it makes a huge difference, if you want me to help. I need this information before I can do anything. How soon can you get this?"

"Tomorrow. I can get you the information tomorrow."

"No, today, I want it today. If you want me to take care of this for you, I need it today."

"Okay, I'll get it as soon as I get back to the hospital. Do you think this is possible? Can you take care of this without anyone finding it out?"

"We can make it happen, but as far as no one finding out, that can become a problem. The more you don't know, the better it is. Just let me handle it. I have no idea what it might cost. If I do this, if I can get it done, I'll never own up to it. I will take it to my grave."

"No problem, I will never ask. Whatever the cost, just let me know."

"Oh, I'll let you know. Believe me, it will not be cheap."

"Never has been," Jerry responded.

Jerry shook his friend's hand and departed the office still confused and concerned about whether to proceed in his deception. He hated being dishonest with Mary, but there was no alternative.

Days had passed since the discussion. The attorney had immediately begun to process the adoption papers. There were many sections that had been deleted from the legal document. The obstacles that they had to endure would weigh on all their shoulders.

The attorney went to the hospital and met with Susan. He discussed in full detail what would transpire. He was blunt about the final signing. He told her there would be no turning back once her John Hancock was on the paper. He backdated all the forms and legal documents to a date before her sickness.

Susan agreed to all that had been read to her. The attorney held out a black ballpoint pen, and Susan signed on the dotted line. Her weakened hand wavered as she scrawled her name, and tears streamed from her eyes. "I am giving away the only child I'll ever have. I am emotionally and physically drained, but I know this is the right thing to do."

"Yes, but they are an amazing couple. You could never have picked more deserving parents than those two."

"I didn't pick them, God did."

19

Donna made rounds and saw all of her patients before clocking out. She knew the decision to leave the hospital would be a big career change for her and hoped it would be her best choice. Whether it was or not, she wanted to remain close to Gracen.

As she filled out the last patient's chart, her focus was on the Gonzalez baby. She began to wonder if his health had improved any. If it had, surely this would be more proof that Gracie was God's healer and messenger on earth. With mounting excitement, she quickly gathered her belongings and headed to the nursery. As the bell rang and the elevator doors slid open, Carmen was standing in the hallway. Slowly, she exited and sauntered toward Carmen. She was hoping that Carmen would say something first. "I've come to tell you that I'm leaving the hospital. I'm going to miss you and all of my patients, especially the babies."

"You mean you're quitting?"

"Yes, quitting."

"After all I went through to get your job back for you, now you are quitting."

"I know, and I am really sorry."

"Sorry. What on earth would make you want to quit? I know your life is probably not what you want right now, but you've been going through some tough times. We all go through them. Things will get better, you'll see, just hang on."

"No, it's not about the bad times. I got another job offer."

"Really, something better than working in hospital?"

"Yes, Mr. Hudson has hired me to help take care of his wife."

"Well, I hope you'll be happy there. He does seem like a very noble man even with the lie he told. You know that lie may make him bitter. He may find it is harder to cope with as the days pass by."

"Yes, I know. I believe he is a great man, Carmen. I believe he really is."

"What about Gracie?"

"What about Gracie?"

"Is he going to tell his wife the truth? Or, is Susan going to let him adopt her and let his wife believe Gracie's hers?"

"I don't know what he's going to do, and that's none of my business."

"But if you'll be caring for her, what are you going to say when she asks you about her?"

"Who's to say she'll ever ask?"

"Of course she'll ask; it's just a matter of time. You had better be able to handle the lie that he has told, that y'all have told. I don't want to see you hurt. You know your heart will be carrying this burden."

"I'm sure I can handle it, but thank you for your concern, Carmen. You have been a dear friend to me, and I'll never forget it."

"Gosh, you're talking like I'll never see you again."

"I'm sorry, it's just a little sad leaving the hospital after all this time."

I'm very concerned about Susan too. If she gives this baby up, I think she will most likely yield to her old lifestyle. And that would be a terrible shame."

"Yes, it would, but I believe she has a plan."

"You talk as if you may know it."

"No, not all of it. I've spoken with her, and she sounds as if she has her life all planned out."

"I hope so. Before you go, Donna, there's something I need to tell you."

"What's that?"

"You were right."

"Right, right about what?"

"Right about the Gonzalez baby. He'll be going home in a couple of days. His lungs seemed to have developed almost overnight."

A great big smile covered Donna's face. She was totally ecstatic.

"So, Gracie healed him. I knew she could do it. I knew she was a real healer."

"Wait a minute, Donna. I never said Gracie healed him. I merely said that the Gonzalez baby was better. Surely it's a miracle, but there's always some kind of scientific reasoning you know."

"This has nothing to do with science and you know it."

"Well, no one knows for sure that Gracie had anything to do with it. There is no proof."

"I know, but he's better and that's all that matters. Proof or not."

"I think you're right, but I am not willing to lose my job over it. Someday, maybe we'll find proof and convince the world. And I wish you all the best with that."

"Thanks, Carmen. I'll stop in and say *hi* from time to time."

"Please make sure you do. I'll miss you."

"Yeah, me too."

The two nurses hugged and went their separate ways.

Now that all the pieces seemed to be falling into place, Jerry had to figure out what to do about Susan. Someone would have to fly out with her and get her set up. The only person who could or would do that was Donna. So after talking with the two women, he got on the Internet and began a search for a house on the water in Santa Cruz. The prices were outrageous, but this was a deal he could not afford to bicker over.

After several grueling hours, he had narrowed his search

down to three possibilities. He printed all three sheets and took them over to Donna at her apartment.

She invited him in, and they sat quietly together discussing all the terms of the arrangements that were to follow.

Her job was to become a full time nanny and nurse to Mary. She also would fly out and help situate Susan when it was time for her release. The other papers she signed ensured she would never tell Mary the truth.

20

It was time for Mary and Gracie to come home. Mary felt as if she had two miracles to celebrate: her recovery and her newborn. Hospital officials knew nothing about the details of the adoption. As far as they knew, Jerry Hudson had arranged for temporary custody of Gracen until Susan could recuperate. They were under the impression the Hudsons were going to provide health care for Susan and her baby. Once everyone was released from the hospital, their affairs were no longer a concern.

Jerry cautiously pulled his Cadillac up to the departure ramp where Mary waited in a wheelchair. Donna was behind her, and Gracie was in her arms. The car rolled to a stop, and Donna opened the front door for Mary. She refused and demanded to ride in the back with her daughter. So, Gracie rode home with her devoted mother on one side and her nanny—who could also be termed a disciple—on the other.

Jerry turned onto Calhoun Street and made his way toward home.

Traveling down Maybank Highway and passing through James Island, he had finally crossed the last big bridge entering Johns Island. Driving down the long stretch of winding rural roads, Jerry had plenty of time to think about what he had done. As he passed Fenwick Hall, he gazed at the ancient oaks that stood watch on both sides of the highway and wished his secrets could be shrouded by their massive branches. With every twist and turn, they got closer to the Hudsons' home on the private island of Kiawah.

He had traveled through the roundabout and now was

passing the shopping area of Fresh Fields. Home was only a few miles away. The closer they got, the more anxiety gnawed at Jerry's mind. Four days had passed since he had literally committed a criminal act by signing the adoption papers. Jerry's blood pressure was skyrocketing. His cheeks were as red as candy apples, and he was breathing like someone on the verge of an asthma attack. His wife and new baby were embarking on a grand adventure, but instead of sharing it with them, he was agonizing.

He had to find an escape. He desperately tried to listen as Mary and Donna made small talk. Their conversation focused on the precious child who sat contently in her little pink car seat. They never tired of discussing how special she was and her angelic behavior. They joked about little Gracen growing up to be a princess like Grace Kelly. Donna kept some things to herself, but Jerry knew she shared Susan's belief that Gracie was even more than an earthly princess.

Jerry continued to drive with his elbow resting on the edge of the car window. He periodically glanced in the mirror and gave them a hollow grin. Mary was alive and it was all thanks to Gracen, Donna, and a lie.

The sky blue Cadillac eased up to the security gate. The guard threw up his hand and the automobile glided on.

Donna gazed at the beauty of this undeveloped refuge. Residents of this understated island were surrounded by a private beach, exclusive shopping areas, golf courses, and unspoiled beauty. There was an abundance of protected wildlife that roamed the streets and yards. With this short drive, Donna had already spotted a deer, a raccoon, and a bobcat.

There were small creeks leading to the ocean that provided great fishing and crabbing. The influential island inhabitants appeared to have it all.

Jerry took a left on Blue Heron Court. He rolled across a small wooden bridge and took a right. He continued for several miles until he pulled into the driveway of a striking three-story mansion.

"Quick, Jerry, get your video camera. We have to have a movie of Gracie's first day home," Mary shouted as they pulled into the driveway.

"Hold on, honey, let's get out of the car first."

"No, I want to video her getting out the car. I want every move we make in a home video, so I can show it to her one day."

"Okay, okay, you've got it. Just sit tight and let me get the camera."

Jerry quickly stepped from the car and hurried to the back where he retrieved a small silver camera from the trunk. He pressed the red button on top, and that's when Gracen's life of privilege began. The first person to appear in the video would be Mary. Still extremely weak, she slowly eased her way out of the car.

"Don't get me, Jerry," Mary laughed, shielding her face. "Get our beautiful daughter and Donna."

"Look here, honey, I'm the director of this movie, and I want my beautiful wife first. Because, without you, there would be no family."

"Okay, okay, you've got enough of me. Now get our baby."

"Yes, your majesty," Jerry replied, turning the camera on the back seat.

Donna bent over, reaching into the car seat, and lifted little Gracie. Mary folded the baby blanket back from Gracie's head so the camera could capture her beautiful face. Donna tilted her forward and helped her wave as they entered the front door of their magnificent home.

"Make sure you get her face, make sure you get her face!" Mary exclaimed, taking slow shuffling steps with reluctant feet.

"I got it, honey. Don't worry, I got it."

"I can't wait to sleep in my own bed," said Mary. "I'm going to savor every minute of this for the rest of my life."

"Your house is beautiful," Donna said, looking around the rooms. "I have never stayed in a place this elegant in all my life. When I became a nurse, I was always hoping to better myself with just a simple home. I'll have to pinch myself every morning to make sure this is not a dream, and I really do live here with you."

"It's not a dream; it's all real. And this is your home now. We built an entire suite on the east wing of our home just for our nanny, and I believe we had you in mind when it was designed."

Donna's lips parted further with a huge smile. She was elated and honored to be living with such nice people in these luxurious surroundings.

She turned to Mary beaming in a joyful haze. "I feel so special and grateful that you chose me to take care of you, and I pray I don't disappoint you. I'll do everything I can to make sure you, Mr. Hudson, and beautiful Gracie will stay healthy and happy."

"We're not worried at all, Donna. You just let us know if there is anything you need. Go ahead and walk around and get familiar with our home. Take the elevator instead of the stairs. You'll wear yourself out just walking from the kitchen to the bedroom upstairs," Mary said with a chuckle.

"Thanks, Mary, I will. Before I do, is there anything I can get for you?"

"Nope, I'll be fine. I am going to hobble to my bedroom and take a nap. I'm worn out for the day."

"What about Gracen?"

"Don't worry about the baby. I'll take care of her," Jerry interrupted. "I'd love to have some quality time with our little angel. I think I'll take her for her first walk on the beach."

"Jerry, she's a little young for the beach," Mary smiled and continued to the elevator.

"Girls are never too young for the beach, are they, my pretty? No they're not," he repeated smiling down, cooing at the infant.

Donna began her tour around the manor. She was star-struck and at a loss for words. She meandered through the halls, opening and closing the large paneled doors. She rode the elevator to the top floor and ambled to her quarters.

She sauntered in, still smiling and floated across the room's walnut floor. Fine Persian rugs were scattered here and there. Opening a set of French doors, she stepped out onto a balcony. It was only then that she felt the essence of her new home.

The yard was precisely manicured with palm trees and an array of beautiful flowers. The house was nestled on the banks of the ocean with a dock that led to the sea. A small pool built into the back deck featured a ripple of blue water that cascaded over small and large stones. There were several umbrella tables with matching chairs neatly arranged on the far left corner. By the poolside were lounge chairs waiting for guests to gather. She could only imagine the parties they must have had there.

The house was stained a natural color with green accents on the shutters and railing. The stairs leading to the back door had landings between three sets of ten steps each. Donna was stunned by the way the structure blended beautifully with nature.

As Gracen settled into her new home, she continued to amaze her parents and Donna. She had the ability to sit on her own at two months. She crawled at four months and had already begun to walk by herself at seven months. Mary and Donna began working with Gracen on the "Baby Can Read" program the first week after bringing her home from the hospital. It began with breakfast. As Mary fed Gracen, she sang the "alphabet song" to her. As baby food was introduced, they began to use flash cards. Every feeding was like kindergarten. Learning was made fun. She could pronounce over forty-five flash cards at nine months old.

With each passing day, Donna was more convinced of who Gracen was. It was abnormal to have the aptitude she had at such a young age. She was exceptionally gifted without a doubt.

The months swiftly passed on. Jerry returned to work, and all of their days fell into a healthy regimen of work and play. Mary's strength was gradually returning. Gracen continued to surprise her parents and Donna daily. She had an interest in everyone and everything. She loved animals, bugs, and most of all, people. She had a passion for touching everything. Any living thing was a marvel to her, and she wanted to stroke it with her fingertips.

One day when she was eleven months old, just beginning to run, Donna was playing with her in the backyard. Gracen scampered across the yard to the property line. She squatted down with her hands on her knees, head cocked to the side, and peeped under the low branch of an ornamental bush. Donna crouched down beside her and glanced beneath the limb. A fledgling bluebird had fallen from its nest and was fluttering along on the ground. A closer look made it apparent one of its wings was broken.

Donna carefully reached in and retrieved the little bird. She cupped her palms around its body to protect it from any additional injuries. Gracie was persistent in wanting to hold the little bird. With quick steps and her hands in the air, she didn't need words to let Donna know what she wanted.

Donna knelt to the ground and opened the palms of her hands to let Gracie touch the bird. Gracie tiptoed, raised her eyebrows high, and peered with excitement at the little bird. She gently stroked the feathers on the broken wing. The scared little creature huddled down and sat defensively without moving a muscle.

After a few minutes of steady stroking, Gracie pulled open Donna's hands. The little bird stood up and incredibly flew away.

Donna stood in disbelief, staring into the face of this innocent child. Gracen smiled with her big blue eyes wandering across the sky with serenity as she followed the bluebird's flight. The powers she held in her hands were remarkable. Donna wondered if there was any end to what she could do. She couldn't wait to tell Jerry.

The hours passed. Donna waited for Jerry, impatient to tell him the news. When his car rolled into the driveway, Donna was quick to rush out and tell him the miraculous story. Her hands were swinging and her head bobbed with excitement as she shared the miracle of his daughter. Jerry was not pleased at all. He told Donna that the bird was probably just stunned and finally came to its senses and flew away. No matter how Donna tried to explain, Jerry was not hearing it. It did not happen and that was that.

21

Days, months, and years sailed by with no more incidents, at least none that had been discussed or documented. Donna had learned, if she wanted to keep her job, any miracles were to be kept to herself.

"Good morning, sunshine. Happy birthday," Mary said sliding the plantation blinds from the windows, releasing the rays that were bursting through the slats.

"Good morning, Mommy," Gracie replied, stretching her arms over her head.

"How's my beautiful six-year-old?"

"Oh yeah, today is my birthday! Mommy, what time is my party?"

"Your party is at one o'clock. Why do you ask?"

"I was wondering if Julie could come over early and play with me. She could help us get ready for the party too."

"Well, honey, since it's your birthday and she is your best friend, you may have whatever your little heart desires, that is, if her mom says it's okay."

"Miss Alice will let her. I know she will. After all, Mom, it's not every day that I am six years old."

Mary laughed, "I guess you're right about that. Well, get out of bed. Let's eat some breakfast, and we'll give her a call."

"Thanks, Mom," Gracie said, leaping from the bed and heading toward the door.

"Wait a minute, young lady."

"Yes, Mom, what is it?"

"The bed—we always make the bed before going downstairs. You know that."

"But it's my birthday, Mom."

"Yeah, Mom, it's her birthday, and since it's her birthday, I'll do it," Donna said, entering the room. She lifted Gracen up in her arms and tickled her tummy.

Mary smiled as she watched Donna playing with her young daughter and thought how blessed they were to have her.

"How about I make the bed, Donna, and you take the birthday girl downstairs for breakfast."

"I don't mind, Mary."

"I know you don't, but you go ahead. I still have a few things to take care of up here."

"How about it, Little Bit, would you like that?"

"Only if you quit calling me Little Bit. I'm six now, and I'm no longer little."

"Well excuse me, Miss Gracen, my mistake. You shall no longer be Little Bit. How about I call you *Princess Grace*?"

"No, just Gracie will be fine."

"You know what? I think you've grown since last night. And you've gotten a little heavier."

Donna and Gracen snickered as they began to descend the stairs. Hand in hand, they promenaded down the stairs and walked into the kitchen where Jerry was waiting, hiding behind the swinging door.

"Boo!" he said jumping out and grabbing Gracie.

She squealed, "You scared me, Daddy."

"I'm sorry, birthday girl," he said, wrapping his arms around her tiny frame. "What would you like for your birthday, sunshine?"

"Uh," Gracie replied with her finger at her lips.

"You name it, whatever you want."

"Whatever I want?"

"Yep, whatever you want."

"I want a pony, a white pony."

"A white pony?"

"Yep, with a pink bow on his head."

"Where would we keep it?"

"In my room."

Jerry laughed, "Well precious, I don't think Mommy would like to clean your room after a pony's been in there. How about thinking on a smaller scale?"

"Does it have to be for me?"

"Does it have to be for you? Who else would it be for? It's your birthday," Jerry said, looking over to Mary as she entered the kitchen. Catching the tail end of the conversation, Mary smiled and shrugged her shoulders.

"Julie. I would like to buy a present for Julie."

"But honey, it's your birthday. That's a very nice gesture, but you are the one who's supposed to get the presents today."

"I know, Daddy, but I have plenty of toys and Julie doesn't. Can't I give my birthday to her?"

"You are so sweet," Mary whispered hugging Gracie. "You are so special. You always want to help and make other people's lives better. I hope your heart will always remain like this."

"Of course it will, Mommy. So, does that mean *yes*? Can I give my birthday to Julie?"

Jerry looked at Mary and then down at Gracie. "How can I say no to such a beautiful little angel? I tell you what. You call Miss Alice after breakfast and see if Julie can go shopping with you. Mommy can take both of you shopping for birthday presents for both of you."

"Thanks, Daddy. You're the best daddy in the whole wide world!" Gracen wrapped her arms around Jerry's neck and kissed his cheek.

"You're welcome, sunshine. Now come on in the kitchen and let's get some breakfast. Your mom made your favorite."

Gracen's eyes grew large with excitement. "Waffles and sausage?"

"Yep."

"Can I have extra syrup?"

"That's a lot of sugar."

"I know, Mom, but it is my birthday, and I'm six now."

"Oh, well, that makes all the difference in the world," Mary laughed, giving her a pat on the back.

They all sat down at the table and began eating their breakfast. Small talk centered on plans for the birthday party. The forecast called for a very hot day, so a pool party was in the works. Gracie's face was beaming as she spoke about how happy she was going to make Julie.

Donna drifted into her own world as she visualized the years that had passed and all the kindness that Gracen always had to offer. She continued to speculate whether she was indeed the daughter of God. The miraculous powers that she once held were apparently in remission. There was nothing to distinguish her from any other generous child. She was smart and considerate, but it was nothing phenomenal. Then again, Jesus did not become known until he was in his teens. The anticipation was still there, and Donna was in it for the long haul.

After the last bite was cleaned up, Mary called Miss Alice and got permission to pick up Julie early. Gracie bustled up the stairs and slipped on her favorite sundress. She scoured her shoe bag and retrieved her blue and gold flip flops from the bottom of the bag. She checked herself in the full length mirror and headed for the stairwell.

Grasping the corner railing, she swung her long, gangly leg over the banister and mounted up as if it were a horse. Slowly she slid, making her descent last as long as possible. She headed to the front door.

"Mom, I'm ready," she called out.

"We're ready. Come on birthday girl, Donna is already in the car. Let's go give your dad a kiss and we'll be out of here."

Julie's house was on the outskirts of town. Donna drove the five-mile route. The anticipation was exasperating for Julie. She had been pacing by the door, watching for the car to arrive.

At first sight, she bolted from the house and called out to her mom that she was leaving. Her mother yelled back, "Be careful and have fun." She waved her hand in the air and skipped on. Her long brown hair was tied up in a ponytail with a pink bow. The long strands swung around and slapped her face from side to side as she galloped toward the car.

Gracen leaned over and pushed the car door open. Julie made a squeaking sound as she slid in on the leather seats.

Securing the seat belt, she exclaimed, "Hey everybody and happy birthday to you, Gracen!"

"Thanks," Gracie giggled with gratitude.

"Julie, what do you think I should get for my birthday? Daddy said I could get whatever I wanted."

"Whatever you want?"

"Yep. I just don't know what I want."

"Cool! I think we should walk around the store and decide there. You might find something better than anything you were thinking about."

The two girls chattered the entire way to the store about all the toys they had seen on television. They went from dolls, to video games, to swimming gear—then from dresses and shorts to swim wear.

The automobile turned into the *Toys R Us* parking lot and rolled to a halt. The girls quickly unfastened their seat belts.

"Hold on girls, wait 'til the car is completely stopped and the ignition is off."

"Yes ma'am," they answered simultaneously with a giggle.

Skipping into the store, they perused each and every aisle. They made sure they examined everything they had discussed, but still, they could not decide. Gracie wanted to let Julie pick the toys. Julie wasn't used to having so many choices. The time had come for Mary to take charge.

"Girls, if you don't decide what you want, we are going to be late for your party. Why don't you pick one thing for yourself, Gracie, and let Julie pick something for herself. Then, pick one thing for each other."

"You want me to pick a toy out for Gracie?"

"Sure, honey. That way, when Gracie comes to your house, she won't have to bring a toy. You'll already have one for her."

"You want me to take it to my house?" she said with excitement.

"That sounds good to me," Gracie added, beaming up at her mom.

The two girls finally made their decisions. Gracie got a new seesaw swim toy for the pool, and Julie got a new movie on DVD, and they chose matching dolls for one another. The two girls were very happy with their decisions, as was Mary.

The shopping cart was filled with party favors that Mary had picked up while strolling down the aisles. They hustled up to the cash register and got their total, which was $159.24. Mary slid her Amex card in the slot and waited for her receipt. The girls laughed and played in the car the whole way home.

The two girls leaped from the Cadillac. Rushing into the house, Gracie went straight to her dad. "Daddy, Daddy," she called out, running into the living room.

"I'm in here, sunshine. Did you find you a neat birthday present?"

"I sure did, Dad. And guess what?"

"What?"

"We bought a movie, too—and some dolls."

"You did?"

"Yeah, but I'm going to let Julie take half of it to her house so we can play together over there."

"Well, that's very nice, honey. Do you need me to help blow up your pool toy?"

"No, I don't think so. You know I'm six now. I am getting really big."

Jerry laughed, "That you are, sunshine."

Gracen kissed her dad's forehead and thanked him again for her birthday gifts. She and Julie skipped to the garage and scanned the area for the air pump. Locating it was easy; making it work was not. After several failed attempts to fill the toy, frustration began to set in. Instead of pitching a fit, Gracie took a deep breath and plopped down on the cement floor. Julie quietly sat down beside her. She stared at the black rubber hose and the brass fixture at the end. She fumbled around with the small machine studying each component. After several minutes, they figured out exactly how to operate it and filled the swim toy with air. They were euphoric with satisfaction.

The guests began to arrive, and the backyard filled with children who quickly headed for the pool. The ground became cluttered with towels, flip flops, shirts, and party favors. The adults relaxed in lounge chairs or gathered around the table and exchanged stories of their children's activities during the week.

The party lasted for hours. There were games, prizes, and a pink, two-layer princess cake with a candle no one could blow out. The children screamed with delight as Gracen blew again and again.

After everyone filled themselves with cake and ice cream and Gracen had opened all the presents, it was time to bring the party to an end. Gracie thanked all her guests for coming and for their thoughtful gifts.

Everyone helped with the cleaning and disappeared one by one until the last guest was gone. Gracen and Julie were excited to go to Julie's house to watch their movie. Donna dropped the girls off at Julie's house and returned home to help put the food away.

Julie's mother and father were divorced, and Julie was the only child. Gracie had become the sister she never had. And Julie was Gracen's "sister" as well.

The two girls hurried inside and let Julie's mom know they were home. Julie placed the corner of the DVD in her mouth and bit at the edge, ripping the plastic coating from the case.

"Why are all those dogs barking next door?" Gracen asked,

peering out of the window and trying to see over the fence.

"That's Mr. Michael's place. He keeps fighting dogs called pit bulls. He's really mean to them. He won't feed them. He beats them, and sometimes, he makes them fight until they die."

"That's terrible. Why doesn't somebody make him stop?"

"My parents tried, but he just keeps buying more dogs. The police make him pay money, but then they let him get more dogs."

"That doesn't make sense. Why do the police let him get more dogs?"

"My mom said it's so they can keep collecting more money from him. She says he pays the police off."

"I want to see. Let's go outside," Gracen responded, heading for the door.

Both girls trotted out the rear door into the back yard. Julie peeped through the fence and saw a dog lying nearby. "Gracie come here," she whispered in a sorrowful voice.

"What is it?" she whispered back to her.

"Look at that little dog lying over there by the fence. He looks like he's dead. He's not moving."

Gracie stared at the skinny, lifeless dog.

"Do you think he's dead?" Julie asked.

"I don't know," Gracie replied, continuing to strain her eyes to get a better look. "Oh look, he's not dead. His ear moved. I just saw his ear move. I bet he's hungry. He looks like he hasn't eaten in a long time. Let's go get him and feed him. We have to save him and take him back to your house."

"I'm not supposed to go near Mr. Michael's house. He's not a nice man."

"Come on, we can sneak over there. No one will know. If we don't help, the dog will die."

"You think so?"

"Yes, I do. He's almost dead now. Look at him!"

"Okay, but we have to hurry."

196

The two youngsters sneaked out of the yard and walked next door. The other dogs were alerted and began barking furiously. Julie's legs quit moving. She stood fast, frozen with fear. She could go no further. Gracie's heart pounded, but she knew she had to go on. She had to save the dog.

She cautiously slipped past the chained dogs. They barked and lunged at her, snapping and rattling their shackles. She plastered herself against the side of the enclosure to stay out of their reach, sliding along the fence line until she made it to the listless dog. Dropping to her knees, she gingerly patted his cold, black nose. The small brown dog lifted his head and gazed up at little Gracie. He gave a quick wag of his tail and dropped his head back to the dirt.

"Don't worry, boy, we're going to help you."

"Like hell you are," an angry voice yelled out.

Gracie jumped to her feet and spun around. Mr. Michael stood behind her with his hands on his hips. His tinted glasses were hanging low on his nose, and his green eyes glared over the top.

"That damn dog ain't worth a shit! He's going to lie right there until he starves to death."

"But that's not right," Gracie shouted. "How would you like to starve to death? Your dog is hurting. Doesn't that make you feel bad, just a little?"

Mr. Michael laughed exposing his almost toothless mouth. "It doesn't bother me a bit. It's his pain not mine. His stomach hurts, not mine. He don't want to fight for me, so he can die. Let's see how hard he will fight for his life."

"You should be ashamed of yourself and help him."

"That ain't none of your business, little girl."

"Well, if you're not going to help him, I will."

Gracie stooped back to her position and brushed her hand across the dog's boney spine. "It'll be all right boy. I'm going to help you."

Mr. Michael stretched down and seized Gracie's arm. Gracie

latched hold of the dog's leg and screamed. She scowled up at the man, scared to death. She tried to pull herself free from him but could not. Her face filled with fright. Her eyes started to water. Her body shuddered as she draped her tiny body over the dog. She shrieked out loud, "No, I won't let him die."

Mr. Michael yanked at her to pull her away from the dog, but she didn't move. She held on to the helpless canine, both lying flat on the ground. He jerked a second time, and again, she did not move. He stood over her, staring, trying to get some response. It was something he really didn't want to do. He tilted his head and looked her up and down.

Suddenly, she reached back to him. She sat up and grabbed his right hand with her left hand. Her eyes rolled to the back of her head, exposing nothing but two white balls. She started to shout in a strong voice. The same strange words were repeated over and over, "EVILA SI DOG, EVILA SI DOG!"

"What the hell!" Michael blurted.

Julie watched in horror. She looked over at Gracie, scared to death, not knowing what to do. She was terrified to leave her alone with this irrational man, but she was also afraid to stay. "What should I do?" she shouted waiting for an answer.

An answer came, but from the wrong person. Mr. Michael screamed back, "Go get help!" He now became the frightened one.

Julie bolted away.

Mr. Michael stared down at Gracie as her blood ran from her hand down to her armpit. The crimson red fluid oozed between her fingers and drizzled onto his. She pressed his hand tighter.

"What the hell," he shouted looking down at the blood.

Gracen repositioned herself with her legs crossed, her eyes fixed to the back of her head, and her body quivering uncontrollably. She held her right hand up, reaching to the sky and swaying back and forth. Her head was now swaying in sync with her hand; drooping to and fro. Again, she mumbled those unrecognizable words.

He jerked at his arm, trying to free himself from this tiny girl's clutches. But this little girl had him in a hold that was unbreakable.

As her hand continued to sway in the air, it too started to bleed. Her head was swaying in sync with her hand. Blood splattered through the air, covering her, Michael and the dog.

The ruthless man was still paralyzed. Her swaying stopped abruptly. Her head tossed up, swinging her blood-soaked hair in the air. She stared at him, blank and emotionless. Not taking her eyes from his face, she gently placed her right hand on the dog's stomach.

"What's wrong with you, kid? Turn me loose."

Gracie's only response was to squint her eyes and tighten her lips.

Mr. Michael's face was as pale as death. His brow had beaded with sweat. He dropped to his knees and fell over. He clawed at his abdomen and began kicking his feet. His stomach was seized by spasms, and as his body was relegated to a fetal position, he screamed out in pain. His lips tightened and began to split. Blood trickled off his chin. His tongue began to swell, and he choked and coughed. Within minutes, this six-foot, 200-pound man had wasted away to no more than skin and bones. The strong body had been transformed to a weakling.

The starving dog hoisted himself up and shook free from death. He began to howl in response to the shrill cries from the fallen man.

Gracie continued her hold, and the strange words came again. The little brown pooch was stationary, not moving an inch. She shouted, "EVILA SI DOG! EVILA SI DOG!"

Julie had rushed into her house and told her mother that Gracie was in trouble. Her mother called Jerry and Mary right away and relayed what Julie had said. They immediately rushed to the aid of their child.

Alice hurried to the neighbor's house. She was horrified by

Gracen's appearance. She thought Mr. Michael had hurt her, and she began to blast him with every breath.

"It's not me; it's her. Please help me, please, she won't let loose," he muttered.

Convinced by his words, Alice squatted down and tried to free his arm, but she couldn't break Gracen's grip on Mr. Michael. She was frantically tugging and prying on her fingers, begging her to release him. Gracen kept repeating the inexplicable words that no one understood. She was uncontrollable and wild. Gracie was covered in blood, irrational and incoherent. Mr. Michael lay whimpering, covered in blood. He had urinated on himself and the gritty dirt that he lay on.

Commotion erupted on the other side of the fence. It was Jerry and Mary, who became hysterical when they saw Gracie covered in blood. Gracen continued to chant. Her trance was obvious to all. Her mother and father screamed her name over and over, but she clutched the man's arm tighter, staring a blank, endless stare.

Julie stood in the background petrified and crying. She wanted to help but didn't know what to do. She had never seen her friend like this before. No one knew if this man was hurting Gracie or Gracie was hurting him.

Julie dashed to Gracen's rescue, screaming at the man to turn Gracie loose. "Let her go," she demanded.

Jerry shook Gracie, screaming her name the entire time. In the middle of all the turmoil, the starving dog had eased his head down and licked Gracie's hand. In that moment, in that very instant, without hesitation, she cocked her head and looked toward the dog. Her parents watched in disbelief. Gracie sat up straight, as if nothing had happened, smiled at the dog, and then fell limp to the ground.

Mary screamed as her daughter lost consciousness. Jerry rapidly reached down and boosted her into his arms. He ran toward his car. Mary and Julie ran behind him. The dog jumped to his feet and followed.

The chaos was just beginning for the Hudsons, but rumor had it that Mr. Michael went to prison for crimes that had nothing to do with dog fighting, and every one of the animals he had tortured made loving pets for local families.

"I'm going to take Gracie to the hospital. I'm not waiting on any ambulance," he yelled out as he raced around the fence.

Jerry dashed across the yard with Gracie's limp body flopping in his arms. He grasped the back door handle with his fingers and staggered backwards until the opening was wide enough to place his daughter on the back seat. Mary was hot on his heels. She ran around to the other side and slid her body beneath Gracen's head.

Jerry slammed the car door, raced around to the driver's side, scooted in under the steering wheel and sped off. Rocks flew as the tires peeled away. Gracie lay limp across the seat. Jerry drove wildly down Maybank Highway, honking his horn as he swerved in and out of traffic.

Gracen was completely silent. Her tiny body was masked by the mixture of black dirt and red blood. Mary cried as she stroked her long blond hair.

"Hold on, Gracie, we're almost there."

The aroma of flowers filled the car, which triggered a sneezing frenzy by Jerry. "Where in the world is that perfume coming from? Did you spill something in the car, Mary?"

"No, I didn't. I don't know where it's coming from, honey, but you need to slow down. You're going to kill all of us."

He craned his neck and peered at Gracie. He noticed the blood dripping from her hands. Both hands were bleeding, and both hands had the exact same marks.

"Good God, Gracie, what were you doing over there? He could have killed you. I can't believe you would go into that maniac's yard. Hold on, sunshine, you'll be all right."

Jerry stared down at his unconscious daughter. He looked again at her hands and thought about the aroma in his car.

The scent suddenly triggered an eerie sense of deja vu. He thought about her birth and what had happened six years earlier in the hospital. The scent, the marks—they had both been present a few days after Gracen's birth. The thing Donna called *stigmata*. Could this be true? Could Gracie have stigmata? Could she be the daughter of God? What were those strange words she was shouting?

"This is nonsense," he said out loud.

"What's nonsense?" Mary asked.

Before he could answer, Gracie sat straight up and screamed, "Dog si evila! Evila si dog!" She then collapsed back onto the seat.

Jerry was startled and swerved his Cadillac, making the vehicle rock. He slammed on the brakes, veered off the road, and came to a screeching halt.

He leaped up on the back of his seat to help his frantic wife. Mary was sobbing to the point of dry heaves while Gracie lay limp, not moving a muscle.

"Mary, you have to get hold of yourself."

"I think she . . . she's dead," she cried.

Fear replaced the worry of Jerry's expression. The corners of his eyes filled with tears.

He reached over the seat and slightly shook Gracen's arm. He felt her wrist for a pulse and quickly reported the outcome.

"She's alive, honey, she's alive. Gracie, are you hurting? What are you trying to say?"

Gracie moaned, but never said a word. Jerry pushed her hair away from her face. Her hand slipped to the floorboard, still dripping with blood. With each stroke he gave to her hair, the fragrance of flowers grew stronger.

"Jerry, drive. I have her; just drive," Mary sniffled and begged.

Jerry turned back to the wheel and drove on toward the hospital. His foot pressed the accelerator and the car sped on. His blue Cadillac was performing well. Jerry swerved, dodged, and squeezed between traffic. There was nowhere the car did not fit.

Saint Francis Hospital's emergency entrance came into view. He roared in, sliding until he came to a screeching halt. He jumped from his car and ran around to the passenger's side and retrieved Gracie from the hysterical Mary's arms.

As he ran through the automatic doors, Gracie flopped, both arms swinging by his side, her hands dripping with blood and leaving a trail on the ER floor. He rushed to the front desk.

"Oh my gosh!" a nurse shouted. She ran out and returned with a gurney. Jerry gently set his little girl on it and watched as they rolled her away. Tears streamed down his face as he turned and saw all the blood that had spilled on the floor.

Mary came running in screaming, "Where's my baby? Where's my baby?"

"They took her to the back."

"To the back? What do you mean to the back? To the back where?"

"I don't know. They just put her on a bed and rolled her away."

"And you just let them!" she shouted. "Why didn't you go with her?"

"I didn't know I could."

Mary stomped up to the front desk. "Could you please tell me where they took our baby? I want to go with her."

"If you could just have a seat, ma'am, someone will call you shortly."

"Have a seat!" she shouted. "I'm not having a damn seat. I want to be with my baby."

"Ma'am, there are papers to be filled out."

"I don't give a damn about your papers. Let my husband fill them out or bring them into her room, wherever that is."

"Let me see what I can do," the nurse said in a frustrated tone.

"Oh my God, Jerry, what do you think happened to her?

I've never seen anything like that in my life. What was she shouting? Do you know what she was trying to say?"

"No, honey, not a clue, and I don't think she knew. I believe she was just mumbling something."

"Mumbling? I don't think so. She was shouting something, some kind of foreign words."

"Where would she learn a foreign language?"

"Maybe Donna taught her." He reached down and grasped her hand. "You really need to calm down, honey."

"Well, good God, Jerry, our child might be dying, and we're just sitting out here and letting her."

"Gracie is not dying," Jerry said with a reassuring voice.

"What was wrong with her hands? Did you see how she might have cut them?"

"No, I didn't. I'm not sure what happened to her, but I know she'll be all right."

"I can only imagine what that man could have done to her."

Stigmata. The word stuck to Jerry's head like super glue, holding it right in the corner of his mind's eye. He saw the word over and over like a flashing neon sign. When he closed his eyes, it only lit up brighter. He could not erase it or make it dissolve.

What would he do if his child had stigmata? What should he do? Would this be a good thing?

He shook his head to clear his thoughts. He had no intention of letting his wife ever learn any of this. He sat down beside Mary and watched as she filled out the papers the nurse had brought over to her.

22

"Where am I?" the little voice asked.

"You're in the hospital, Gracie. I'm your doctor. Can you tell me what happened?" he asked anxiously, desperate to know.

Her eyes blinked several times as she gazed around the dimly lit room looking for something familiar. She glanced at the bright eyed, bald doctor but quickly turned back toward the window.

"No, I don't know," she answered with fright.

"I need you to think real hard and try to remember."

Gracie looked around the room and then back at the doctor. She put her finger up to her mouth, as she always did in deep concentration.

"It's my birthday. I'm six today."

"Well, happy birthday. Were you having a birthday party?"

"I was. I was having a pool party," she said with excitement in her voice.

"Well what happened? Who hurt you?"

Gracie glanced down to her hands. Her eyes whizzed back and forth, and her mind was traveling a mile a minute.

There are dogs next door, and Mr. Michael is really cruel to them. My friend Julie and I wanted to help one. We thought it was dead at first, so we went to see. Mr. Michael came out and was very angry because we wanted to comfort the dog."

"Why was he angry?"

"Because he wanted the dog to die."

Gracie looked terrified.

"He grabbed my arm and I tried to pull away, I really did. I screamed, but he kept pulling me. I heard a voice tell me, 'Just hold on.'"

"Was it your friend?"

"No, not my friend. It was someone else."

"There was another person there?"

Without a reply, she continued to relate the details. I held on tightly to the dog. The voice told me to grab Mr. Michael's hand, so I did."

"What happened then?"

"He tried to get away, but I wouldn't let him." Gracie continued to tell her story. She explained in great specifics, word for word, exactly what had happened. She was on play-back mode and she had rewound perfectly.

"I held on to his hand with one hand and the other was on the sick dog. The voice told me to concentrate on the dog and I did. The voice said for me to feel the dog's pain and I did. I took the pain from the dog and gave it to the person that was responsible for it, Mr. Michael. I made him feel what the dog felt. He had to know how it felt. He screamed in pain, just like the dog had. Mr. Michael had to become his sacrifice."

"Whose sacrifice?"

"The voice."

Gracie cocked her head, relaxed her body, shrugged her shoulders, and replied, "That's all I can remember."

"That's it?"

"Yep, that's it."

The doctor could not believe what he had just been told. He had heard a lot of stories from children, but nothing as bizarre and unimaginable as this one.

"So that's all you can remember? Do you know who the voice was?"

"Nope, just a voice."

"How long have you been hearing this voice?"

"Forever."

"Has this voice made you do anything like this before?"

"No, not like this."

"What do you mean *not like this*?"

"Sometimes it tells me to hold Mommy's hand to make her feel better. That keeps her well."

"What keeps her well?"

"Me holding her hand. The voice keeps her from getting sick again."

"The voice keeps her from getting sick, huh? Is there anything else you or the voice needs to tell me?

"Nope. Can I see my mommy and daddy now?"

"In just a minute. I need to bandage your hands first."

"Okay," Gracie said displaying her hands to him.

The doctor reached out and gently flipped them both over. His subconscious mind told him that he was perhaps dealing with a schizophrenic little girl, who might have multiple personalities.

Just then, her physical symptoms—or lack thereof—caught him off guard. He witnessed her healing. The wounds that had marred her hands were closing and disappearing. He rubbed his finger across the ridge of the hole in her hand and felt unnatural warmth emanating from it. The more he rubbed, the warmer it got.

Gracie extended her fingers straight out. She was straining to open her palms as fully as possible. The doctor asked if he was hurting her. She did not reply. The wounds reappeared. He was bewildered. He looked directly into the innocent eyes of the child. His mouth was agape, but no words escaped. She journeyed deeply into his mind, holding him tightly with her hands, paralyzing him. With a quick jerk, she wrapped her fingers around his knuckles. She connected to someone trying to call out to him. She could hear a voice that was neither hers nor his. She listened closely, and her subconscious mind followed the sound to a house. She verbally described what she heard and saw.

"There is a voice trying to call out to you for help. Something is wrong. It's a woman, I think she's hurt. I'll take you to her. You must listen to what I say." Gracie took a voyage to the sound of the unknown voice.

"I am standing outside a house. The house has a bright red door. I am going to go inside." She cautiously turned the doorknob and stepped inside.

"I think this is your house. I see a picture on the wall of you and a woman with short black hair. Your house is very beautiful. I am walking past an orange colored room, and now I am going down the hallway. I see pictures of three different boys on the wall. They must be your sons. There is something wrong at the end of the hall. I hear crying. The voice is soft and weak."

Gracen took in a breath of air and slowly exhaled. "There is a door that is closed. I cannot get in. Something is wrong. I think I hear your wife. She needs you. You must get your wife help immediately. There is something wrong with her. You must send an ambulance. If you don't, she will die."

The door to the hospital room swung opened. Jerry and Mary rushed in. They were hysterical and demanding to know if Gracie was all right. They stopped abruptly when they saw their daughter.

"Oh my God," Mary said, running up and putting her arms around Gracie.

Jerry grabbed the doctor by the shoulders and shoved him. He stumbled across the room, blood dripping from his hands. He glanced back to Gracie sitting on the edge of the bed, immobile, staring into space, lost inside an unfamiliar house. Her light yellow blouse was covered in blood.

"What's wrong with you?" Jerry screamed with fury. "What have you done to her?"

The doctor said nothing. He looked down at his hands and wiped them across this chest. He mumbled incoherently and scurried from the room, leaving the Hudsons standing in confusion. He ran down the hallway to the nurses' station and snatched the phone from the wall. Panicking, he tried to dial the number. He called his house repeatedly, but no one answered. He dialed 911, identified himself, and asked that someone get to his house right away. He relayed the information Gracen had given him. He said his wife may be hurt and she may be locked in the room near the end of the stairwell.

The operator wanted to know how he knew this, and the only answer he could come up with was a lie.

"My neighbor called and said they heard noise coming from my house," he replied. The dispatcher immediately sent out an ambulance.

The doctor raced down the hallway to the emergency door exit. His house was just a few blocks from the hospital, so he believed he might be able to get there first. Without saying a word to anyone, he rushed out and hustled to his car.

Speeding through the crowded streets, he continued to call from his cell phone. There was no answer. Was it really possible for this child to have seen his wife? She described his house perfectly. She had never been there before. He had never met her until today. Was she psychic? He shook his head in disbelief.

Veering into his driveway, he noticed that the red front door was half open. He leaped from his car and ran up the walkway. He called for his wife but did not hear a word. He rushed to the master bedroom and pushed on the door. It was stuck. There was something behind it. He pressed with his shoulder, bumping the door until it finally gave a little. Inch by inch, he gained an opening wide enough for him to squeeze through.

Just as Gracie had said, his wife lay unconscious behind the door. He hurried to the nightstand and fumbled with a diabetes test kit. He rushed back and checked her sugar level; it was up to 1000. She had slipped into a coma. He gently raised her up and placed her on the bed. Trying to stay calm, he hurried to the kitchen for some insulin. He rummaged through the refrigerator, pushing food out of the way and trying to locate the small bottle.

"Where is it?" he shouted.

Someone was pounding on the door. It was the paramedics. They were in the foyer when the doctor ran out to point them toward the bedroom. His professional demeanor had disappeared.

"Do you guys have insulin? My wife is in a diabetic coma, and I can't find her insulin. You have to hurry."

"How are her vital signs?"

"Look buddy, I don't have time for questions right now. Just get in there."

Stabilizing the doctor's wife seemed to take forever, but in fifteen minutes, she was placed on a gurney. The paramedics secured belts around her and hoisted her up. Carefully making their way back to the ambulance, they slid her body through the double doors, flipped on the sirens, and headed for the hospital.

An hour later, the doctor had confirmed that his wife was okay. He headed back to Gracen's room. Jerry and Mary sat on each side of the bed holding their daughter's hands.

"Excuse me young lady. How are you feeling?"

"I feel great. Can I go home?"

"We'll see. Let me talk to your mom and dad for a minute and I'll decide.

"Okay," Gracie replied with her musical voice.

"Let's step out into the hallway."

"Honey, we'll be right outside the door if you need us."

"Okay Mommy."

Concern immediately swept through their minds. Something was wrong with Gracen. Mary trembled while Jerry draped his arm around her shoulder and pulled her close. They stepped into the hall and waited for devastating news.

"So what is it, Doc? What's wrong with our daughter?"

"I'm not quite sure."

"Oh no," Mary wailed.

"Oh no, no, no. There's nothing physically wrong with your child, nothing that I can determine. We still may need to run some more tests on her."

"What do you mean—*physically*?"

"Mr. Hudson, your daughter seems to possess special powers. I believe your daughter is gifted."

"Gifted?" Mary said.

"I mean she can see things before they happen."

"No, she does not," Jerry snapped.

"Are you sure you've never seen her do anything strange?"

"No we have not," Jerry stubbornly countered.

"Define strange," Mary said in a puzzled tone.

Both men turned toward her. "I have seen her do several things that I think are unique."

"Like what?" the doctor quickly asked.

"Like she told me the phone was going to ring before it did. She's talked about people in great detail, people she's never met."

"And that's enough," Jerry declared. "There is nothing abnormal about our daughter, and I do not want you making up things or putting things in my wife's mind."

"I haven't even said anything yet. But you must know that little girl in there saved my wife's life. Had she not seen what she saw, my wife would be dead."

"Oh no, what happened?" Mary asked in a concerned voice.

""Nothing happened," Jerry exclaimed again.

"What are you so afraid of, Mr. Hudson? I haven't even

begun to tell you what your child did for me."

"What are you so worried about, honey? If Gracie did something that helped his wife, I'd like to know, wouldn't you?"

Jerry kept silent and the doctor began his story. Mary's eyes grew large as she hung on every word. Jerry began to pace the hallway, knowing the secret of his daughter was about to be exposed.

"Oh my Lord, is Little Bit okay?"

All three turned to see Donna bustling toward them. "What happened? Julie called me and told me some kind of crazy story about the neighbor's dog."

"Gracen is fine, Donna," Jerry replied.

"I would be interested in hearing the crazy story," the physician interrupted.

"There's no story," Jerry growled.

"Jerry, what has gotten into you? Why are you so rude to the doctor? He's only trying to help."

"I'm sorry, Mary, you're right. I apologize for my behavior; it's just been a long day. And to top it off, it's her birthday."

"Yes, she told me."

"Well, you can understand my short temper. If you don't mind, can you just discharge her so we can get home and finish the cake?"

Donna scooted past and into the room. "How's my Little Bit doing? Are you all right?"

"Hey, Miss Donna. I'm fine, but can I go home?"

"Your dad is working on that as we speak. What happened to you today?"

"I don't know. I think I'm weird."

"You are not weird, and don't you think that way."

"The kids at school say that."

"What do they know? You're different, baby, and that's what makes the world so unique. If all of us were the same, it would be boring, now wouldn't it?"

"I guess. Miss Donna, how do I know things?"

"What do you mean?"

"I know things."

"What kind of things?"

"I know when people are sick and they need help, like the doctor's wife."

"He probably was thinking real hard about it and you picked up on it, that's all, sweetie."

"No, that's not all. I know the little girl in the next room has something wrong with her heart."

"Maybe you overheard someone talking."

Gracen downed her head and begin to speak a little above a whisper. "She will die in two days," she said in a saddened tone.

"Little Bit, you shouldn't say things like that."

"But it's true. I'm not allowed to help this time. I have to let her die. That makes me very sad."

"What do you mean?"

"The voice said so."

"What voice?"

"You know, I've told you before. It's the voice that tells me when to help and when not to. I don't know where it comes from, it's just there. I am weird," Gracen began to cry."

"Don't cry, baby, you're not weird. You are very special. God gave you this gift, and you'll have to learn how to use it. Take your time. It will come to you."

"What are you telling her?" Jerry shouted.

"Nothing, I was trying to console her."

Jerry glared, "We're not having this discussion, Donna. Do you understand?"

Donna did not understand, but she did not say another word to him. She acknowledged with a shake of her head. The fury in her eyes spoke differently. Why could they not have the conversation? Gracen was in turmoil. This was surely too much for a six-year-old to understand. It was too much for the adults to understand, which was why Jerry did not want to debate it.

Mary continued to talk with the doctor in the hallway. She wanted more information. The doctor placed his hand on her back and directed her to the nurses' station. Side by side, they took the short stroll and discussed Gracen's mysterious ability.

While they talked, the doctor signed Gracen's release papers. He advised Mary to contact a specialist in the field of psychic phenomena, a psychiatrist, or maybe even a priest.

"Thank you so much, Dr. Drake. You have been very helpful, and I hope your wife continues to improve. I see the wheelchair is headed to Gracen's room, so I must go."

"Please keep in contact with me. I would love to hear about her progress."

Mary nodded and retreated to Gracen's room.

"I heard that someone is ready to leave us and go home to birthday cake," said the candy striper, smiling as she stood behind the rolling chair.

"Yes ma'am, it's my birthday."

"Well, happy birthday to you. No one needs to be in the hospital on their birthday, so let's hurry and get you out of here."

Jerry helped Gracen from the bed and put her in the awaiting wheelchair.

"Your chariot has arrived, sunshine, and we're going home."

"Hooray! Can I have some more ice cream and cake?"

"It's your birthday, and you are six years old. I think we can arrange that for you," Mary answered, reaching down and giving her a tickle.

"Hold on. We're going for a ride."

Gracen's big blue eyes gleamed with excitement. She waved as she passed the nurses and other patients who stood nearby.

The candy striper pushed the down button and waited for

the elevator doors to slide open. She turned the wheelchair around and backed inside. Jerry reached out to the panel and pressed the first floor button. The metal doors slid with a rumble and clamped closed. The big box jolted and descended downward. When the doors opened, Jerry pushed past and darted to the parking lot to retrieve the car.

Gracen scoured every inch of the first floor in search of something and when she found it, her eyes were fixed.

While passing down the hall, she glanced in a room with a half open door and saw a boy dressed in a baseball uniform. He sat by a shaded window and appeared sad and lonely.

"Please take me in there," she said grasping hold of the door frame.

"Why on earth would you want to go in there, Gracen? That's someone's private room."

"I know, Mommy, but I need to talk to him. Donna, please tell them to take me in there," she begged.

Donna stared into her pleading eyes. "Stop, let me see if it will be okay."

"Do you think that's a good idea, Donna? Gracie has been through an ordeal today."

"I'll be fine, Mom."

"Knock, knock, excuse me." Donna stepped into the room. "May we come in for a second? Our little one here has something she wants to say to you. I know this is a strange request, but it's her birthday today."

The brown-eyed teenager nodded. Gracen sprang to her feet and waltzed toward him.

"May I hold your hand for a minute?"

"Gracen, honey, no," Mary grabbed her by the shoulders and tried to turn her back around. Donna gripped Mary's hand to stop her. Gracen continued on.

The utter passion in her voice was profoundly righteous as she spoke to the boy. She held his hand tightly. As strange as it seemed, the boy welcomed the girl wholeheartedly.

Her smile consoled him. Everyone watched and waited until she spoke.

"Your father will be fine. He will make a full recovery. Your mom is on her way, and you will all be reunited as a family."

"Gracen, what are you doing? You don't know these people. I'm so sorry for the intrusion."

"No, please, she's right. I'm not sure how she knows, but she's right. My father and I were in a bad accident on our way to the ball field. My mom's been working overseas. It's been hard on all of us."

The phone on the bedside table rang. "Please excuse me."

The boy lifted the receiver and began a conversation. Mary was trying to coax her daughter back to the wheelchair when the boy held up a finger motioning for them to wait.

A moment later, he turned with a tear streaming down his cheek. "That was my mother. She quit her job, and she's flying home tonight! How did you know?"

Before she could answer, Donna stepped in. "Gracen is a very special little girl. She speaks to God, and He answers her. It's her gift."

"What a gift," the boy said with enthusiasm. "By the way, my name is Justin. But you probably already knew that, huh?"

"No, I didn't. My name is Gracen, and I'm six today."

"Well, happy birthday, Gracen. I wish I had a present for you."

"Oh, that's okay, I got plenty of gifts earlier today."

"Here, take my hat. Justin removed the hat from his head. "Maybe one day we'll meet again, and I'll have a gift for you and we can trade."

"Cool," Gracie replied, situating the cap on her head.

"We really have to go, honey. Your father will be looking for us."

Gracen plopped back into her chariot and said her goodbyes.

The young boy thanked her again, and the candy striper backed out the doorway and headed for the exit.

Rolling through the glass doors, they saw Mary had been right. Jerry was searching for them.

"Where in the world have y'all been? I've been looking all over for you. I thought Gracen had another incident."

"Incident, is that what you are calling it?"

"Not now, Donna," Jerry spoke aggressively as he opened the car door.

The candy striper helped Gracen from the chair, and Mary fastened her seat belt securely.

"Are you coming with us Donna?"

"No, Little Bit, I have my own car here. I'll be close behind."

The ride home was quiet. Gracen was tired. She gazed out the window and sang quietly. Her angelic voice was barely audible.

Mary noticed the frustration on Jerry's face. She was not pleased. Jerry ran his fingers through his hair and rubbed the tense muscles in his neck. Very little conversation was shared between the two. Over the years, it had become so natural for him to be cautious and to repress all emotions. He did not realize how much he had deprived himself of because of his foolish fears of the betrayal. He was ashamed because he was so weak from the burden of guilt, but he had carried the sham this far. It was far too late to turn the clock back now.

"Look, Mommy, Donna beat us home."

"That's because she drives like a maniac."

"Jerry," Mary scolded. "What is wrong with you?"

Jerry never answered as he stepped from the car and continued inside.

"I'm sorry, Gracen; Daddy's had a bad day."

"It's okay, Mommy, I know he still loves us."

"Come on, Shortcake, let's go inside and see if we can scrounge up some birthday cake."

Hand in hand, the two skipped inside. Gracen retrieved some party plates and placed them on the table. Donna removed the cake from the cupboard, the ice cream from the freezer, and silverware from the drawer. After scooping the desserts onto their plates, they sat down and made up for lost time.

After the last morsel was consumed and the kitchen cleaned, it was off to bed. Gracie kissed her parents, and Donna walked her to her room.

Gracie was full of questions about the day's events, and Donna had to be careful with her answers.

"You know, Little Bit, you should ask Father Wilkins at your church to teach you more about God. He is a lot smarter than I am. God has special people to whom He gives gifts, and you are one of them."

"Donna," Jerry called from the doorway. "Gracie needs her rest. Give her a kiss and come downstairs, please."

"Good night, Little Bit, I love you."

"I love you too, Miss Donna," she replied blowing kisses in the air.

Donna closed the door behind her and sauntered downstairs. As soon as her foot touched the bottom step, Jerry blasted her.

"Just what do you think you are doing?"

Jerry wasn't yelling, but his anger was evident. He was gritting his teeth and shaking his finger.

"What are you talking about?"

"I heard you. If I had not come in that room, you would have filled her head with all that stigmata crap. I can't trust you anymore. I need to do something different here," he replied."

"You're getting a little paranoid, aren't you? Don't like what you're seeing?"

"No, and I don't like what I'm hearing. You just need to keep your mouth shut!"

"She needs to know. I wasn't going to tell her, but she needs to know. I think someone should explain what's happening to her; she's confused. She knows she's different. The kids are teasing her, and she's beginning to believe she's strange. Why don't you let me tell her?"

"Absolutely not."

"How cynical can you be? You know, Jerry, I used to think you were the most honorable man I had ever met. The things you did to keep Mary alive were incredible. But this lie that has been shrouded by secrecy has destroyed your integrity. You have lost what made you desirable. You have become a selfish, paranoid little man full of suspicion and anger. I made a promise that I would never reveal what I know, and I will stand by my word."

"You surely will. I am going to make sure you don't say anything."

"How are you going to do that?"

"Don't you worry, honey. I knew this day would come, and I'm prepared."

"Prepared, what does that mean?"

Without replying, Jerry stomped from the house. Donna eased to the window, moved the drape slightly, and watched.

Jerry retrieved his car keys from his pants pocket and popped open the trunk. He lifted a manila envelope from his car and entered the garage. She leaned into the glass, tilting her head side to side, trying to see the contents.

"What have you got up your sleeve, Jerry old boy?" she muttered to herself.

Totally oblivious of what was in store for her, she gave up and retired to her room. She knew he would go to great lengths to keep his secret from being revealed. Protecting the innocence of his daughter and keeping her normal were noble motives, but Donna feared Jerry's methods.

23

The following morning, Gracie leaped from her bed and raced to Donna's room, but it was empty.

"Donna," she called out, but no answer came. She slid on the banister to the bottom of the staircase and called once again. Skipping through the doorway of the kitchen, she saw her father sitting alone at the table.

"Good morning, sunshine."

"Good morning, Daddy. Do you know where Miss Donna is?"

With a slight hesitation, he answered. "Miss Donna had to leave us."

"Leave us?"

"She had to move out."

"Move out! Why?"

"Her mother is sick, and she had to fly out to Canada last night to help her."

"When is she coming back?"

"I don't believe she will be coming back."

"She's not coming back ever?"

"I don't think so, honey."

"I don't believe you. She wouldn't have left without telling me. Did you do something to her?"

"Of course not. Why would you think such a thing?"

"I heard you arguing with her last night."

"Don't be silly; that had nothing to do with her leaving."

"Donna can't leave me, she can't," she burst into tears. "She is the only one who doesn't think that I'm weird. She's the only one who understands. Why did you make her leave?"

she yelled with tears flowing like a raging river.

"What's wrong, Gracie?" Mary squatted down to Gracie and took her by the hands. "Why are you crying and shouting at Daddy?"

"He made Miss Donna leave me," she sniveled.

"What is she talking about, Jerry?" Mary stood back upright and scolded in a demanding voice.

"Her mother was sick and she had to leave. What's the big deal? We'll get another nanny, a better one."

"I don't want another nanny!" Gracen screamed to her father and ran from the room. The stomping of her feet thundered throughout the mansion.

"What's the big deal? Really! Have you lost your mind?"

"Donna had to leave, honey. You didn't think she was going to stay here forever, did you?"

"Yes, I did. And don't think you can replace Donna! There is no better nanny than Donna. I suggest you get on the phone and find her. She is part of this family, and we want her back."

"She's not coming back."

Mary stomped over to the counter and snatched the phone from its receiver.

"I'll call her myself," she shouted dialing Donna's mobile number.

Jerry put his head in his hands. He slowly looked up with his hands still clutching his face.

Mary's eyes glared with rage. She slammed the phone down and shook her head.

"What have you done, Jerry?"

"I haven't done anything."

"Donna would never leave us without saying goodbye, especially to Gracen. You've done something to her, haven't you?"

"No. I swear, I haven't."

"If you don't give me some explanation for why Donna left

this house, without saying a word to me or our daughter, I will pack our clothes and leave you this instant."

Jerry leaned back and sighed. He rubbed at his forehead and gritted his teeth.

"I never wanted you to know. You'd better sit down."

Mary's face conveyed her shock. She shuffled over to the table, took a seat, and waited.

"When you were so sick in the hospital and I thought you were going to die, I did a terrible thing."

A tear seeped from the corner of Mary's eye. Jerry bowed his head and rested it in his palms.

"I felt lost and scared. I would have done anything for you, you must believe me. Then I met Donna, full of life, fun, and most of all compassion. We spent hours together." He pulled Mary's hands to his. "We spent hours discussing you and the baby and how much this baby was making a difference in your well being. She was healing you right before our eyes. Donna didn't want to do it. It was my fault entirely. I begged her until she finally gave in. That is why she got fired."

"You had an affair with her? How could you? And to bring her into our home and trust her with our child and me. For all the times I confided in her, things I would only tell a friend. Did you make fun of me and laugh behind my back at my ignorance?"

"No, God no! You have it all wrong. That's not what I was trying to say."

"I remember in the hospital you were trying to tell me something then. I remember the nurse coming in and you were very upset. You were going to tell me then, weren't you?"

Jerry stared at his wife. She jerked her hands free from his and leaned back in the chair. Eye to eye, rage to fear, his eyelids slowly closed and he shook his head with a slight bounce up and down.

Quietly, Mary slid the chair backwards, stood tall, and began to walk away.

"Honey, I don't know how to apologize for the things I've done. I would do anything to make things right—to take back the deceit and the pain I've inflicted on this family. I wish with all my heart that I had done things differently."

With one hand covering her mouth, muffling the sounds of her whimpers, she tossed her other hand in the air and ran out of the room.

24

That terrible morning in June, the day after Gracen's birthday, Mary packed suitcases for her daughter and herself, and without further ado, they moved out of the mansion. Jerry begged for forgiveness, but the damage was done; his castle had crumbled.

Few words were exchanged. All eyes were swollen and hearts were broken. Mary didn't know how she would begin to recover. She had been betrayed by both her husband and her best friend, a friend she had entrusted with her child.

Jerry stood at the doorway in despair as his beloved wife and innocent child drove away.

Many sleepless nights would pass as Jerry lay in his bed alone. A thousand times he regretted the lie that started it all, but without it, he would not have his wife or child. Even though they were out of sight, they were alive, and his love for them both would have to be enough to comfort his troubled heart. He would never influence Mary's choices by telling her the truth. Their future was totally in her hands.

The newest deception about the affair was never intended, but, at the time, it seemed to be more logical than the truth would ever be. When Mary accepted the idea of an affair, he decided to go with it.

He prayed in the darkest night to regain the strength and courage to do what was right, but a solution never came. His family had not returned.

Jerry seldom left his home. He shifted his money around the stock market and invested in several real estate repossessions. The money kept flowing in. He had doubled almost all of his new investments. Everything he touched seemed to turn to gold, all except his family. The separation from them was driving him insane.

Every morning, Jerry sat on his back deck and watched the beautiful wildlife that gathered on the beach. The seagulls soared and called to one another as they circled the sky, keeping a keen eye on the dark water in search of food. They screamed and squawked as if to call family members to share their findings.

The fiddler crabs scurried to the water's edge, pinching their unsuspecting prey and scooting back to their holes in a flash.

The dolphins epitomized freedom and joy. Everything seemed to have a mate, a family. All life appeared to be united—all but his.

25

On a cool morning in November, the ground was crisp with the frozen dew. The ice crunched with every footstep as Mary approached the doorway. Four months had passed, and the holidays were coming up sooner than she would like. Mary straightened her skirt, ran her hands across her buttocks, then lightly pressed one finger on the doorbell and waited. Only a moment had passed when the door eased open.

Jerry was speechless. With one hand on the door and the other on the casing, he stared with uncertainty into the eyes of his beloved wife.

"May I come in?" she asked.

"Of course, this is still your home. You're always welcome here. How have you been?"

"Fine."

"And Gracen, how is she?"

"She's doing great."

"Would you like some coffee?"

"No, I can't stay long. There are some things I would like to discuss with you, some questions."

"About?"

"About Donna."

Jerry became nervous. He knew anything that involved Donna could not be good.

"Mary, that was a long time ago. Can't we just forget all this and start over again?"

"How long did it last?"

"How long did what last?"

"You're going to make me say it, huh? She reached into the

depths of his worried soul and without a blink of her eyes, she said, "The affair."

"Mary, I really didn't have an affair. Donna was kind of like a companion. She helped me with things."

"Oh, I bet she did."

"It wasn't like that. Look, Donna and I got drunk one night after all hell had broken loose in the hospital. That was all it was. I felt terrible. She was mortified, and we promised each other it would never happen again, and it didn't."

"If that was all it was, why did she leave?"

Here came another lie; he knew it. He became agitated and squirmed in his chair. His joints popped as he twisted his fingers. He scanned his mind for an answer, a plausible answer that wouldn't result in her leaving again.

"She told me she was in love with me, and she was going to tell you everything. I knew it would destroy you . . . us, so I had to do something."

"What did you do?"

"I gave her a year's salary and made her sign some documents guaranteeing that she could never return. I couldn't live with this hanging over my head."

"It is so hard to understand why she would do such a thing. I can't believe I could have been so blind . . . that I misjudged her character like that. I trusted that woman with our child. I brought her into this house, into our family."

"I'm truly sorry, and if I can do anything to make our situation right again, I will. I love you, honey," he said, clutching her hand. "I mean it: I'll do anything."

She didn't pull back, and he knew that was the first step.

"Tell me what to do and I will do it. I miss you and Gracie. My heart aches for you."

"We miss you too."

"Will you please come back home?"

"Yes."

That was the three-letter word he had waited and prayed for. His blood raced through his chest as his heart beat profoundly. He pulled Mary to him and kissed her relentlessly all over her face. She wedged her hands between them and pushed him away.

"I'm not ready to commit to our marriage just yet. I would like to take it slow and see how it goes."

"Not a problem," Jerry replied. "I'm just glad you and Gracie are coming home."

"Me too," she replied.

Jerry wasted no time in retrieving their belongings and bringing them back home.

Gracen was exploding with joy. She had missed her father, and although she was sad over the dismissal of Donna, she forgave him.

Donna's name rarely came up. Mary had done a good job of filling the void in Gracen's heart. The months spent away from her familiar territory made it easier for her to accept and to cope.

Gracie did keep pictures of Donna, and in the secrecy of her room, she would talk to the image of her friend from time to time and tell her how much she missed her. She was too young to understand the reason for Donna's sudden departure, but she understood her parents well enough to know it would be an uncomfortable conversation if she brought it up. She kept her feelings bottled inside and continued on with life.

Thanksgiving and Christmas brought gifts, joy, and laughter. Everyone in the household appeared to be exuberant and thankful for their togetherness, but sometimes things aren't as they seem.

Although Mary desperately tried to forgive Jerry, their love was not the same. She was hiding behind an artificial smile. Jerry went to great lengths to make her happy, but neither money nor his constant declarations of love could buy happiness.

A few years came and went, and with each passing of the moon, it seemed their life was the best that it could be.

Gracie attended private school at Sea Island Academy and had many friends. Julie was still her closest and best confidant. They continued to have sleepovers and share secrets as friends always do.

One bright warm Sunday morning, Gracen sat down at the altar with Father Wilkins, something she loved to do after church.

"Father Wilkins, can you tell me who God is?"

"Who is God? God is the Father of the world. He is our salvation."

"What is salvation?"

"Salvation means He is our escape, our deliverance from evil. He is our protector, the one that we should go to if we are in need.

"Why does God not let people see Him?"

"I don't know, dear. But I believe if you really try hard enough, you can see Him."

"I look for Him all the time. I do try really hard, but I haven't ever seen Him. Do you think he could He be a woman?"

"A woman? I don't know. Why do you ask?"

"Because I see a woman with long yellow hair, like mine, but she isn't real."

"What do you mean she isn't real?"

"She always fades away when I look at her. I believe she's a ghost. I have been seeing her for a long, long time."

"A ghost, huh," he chuckled at her. "Come on, give me your hands."

Gracie held her hands out and the priest cupped his around hers.

"Now close your eyes. Think about all the beautiful things in the world, all the beautiful and unique animals. Think about all the beautiful flowers, how wonderful they smell. Can you envision all the beauty that the world provides for our pleasure? Doesn't it make you feel good inside?"

Gracie sat quietly and very still, holding Father Wilkins's hands. A smile came across her face.

"Yes, it does. I feel very good inside. I can smell the flowers."

"Well, that is God. God is everything that is great and good. God is everywhere and everything."

Gracie stared up at Father Wilkins with a strange look on her face. "Oh, I understand now. We really do see Him, but, He is not a real person. We can feel Him and talk to Him, but He only answers us through our minds. We just have to have our minds clear and listen."

"Very good, and I think that pretty well sums it up. So every time you get lonely, scared or just need someone to talk to, you know what to do."

"I sure do. Thanks."

"Excuse me, Father Wilkins, there is someone who would like to talk to you."

"Thank you, Father Marlo. Father Marlo, have you met our little Gracie?"

"No, I don't believe I've had that pleasure."

"Well then, Gracie, this is Father Marlo. He is visiting from Kentucky. He came down to see his sister."

The short, overweight priest walked closer to Gracie. He had a smarmy smile on his face. His eyes were empty, almost black. He squatted down in front of Gracie and reached for her hands.

Gracie in return, smiled and held her hands out to his. As their fingertips scarcely touched one another, Gracie had a strange feeling. She quickly jerked her hands away from his.

"What's the matter, child?" the priest asked.

Gracie did not say a word. She backed away, sliding behind Father Wilkins's legs. "What's wrong, Gracie?"

Gracie never took her eyes away from Father Marlo. She

clenched Father Wilkins's pants leg and looked around to Father Marlo.

"Gracie," Father Wilkins called out to her, smiling, trying to tug her away from his leg. She held on tightly as he gently nudged her in front of him in sight of the other priest.

Father Marlo reached out to her again. "No," she screamed at him. "Don't touch me."

"Gracie, what has gotten into you? I have never seen you act this way."

Gracie's brow was furrowed. The look on her face was one of unyielding anger. "You are not a nice man. You do bad things to boys."

"What? What is wrong with you, little girl?" The priest sneered with a half-cocked grin.

Gracie stood erect with both hands on her hips, "God shows me things and He showed me what you do. But I'm not scared like those little boys. I'll tell on you, and God will protect me. You are an evil man. God will punish you."

"Gracie, what's gotten into you? You need to apologize to Father Marlo, this instant."

"I will not," she said sternly. She rose up tall and glared at the priest, and then, she quickly backed away and ran off to find her mother.

Father Wilkins apologized for Gracie; he had never known her to be rude and disrespectful. He assured Father Marlo that she was normally one of the sweetest little girls one could ever hope to meet.

"You know how kids are," Father Marlo replied. "I'm sure she didn't mean any harm."

Father Wilkins left the room to meet with some people who were waiting for him. He could not help but be concerned about what Gracie had said. He knew Gracie too well to think her imagination would ever travel to those wild and depraved depths.

During his meeting, he smiled and shook his head as his visitors talked, but their words were wasted. Their comments were an incoherent bundle of letters rolling from their mouths. They might as well have spoken an unrecognizable language. His mind was elsewhere.

With anticipation prying at his mind, he finally apologized to his guests and cut the meeting short.

A few hours had passed when Father Wilkins was finally able to leave the church. Those hours had seemed to last forever. All he really heard was Gracie. Her words flooded his brain. He was hanging on for the ride, but knew not where he would fall.

Pulling into the Hudsons' driveway, he wasn't sure what to say. He knew he had to talk to Gracie alone, but he wasn't sure how to ask. He straightened the collar on his shirt and reached for the shiny brass knocker on the front door and tapped it gently. After a few moments passed, he noticed the doorbell hidden behind a stunning yellow, flowering bush. He pressed it and heard the chime from indoors. Mary opened the door and greeted him with a smile.

"Father Wilkins, what brings you here?"

"How are you Mary? May I come in?"

"Of course, please do."

"I hate to intrude without calling, but I would like to talk to Gracie if I may."

"Gracen? Is anything wrong?"

"I hope not, but Gracen was a little upset today when she met Father Marlo. It was completely out of character for her, and I just wanted to make sure she's all right."

"Gracie told her father and me what she learned in Sunday school and how you had taught her how to talk to God. She said she couldn't wait to tell Julie. But she said nothing about Father Marlo."

"May I speak with her?"

"What's going on?" Mary and Father Wilkins turned to see Jerry standing at the bottom of the stairs.

"Nice to have you visit us, Father, but is there a problem?"

"No, honey, it's not a problem. He just wants to talk to Gracen."

"Why?"

"She seemed troubled today when I introduced her to Father Marlo. She acted out in a way that surprised me, and I just wanted to know why."

"I don't mean to be rude, Father, but Gracen is a kid, and I don't think you should make anything of this."

"I know, I know, but Gracen is different. She's not like most children."

"What do you mean?" Jerry replied angrily. "She is just as normal as anybody else's kid."

"I don't mean to be disrespectful or to imply that something is wrong with Gracen, but she knows more than most people. She has a genuine, gentle, caring allure to everyone. People just want to be around her, and she reaches out to them. She always wants to help, especially those who are sick. It almost seems that she heals folks. You must have realized that by now."

"That's nonsense," Jerry snapped.

"I have noticed it," Mary said stepping beside the priest. "Please come on in and have a seat. I'll get Gracen for you."

"No, you won't. Gracen does not need to be questioned by anyone. She hasn't done anything."

"I'm sorry, I shouldn't have intruded. I'll go."

"No, Father, please come in. Gracen loves talking with you. Jerry is being overprotective of our daughter."

Father Wilkins turned in Jerry's direction for approval. Jerry hesitated but nodded and stepped aside.

Gracen came bouncing down the stairs as her mother called out to her. Surprised, but excited, she ran and gave Father

Wilkins a hug.

"What brings you to our house?" she asked.

"You, little one."

"Me? Why?"

"I was concerned about your reaction to Father Marlo, and I thought you might want to explain."

"I just don't believe he's a nice person."

"Why would you say that, sweetie?" her mother asked.

"Sometimes, when I touch people, I can see what they do. God shows me things."

"That's enough," Jerry shouted angrily.

"No, it is not," Mary said. "We're talking about things I have felt for years now. I just wanted someone else to say it." Mary consoled Gracen and prompted her to continue. Jerry was frustrated and concerned about what would be revealed. He was strongly opposed to hearing the words *stigmata* or *the daughter of God,* and he assumed they would be at the core of this conversation. Father Wilkins knew in his heart that was exactly who she was. Mary was naive and had no idea of the power her daughter possessed. She had watched Gracen bring dead birds back to life before, but she always convinced herself that the birds were not really dead. Things were now changing. More people were seeing what she thought was her imagination.

Father Wilkins discussed the fact that she might be exceptional. He pointed to her ability to help the sick and needy. God seemed to intervene through her small body. "Miracles are for all ages and colors," he said. "God does not discriminate."

"This is ridiculous," Jerry blurted.

"No it's not, Dad. I can heal sick people. That is why I always like to touch people. God tells me whose hand to hold. I have being doing it as long as I can remember; I just didn't know it was God's voice that I was hearing. I was ashamed of it, so I didn't tell you and Mom. I thought it was just a voice in my head. I used to think I was crazy, but Miss Donna always told me I was a special person and not to doubt the voice, so I didn't."

"Miss Donna," the priest attentively asked.

"Yes, Miss Donna used to be my nanny. She taught me a lot about God. She always told me I was special, and one day I would have a message to deliver. I don't know what the message is, but I'm sure it will come."

"I believe I met your Miss Donna many years ago when you were just born. She told me then that you were special. I remember her well."

"I think I have heard enough. I would like you to leave now," Jerry said in a demanding voice, walking to the door.

"I am very sorry, Mr. Hudson, for the intrusion. I will be on my way."

"Father, may I come by and talk about this with you tomorrow?"

"Of course, Mary, anytime you would like."

"Thank you for stopping by. I'll see you tomorrow."

Jerry stood tapping his foot, leaning on the door and holding it open, waiting for him to leave. Mary was not pleased with his assertiveness. She glared up at him as she escorted Father Wilkins to the driveway. She stood with agitation as she watched his car back away. Before it was completely out of sight, she turned and stormed back to the house. Jerry saw the fire in her green eyes.

"Honey, I know you're upset, but that was nonsense. There is nothing wrong with Gracen."

"That is the first sensible thing you've said. He never said anything was wrong. Actually, it's just the opposite. He was saying how right she is. She is special, very special."

"I'm sorry, Daddy, that I'm a disappointment to you. I never asked for this."

"No, you are not a disappointment. I am so sorry if I made you feel that way. You are just a little different."

Jerry quickly stopped. He feared those words were coming, the words that she was blessed with stigmata. He stared into the lost eyes of his child. He could see she was conflicted. Something had to be done. He lifted Gracen's hand and gazed over at Mary.

"Mary, how about taking our daughter upstairs and start packing?"

"Packing? Where are we going?"

Jerry smiled, "Rome."

"Rome, really Dad? We're going to Rome?"

"Why would we go to Rome?"

"To find answers for Gracie. I think we should visit the Pope, the Vatican or whatever it takes to get answers about this . . . this gift."

"Oh, Daddy, thank you, thank you."

Gracie jumped up and kissed her father with gratitude. Mary grinned and nodded her head with contentment. It was the first time Jerry had admitted his child was extraordinary and needed guidance.

"I'll get in touch with everybody at the office and let them know we'll be gone for a while. I can take care of everything else on the computer. Thank God for technology."

"Thank you, Jerry."

"No thanks necessary. Now go, start packing. We've got a plane to catch."

"What about school?"

"We'll home school you," Mary replied.

"Great, can I call Julie and let her know?"

"Yes, it will take several days before things will be in order."

"You're the best, Dad."

Jerry smiled with contentment. All the years of denying the truth had made him miserable. Now it was finally coming to a head. And after every plausible excuse, Jerry was all out of ideas for denial. He felt fifty pounds lighter. The burden had been lifted.

In the days that followed, Mary and Gracen searched the Internet for answers. Rome seemed to be the most likely place to find them. The three of them left for an extensive stay in Italy.

When they arrived, the countryside was beautiful and unlike anything Gracen had ever seen. Jerry and Mary had spent their honeymoon there and had always wanted to return. Visiting the villages surrounding Rome seemed to rekindle their marriage. They laughed and played like youngsters.

They began learning more and more about lives dedicated to religion, stories Gracen craved. She was very receptive to teachings in the cathedrals they had visited.

They learned little at Padua. The village was an easy day trip from Venice. They saw Europe's first botanical garden, Giotto frescoes, and a cathedral called Basilica di Sant'Antonio.

Matera, in southern Italy, was a little off the beaten path, but Mary thought it might be worth the effort go there. There they saw the sassi of Matera, cave houses and churches cut into the rock walls of a large ravine. From there, they went to Ravenna, near the Adriatic Sea in Emilia-Romagna, a town known for its mosaics. The small town still has Roman remains and museums dedicated to their preservation. Again, they enjoyed the tours, but gained no insight into Gracen's calling.

They spent several months visiting the small villages and speaking with many, many priests. One Sunday, a young Italian girl with a rich olive complexion quietly sat beside them in church. She never spoke a word until the services were over. She gently grasped Gracen's hand and smiled. Her long black hair shined like silk and her eyes twinkled like stars as she spoke.

"You must go to Rome and visit the cathedrals. The answer

to your search lies there."

"How do you know what I seek?"

"God will guide you. Do not give up, for it may take a while to receive the answer to your quest."

Without another word, she smiled, nodded to Mary and turned away. Lowering her head, she sashayed down the aisle and disappeared into the street, never to be seen again.

Mary and Gracen stood dumbfounded.

"So, Mom, should we go to Rome?"

"Definitely, we are going to Rome. Let's go to the cottage and tell your dad."

Mary and Gracen were overjoyed. Even though they had no idea who this mysterious woman was, they believed her.

Jerry was pleased to receive the news, but he too had a plan.

"I'm glad to hear that you may be on the right trail now, but I have to return to the states for a while. I can't take care of everything from here."

"But Jerry, this might be what we've been waiting for. We can't leave now."

Jerry looked over to Gracen and saw the desperation in her eyes. Mary was pleading too, without saying a word.

"Okay, already, you can stay. Take as much time as you need. Just keep me posted."

"Thanks, Dad!"

"You're welcome. Anyway, think about all you're learning here. You are learning a different language, which will help you in the future. Make the most of everything you find out— even if it's not what you thought you were looking for. I'll be leaving in a few days. Do you girls think you can spend some time with me?"

"Oh yes," they both replied.

26

Jerry stayed two more weeks before he left for the states. Mary and Gracen, anxious to get started on their own trip, saw Jerry off at the airport. They returned to the hotel, packed their clothes, and took a taxi to the train station. They had not a clue where to begin, but they were sure this would be the climax of their adventure.

Just before they arrived, Gracen got an e-mail from Julie:

"Hey, girlfriend, I found this for you on the Internet . . . kind of silly to send you a tourist's guide, since you are right in the middle of it already, but I wanted you to know I was thinking about you, and I thought this could help with your questions. It has a lot of info that makes me envious of you. I hope one day I can come out and visit you if you plan to stay for a while. Check out the listing below."

Rome is the city known as the wellspring of the Roman Empire and for the breadth of political and cultural innovations that derived from this unique period of history. In addition, Rome is known as the fount of the Roman Catholic religion, which has also had a worldwide, dramatic impact on culture and politics.

Many of Rome's churches are places of almost indescribable beauty and contain impressive artwork that can be found nowhere else in the world. The history of the churches in Rome mirrors the ebb and flow of political power wielded by the Catholic Church and its popes.

There are over 900 churches in Rome and each offers a unique snapshot of history, and, in many cases, stunning architectural and artistic treasures. Touring Rome's churches can be complicated, as there are so many to see that you will run out of time before you run out of opportunities to explore unique and, perhaps, unanticipated treasures. In order to simplify things a bit, we have selected only a few of Rome's churches to try and whet your appetite to see more.

There are four Papal Basilicas in the world and all are in Rome. The Papal Basilicas include Saint Peter's in the Vatican, the Basilica of Saint John Lateran, the Basilica of Saint Mary Major and the Basilica of St. Paul Outside the Walls.

Saint Peter's Basilica is regarded by many Catholics as their most important church. St. Peter, one of the Twelve Apostles, was selected by Christ to lead his religion and, after Christ's death, he migrated to the heart of the Roman Empire to continue this task. St. Peter, who was the first bishop of Rome (and Pope), was martyred during Nero's reign in the mid-first century and is believed to have been buried with great secrecy in a crypt that is some distance beneath what is now the main altar of Saint Peter's Basilica.

Saint John Lateran is the official cathedral of the Church of Rome and the official seat of the Pope in his role as the Bishop of Rome. The church was built to honor both Saint John the Baptist and Saint John the Evangelist. Be sure to view the Scala Sancta (the Holy Steps), which are believed to include original components of the staircase ascended by Jesus Christ during his judging and sentencing by Pontius Pilate.

Saint Mary Major is one of the most visited churches in Rome, as it is the major Papal Basilica dedicated to the Blessed Virgin Mary, mother of the Christ. Portions of the basilica date back to the 5th century and the initiative to build the basilica dated from the Council of Ephesus, which proclaimed Mary the mother of God. Later in life, after the Crucifixion, Mary migrated to Ephesus, which became her final home.

In the fourth century, the Emperor Constantine built a basilica outside of the Aurelian Walls at the purported location of the grave of Saint Paul the Apostle, who had been martyred during Emperor Nero's reign in the mid-first century. The basilica was enlarged, expanded, restored and redesigned a number of times, with each action contributing an important addition to the church. The new mosaics, cloister, altars and frescos contributed to the beauty and mystique of St. Paul's Basilica.

Mary and Gracen delighted in Rome's treasures. A particular favorite was Santa Maria in Trastevere, which houses a relic known as the "Holy Sponge," reputed to be a piece of the sponge that was used to offer Christ a drink during his crucifixion.

However, many more months had passed without any new information. The months were now becoming years. Jerry requested for them to return home, but they felt as if this were their home now. They both loved it and found much peace and contentment in Italy, so he played the role of dutiful husband and father and flew back and forth for visits.

As the years went by, Gracen had no more episodes of healing or unexplainable bleeding. Mary was beginning to believe her daughter was no different than anyone else's. She was a typical teenager. She loved to listen to music and to dance—and she spent hours on Facebook. She always e-mailed Julie and a few more friends to make sure she wasn't missing anything.

One day, Mary and Gracen attended mass at the St. Mary's Major cathedral. Gracen felt an unsettling connection with the priest. She listened intently as he spoke. She consumed and devoured every word.

As the service was coming to an end, and the visitors began to leave, Gracen felt compelled to approach the altar. As the last person exited, she rose from her seat and cascaded to the front. Mary followed but stopped at the front pew. A force drew Gracen to the feet of the Archbishop. She dropped to her knees, bowed her head, and reached up for his hands.

He acknowledged and accepted. As their fingers touched, harmony transpired. Static electricity sent rays of light, which sparked at the tips of each hand. The priest smiled and looked to the heavens. Gracen's ankle length dress illuminated with sheer beauty. A golden ring embraced both bodies.

The display lasted for a few minutes. The Archbishop asked

Mary and Gracen to join him for a glass of wine and some bread. They followed close behind as he led them through the breathtaking cathedral. The windows were filled with colorful, mosaic stained glass with depictions of Jesus and his disciples. The hallway walls were lined with portraits of priests from the past. Religious statuettes stood in each corner, welcoming them through the large door that was held open for them to enter.

Behind the door was a quaint little room where the Archbishop scurried over to an oak desk and slid out a piece of paper from an ancient looking book. The portly man teetered to Gracen and held up the paper.

"I have been waiting for you," he spoke softly.

"Me, why me?"

"I received information that you would be coming. You are the chosen one of this decade. You have been born to carry the message."

"What message? And how do you know who I am?"

"It is the message that God lives. And I know from this note that I received some time ago."

"May I see that?"

"Yes dear, you certainly may."

The paper read, "The chosen one will be coming. This is the year that she will be revealed. Her hair is golden like the sun and her eyes as blue as the sea. Her touch is soft and warm. Without a doubt, you will know who she is."

Gracen flipped the paper over and back again. There was no more than that, no date or signature.

"So, who gave this to you?"

"A young woman with black silk hair. I had never seen her before or since. But she knew you were coming. She said it several times. I didn't know what to make of it until I saw you. Please, have a seat," he said pulling two chairs away from the wall.

Mary and Gracen sat down on the antique, straight-back chairs. Mary shifted and made herself comfortable. Gracen sat at the edge, eager for more information.

"May I offer you something to drink?"

"No thank you, we're fine. I would like to know what you meant when you said I was chosen one."

The Archbishop smiled, "God chooses certain people to carry His message, and you may be one of those people."

"I'm not sure I follow you, Father. No disrespect to you, but don't you think someone with more of a religious background would be the one you are looking for? Someone older perhaps?"

With a chuckle in his voice he replied, "There is no age to holiness."

"Holiness," Gracen laughed. I am not holy. I mean I believe in God, but I am far from holy."

"Do you remember Father Wilkens from the states?"

"Of course, he was our priest. Why?"

"He contacted us almost sixteen years ago. Not long after Gracen was born, she had unexplainable bleeding of the hands and feet. The wounds miraculously healed as fast as they had appeared, leaving no trace at all."

"I remember that," Mary anxiously replied.

"You never told me any of that before."

"I was really sick at that time. When I saw all the blood, I thought I had hurt you in some way. Donna and Jerry convinced me that it was nothing and removed you from the room, and when you were returned to me, there were no marks, so I just assumed that they were right."

"We have had someone checking in on you from time to time. You know, just to see if it had returned."

"What returned?"

The priest stood from his seat and gazed down at Gracen. "Would you and your mother be so kind as to follow me down the corridor?"

"Sure," Gracen leaped up with enthusiasm.

The priest motioned for them to follow as he went on. The two shadowed close behind and were overwhelmed by the beauty of the building. The relics were spectacular. The pastor stopped at a large bronze colored door and retrieved a set of skeleton keys from the pocket of his cloak. He jiggled the keys into the lock until it clicked. Slowly, he pushed opened the door revealing a dimly lit passage. Several antique light fixtures hung from the ceiling. The faint glow came from twenty-watt bulbs, which created a golden allure.

Mary and Gracen stepped from behind the priest and stood in awe. The corridor appeared to extend as far as the eye could see. The walls were lined with portraits each labeled with a brass plaque.

The Archbishop smiled as he noticed the gleam in their eyes.

"These would be the saints who have passed on before us. They are the few worthy of this honor. They performed many phenomenal miracles of all kinds, each one different but the same in the end. The one thing they all did was worship and believe in our Lord. They carried His message until the day they died, just as you will, Gracen."

"I am honored, but I am not a saint. And I don't have a clue about how to deliver a message."

"It will come. You have already had the wounds of Christ on two different occasions. More will follow."

"How do you know so much about my daughter?"

"We have observed her from birth. When you left the states, we lost track of her. I am pleased that our Lord brought you back to us."

"Was it a young, blond woman who watched me? I've seen her since I was very young. She actually looked a lot like me."

"No dear, it was Father Wilkins. He kept us informed."

"What woman? Why haven't you ever told me or your

father?"

"I thought it was a ghost. Every time I tried to get close to her, she disappeared. I didn't want you to laugh at me. Dad already thinks I'm crazy."

"Your father does not think you're crazy. Why would you even think such a thing?"

"He's always trying to protect me from things instead of finding the answers. Just like this . . . sainthood. No disrespect, Father, but he would probably tell you that you were crazy for saying such a thing."

"Your father is just worried about you, Gracen. This is a big responsibility to be burdened with. People are not kind to those who are different. And if you do carry the wounds of Christ and the stigmata returns, which most likely it will, the media will come and invade any privacy that exists in your life."

"Stigmata?"

"Yes, Mary, stigmata."

"What is stigmata? It sounds scary."

"Please follow me back to the office. I have literature that will explain and help you both."

They took a few moments to admire the portraits before returning to the priest's office. The Archbishop removed loose papers from his desk drawer, secured them with a large paper clip, and handed the stack to Gracen. She expressed her gratitude and left the church with great satisfaction.

27

Returning to their villa, the Mary and Gracen began to scour the pages. Weeks went by as they read the papers and searched for more information the Internet. One of the most helpful descriptions of "stigmata" came from a passage written by Stan Griffin:

According to the Bible's New Testament, the last days of Jesus on earth included the following events:

" ... Pilate scourged him (whipped or otherwise applied punishment). And the soldiers platted (braided) a crown of thorns, and put it on his head ... "

" ... they smote him (inflicted heavy blows) with their hands ... "

" ...they ... led Jesus away ... bearing his cross ..." (to be crucified—put to death by being nailed to a cross)

This was one method of capital punishment in the ancient world. Nails would be driven through the wrists and the feet. Death would come as a result of blood loss and heart failure.

" ... When they saw he was dead ... one of the soldiers with a spear pierced his side and forthwith came there out blood and water."

Through the centuries these passages have been read and re-read. Christians everywhere have been momentously affected by what happened to Jesus. The impact of his death for the sins of others and his defeat of the kingdom of evil still reverberate throughout the world.

St. Paul in the years after Jesus' death (first century A.D.) wrote in Galatians 6:17:" ... I bear in my body the marks of the Lord Jesus." In the original Greek, 'marks' was written "stigmata." (stig-MAH-tah) Paul's statement is generally interpreted as referring to the sufferings that branded him Jesus' soldier and slave and perhaps highlighting actual marks on his body as evidence of what he endured.

Sometime in the early 300s A.D. a few Europeans reported wounds that mysteriously began to appear on their bodies. The word "stigmata" was used to describe those situations. Taken from the Greek, it means "sign" or "mark." Both Greeks and Romans used the word to involve a brand: sometimes on slaves, sometimes on soldiers, and very widely on cattle to identify their owners.

As it began to be used by Christians in the fourth century, "stigmata" was defined as marks found on people, which resembled the wounds (and the pain) that Jesus sustained during his crucifixion. Those so afflicted (called "stigmatists") developed injuries on their hands, wrists, and feet where the nails were driven in, on the sides where the spear had penetrated, on shoulders and back where the scourging had ripped the skin, and sometimes on the forehead where the crown of thorns had been placed.

Often accompanying the marks was blood (or at least what appeared to be blood), in small or large amounts, sometimes on the skin and other times visible just beneath it.

There were not many such claims during this period, and very little official notice was taken of them. It wasn't until the 13th century that the number of such reports began to increase.

It was 1224 when the first undisputed and best-known case of stigmata surfaced on the person of St. Francis of Assissi, one of the great Roman Catholic Church saints.

Two years before his death, St. Francis was praying on Mount Alverna, a place in central Italy where he often went to be alone. He was in the middle of a 40-day fast, feeling weak, and his eyes were burning. While he was praying and concentrating on his meditations, a vision appeared to him: an angel who was carrying an image of a man nailed to a cross.

When the vision disappeared, St. Francis felt sharp pains in various places on his body. Looking to find the source, he saw that he had five marks like those on Jesus' hands, feet, and sides. Observers described them as "fleshy" and "nail-like ... "round and black, standing clear of his flesh." His side appeared to have been lanced; his companions actually saw that wound appear, as though his skin had been slashed. During the days that followed, St. Francis' trousers and tunic were often soaked in blood. The marks remained until his death and reportedly caused him much pain.

Church authorities have not recognized St. Francis' stigmata as "divine intervention." Pope Benedict XIV (1740-1758) said he was "doubtful." St. Francis de Sales (1567-1622) at first believed the marks were the result of heavenly action but later came to judge them as "a product of strong compassion in a person thinking about Jesus' suffering." Pope Pius (1846-1878), like many of his predecessors, believed that St. Francis' stigmata were "historically certain but not an article of faith."

The Church's opinion is that this phenomenon occurs only in ecstatics, persons in a state of "ecstasy," reportedly a common denominator in all stigmata claims. This is described as an intensely emotional state in which rational thought and self control are absent.

The question arises: Why did God start to intercede in human affairs after 13 centuries? If stigmata are intended by Him to inspire and encourage the faithful, it is puzzling that for the first 12 centuries there were only a handful of occurrences.

To explain why, we might consider the Church of that period. It was being criticized for various abuses and for ignoring the average man and woman. It was on the brink of some important changes. The "common people" wanted some direct communication with Jesus, but the Church required them to obtain permission for that contact. So to bypass an un-yielding church, individuals began to suffer with Jesus on their own, feeling that body on the cross within their own bodies.

There are some interesting statistics concerning stigmatists through the past centuries. A reliable, approved list does not exist; but an "unofficial" roster has been assembled (one that is not recognized by the Church). There are approximately 300 names on it.

Thirty of the people listed are currently living. Most of those on the list come from Roman Catholic countries and follow that religion. There are a few from other churches, including the Baptist and Anglican—to name only two. Seventy percent come from the same country: Italy. Ninety percent of the stigmatists are women.

A significant proportion of the cases are to be found among members of religious orders; in particular, the Dominicans and the Franciscans have 100 each. A considerable number have exhibited a wide range of symptoms from "mystical" to "hysterical." Many achieved reputations for their holiness and were later canonized (declared to be saints). However, many instances of stigmata have occurred to very ordinary people.

A number of the stigmatists reportedly died at the age of 33, Jesus' age when he expired on the cross. Many of them were fasting and having difficulties in eating. Quite a few of them allegedly had difficult childhoods . . .

"Wow, Mom, do you think I have this? I don't recall hurting like some of these people did."

"I think maybe this is all a big misunderstanding, but if it is true, we now know what to expect."

"So, are we going to mention it to Dad?"

"No, not just yet. What do you think about going back to the states?"

"I think I'm ready to go home for a while. We don't have to stay forever, do we?"

"Forever is a long time. Why do you ask?"

"This seems like where I belong now. If I want to return, may we?"

"Of course we can."

"When do you want to leave? I can't wait to tell Julie."

"How about Wednesday? That gives us three days to pack and make the arrangements."

"Great! I'll call her now."

28

Mary and Gracen flew into Charleston, arriving on a Wednesday as planned. Jerry had picked up Julie so she could greet them too. Many hugs and kisses were exchanged. Although Julie and Gracen had stayed in contact, they still had a lot to catch up on.

"Hey Gracie, there's a party Friday at Cody's house. Want to go?"

"Cody? I haven't seen him since I was ten."

"Yeah, he's the one you had a crush on," Julie chuckled.

"I did not. Anyway, he called me a freak, remember?"

"So did a lot of our so-called friends, but that never mattered before."

"And it doesn't matter now. Do you think Cody will mind if I come with you?"

"No, he won't mind. Look at you. You're gorgeous. He would love for you to be there."

The two girls laughed and talked for hours. When night fell, Julie went home and Gracen settled back into her old room. It was still decorated with childlike posters and frilly things. Gracen couldn't wait to go to town and shop for things to redo it. She e-mailed Julie and the two planned to leave early Thursday morning.

29

After a fun day of shopping, the two girls spent the rest of the evening redecorating Gracen's room. Julie stayed overnight, and they spent the majority of it gossiping.

"So Gracen, did you date any of those tall, dark, and handsome Italians I heard so much about?"

"Nope, I was too busy studying and touring Europe. What about you? Who is your current beau?"

"You say that like it there have been many."

"Well, you did e-mail me about several different ones."

"Well, I am unattached at the present time. I think I like it this way."

"Why is that?"

"I don't know. I guess I don't have to answer to anyone, and I can make any plans to go anywhere I want to."

"That's the way it should be, even if you were dating."

"You've got a lot to learn, Gracie."

"I know, I know. So tell me, how does Cody look?"

"He's still hot. I told him you were coming tomorrow."

"You did? What did he say?"

"He said, 'I can't believe you're bringing that religious freak to my party.'"

"Oh no, I'm sorry. I won't go."

Julie threw her pillow at Gracen. "Get real; he didn't say that. I was kidding. He said he couldn't wait to see you again."

Gracen downed her head and smiled. She was excited to see her old friends, even those who did think she was a freak.

After many interesting stories were shared, the two drifted off to sleep in the early morning hours. Mary entered the room at eleven o'clock and woke them.

Julie quickly got dressed and drove home. She was supposed to have been home by nine.

As the day crept by, Gracen's anticipation became unbearable. She changed her clothes a dozen times before she finally decided on a pair of designer jeans from Italy and a button up white shirt.

At eight, Julie rang the doorbell. Gracen leaped up on the handrail and slid down like old times. Jerry and Mary heard a loud thud as she landed on her butt. She chuckled, pushed herself up, and ran her hands down her hips.

"Dad, Mom, I'm leaving."

"Have a great time," they shouted from the den.

Gracen hurried out the door, and the two girls raced down the steps to a red convertible.

"Cool car," Gracie said, buckling her seat belt.

"Thanks, my mom let me borrow it. Someday, it will be mine."

"I hear you."

Cody's house was not far from Gracen's. When the girls arrived, there was a welcoming committee for Gracie. She was very pleased that her friends remembered her after such a long time away.

She played catch up with a few girls. Then Cody walked in, still looking as hot as Julie had promised.

"Well, look at you," he said, reaching for Gracie's hand. "You are beautiful."

She blushed, showing the innocence she had never left behind. Her long hair fell to her face as she lowered her head and giggled.

"Still shy, huh?"

"A little," she softly replied, looking into his eyes.

"I know this sounds corny, but your eyes tell a story. You should never have to talk. You could say everything just by looking at someone."

"Huh?"

"Never mind, you just have beautiful eyes."

"Thanks."

"Come on in and have a good time. Hey everybody, remember Gracen from elementary school?" he shouted, walking in front of them and holding up a beer.

The crowd yelled greetings to her and continued what they were doing.

She and Julie mingled for a while, and then Julie disappeared with a former boyfriend.

Gracie slipped away from the party to get some air. Making her way through the crowd to the kitchen, she found Paula with Billy and Cody guzzling Jell-O shooters one after another. Paula stumbled and almost fell over a stool.

"Come on, girlfriend, let's get you outside and get some air. You need to sober up before you go home."

"Sober up. What for? I'm having fun, and I don't care if I even go home," Paula slurred.

"Come on now," Gracie said, pulling her along and supporting her weight.

Paula was a school friend from her elementary school years. She was petite with shoulder length brown hair and big brown puppy dog eyes. Her friends Billy and Cody were football stars. Both were very popular in the school.

The two girls, arm in arm, staggered from the house. They both stumbled around in laughter. Gracie tried to keep Paula balanced as they wobbled down the steps from the porch.

"Hey Gracie, who's house are we at?"

"It's Cody's."

"I didn't know he lived on the beach."

"Yeah, he's been living here for a while. The view is awesome."

"Gracie?"

"Yeah."

"I think I'm drunk."

"You think so?"

"Yeah, I think so. Gracie?"

"Yeah."

"I think I'm gonna be sick. Hurry and get me to the bushes. I'm gonna be really sick."

Gracie put her arm around Paula and helped her stagger to the edge of the yard. Paula dropped to her knees and started to vomit.

Gracie turned her head away and started to gag. "So, this is fun."

"It was ten minutes ago," Paula stammered.

"Hey, are you all right? I need to step away from you before I get sick too. Can I leave you alone for just a minute?"

"Sure, yeah," Paula replied, spitting the leftover residue into the bushes.

"I'll be right back. I'll see if I can get you a washcloth."

"Thanks, girl. You're the best."

"I'll be right back. Don't go anywhere."

"Go anywhere? Hell, I can't even stand up," she said, plopping down on the ground, crossing her legs, and sitting Indian style.

Gracie laughed and walked through the thick white sand toward the house. Making her way back up the wooden steps, she took a quick glance over her shoulder and saw Paula in the same position with her head and shoulders drooping.

Gracie noticed Billy, an old classmate, staggering toward Paula. She felt better heading into the house now that Paula wasn't alone.

Everyone was laughing and dancing. The party was a hit, but no one was out of control. Gracie reached the bathroom door, tapped gently, and turned the knob to enter. As she stepped onto the marble tile, someone grabbed her arm. She whirled around and smiled at Cody.

"Cody! What are you doing?"

"Come on, Gracie, dance with me."

"I've got to use the bathroom. Let me go."

"If I let you go, will you dance with me when you come out?"

"Maybe, but if you don't let me go, I'm going to pee in the floor."

"Oh baby! By all means, go pee," he said releasing her arm and meandering away.

As she was washing her hands, someone pounded on the door. Surely Cody hadn't come back. "Come on, hurry up. Who's in there?" a voice sounded in tandem with pounding from the other side of the door.

"I'm coming. Give me a second," Gracie replied. She looked in the mirror and ran her hands through her hair.

"Come on," the voice shouted with another hammering of the door.

Gracie turned the knob and stepped out to see an unusual looking girl. A tall, slender girl with grass-green eyes leaned against the wall waiting her turn. Her short hair was dyed coal black; her face was a pin cushion with piercings in her eyebrows, nose, and lips. Gracie stood gawking at the unfamiliar female.

"What is your problem? Do you want to take a picture? Are you gonna let me take a piss or what?"

"Oh, I'm sorry. Gracie stepped from doorway with her big blue eyes focused on this wild child.

"Hey Gracie, what about that dance? Come on, this is a jamming song."

"Go ahead, Cody," Gracie chuckled. "You look like you are doing an awesome job by yourself."

"You like that." Cody danced across the floor toward her.

"Yeah, I like that, but I need to go check on Paula. I'll be back in a minute." Gracie waved her hand and trotted out the door.

Snickering and dancing down the steps to the beach, she felt a cool breeze from the crashing waves wash across her face. She settled on the bottom step for a brief moment to enjoy the view. The tranquility of the ocean temporarily erased her concerns for Paula. The full moon lit up the magnificent, endless sea. The waves rolled high and ravished the sand.

She slid her feet deep into the warm sand and wiggled her toes. She closed her eyes, and her long blond mane blew in the wind; she swayed from side to side as the faint sound of music ricocheted in the wind.

The music soothed her soul until an indistinct cry resonated through the breeze. She opened her eyes and turned in the direction of the sound. She heard nothing but felt concerned enough to look around.

"Nooooo," someone screamed loudly.

Gracie jumped to her feet. "Paula," she shouted. "Paula," she called leaping to the dense sand.

She ran to the bushes, but there was no Paula. She ran further on the beach. She looked in both directions as far as her eyes would allow her to see. Still, there was no one.

"Pau . . . la," she screamed. "Billy," she yelled louder. No one answered.

Gracie was scared and became frantic. She stroked her wildly blowing hair from her face and twisted it to one side. "Pau . . . la," she screamed again.

She heard a faint cry and stopped to listen more intently.

"Nooooo," Gracie heard it clearly.

At the edge of the sand dune, she caught a slight glimpse of movement. Immediately, her long legs leaped across the brush and ran toward it. The thick sand sucked at her feet, straining her calves, the muscles that gave her speed. She felt as though weights were strapped to her ankles, pulling her deeper into the sand as she climbed to the top of the dune. She peered down into the valley of the dune and the moon cast light on a menacing scene. Billy lay on top of Paula, while she begged, fought, and pleaded for him to get off of her. She was helpless underneath his weight.

Gracie stumbled down the sand dune, and Billy never knew she was there. She drew her arm back and delivered a blow to the side of his head.

"Shit!" he shouted as he regained his balance. "You little freak. You want some to?" He soared to his feet and grabbed Gracie's arm.

"What's wrong with you, Billy? Don't you know what *no* means?"

"Hell no, I don't know what *no* means, unless it means *yes*. It means *yes* in my book," Billy said. He grabbed Gracie and roughly kissed the side of her neck.

"You bastard!" Gracie exclaimed, looking down at Paula. Her shirt had been ripped from her chest. "You need to go sober up, boy."

"That's not what I need. I need you." He threw Gracie to the ground and fell on top of her.

"Get off me! Get off me!" she shouted.

"Not a chance. You know you want me."

"You bastard! You're a sick bastard!"

Billy tugged at Gracie's clothes. Paula sat up and pulled her shirt back up to her shoulder. She rolled over to her knees and staggered to her feet. She stood for a brief moment then lurched away to get help.

Billy never noticed Paula's departure. He continued to grope at Gracie's shirt.

"No," Gracie screeched. Her demeanor changed. Her arms flared out. Her body stiffened flat to the ground. Her legs spread, and her convulsions created a tremor.

"Oh yeah, baby, that's it," Billy said.

Gracie took a deep breath. Her body shook furiously. In a split second, she flipped Billy over and pinned him to the ground, ripping off his shirt.

"Oh yeah, baby," Billy exclaimed. "I knew you wanted me."

"I said *no*," her voice deepened. "What part of *no* don't you understand? Did you not hear Paula say *no*?" she said in a commanding voice.

Lightning struck the white sandy dune and lit up the sky. The wind danced across the sand as Gracie began to rant over and over, "We said *no*!"

With the flash of the lightning, Gracie's face was revealed. "Oh my God," Billy shouted. Her long blond hair thrashed wildly in the wind. Her blue eyes were turned to the back of her head, so nothing but the whites were exposed. Sitting up straight, still on top of him, she stretched up toward the sky. Lightning struck and skated across the water. Horrified, Billy was unable to move.

"No!" he implored. "Come on, Gracie, that's enough. Stop." She never responded.

"Somebody help me!" he shrieked with fear.

"How does it feel?" she queried in a strange deep voice.

"I'm sorry. I'm sorry, Gracie."

Paula and some friends from the party climbed to the top of the dune and were astounded by what they saw. Everyone stood cheering on the mound as they saw that the roles had been reversed, with Gracen dominating Billy, but they were unaware of what was really happening. Her head was lowered over Billy's face, so the unsuspecting friends were unable to see her eyes.

Slowly, Gracie arose and stood erect. She stretched both hands to the sky. Her eyes were closed. Her arms jerked feverishly. Lightning bolted from the heavens to the ground and traveled up her legs to her fingertips. She screamed a crucifying squeal and expelled the strange language she had uttered as a child: "DOG SI EVILA! EVILA SI DOG!"

"Oh no," Julie yelled out. "Someone needs to help her!" she shouted.

"Help her? Someone needs to help Billy," a bystander yelled.

Gracie turned to the crowd and they got a full view of the hideous scene. The strands of her hair swirled like tiny branches in a whirlwind. The group huddled in disbelief.

Gracen turned back to Billy and stepped to his side, her arms stretched out, with fingers spread wide. Slowly, her palms began to droop, but her arms remained outstretched. Blood flowed down and hung at the tips of each finger. Her head bowed, her shoulders sagged, and without effort, she crossed her feet. She was sprawled, slumped, and appeared to be perched, hanging limp in the air. The lightning bolts caressed the sand around her feet. The blood drizzled and dripped to the white grit. It was a striking image of a female Jesus on a cross.

Julie ran down the dune to Gracie's aid.

"Gracie." Softly, she called her name. Julie lifted Gracie's head and brushed her hair away. She was startled by the sight.

A thin strand of her hair was embedded in Gracie's forehead. Her eyes were shrouded by the blood from her brow. Her weary lids with the slowly seeping fluid displayed sorrow and disappointment.

The silver bolts from the universe fired with fury and knocked Julie to the ground. Light encircled and elevated Gracie's body. She seemed to be unaware that her body was rising. Her body ascended far above Billy.

Julie jumped to her feet and leaped to save her friend. Gracie's arms were still stretched, her head drooped low, and she was hanging in midair with her feet crossed.

Julie wept like a baby. "Somebody get down here and help," she pleaded.

Their friends, one by one, stumbled down the dune. They

gathered around and observed, but no one touched her.

The wind blew swiftly through the crowd. Gracie's blond mane lashed in the wind, except the stationary piece that was plastered into her forehead.

Gracie began an incoherent chant. They all covered their faces as the wind swept the beach.

The buttons on Gracie's white shirt popped and sailed through the air. The blouse flared behind her like wings holding her aloft. The bloodstained sand twisted, snaked, and rose to her side. It twirled like a funnel, holding her high above the others. She continued to chant her broken words.

"Jesus, she looks like Jesus!" someone shouted.

"Oh God, she does," another responded.

"What's going on? We have to help her," Julie screamed. "Help me get her feet," she screamed, jumping in the air.

No one moved. Everyone was paralyzed by fear and disbelief. Mouths dropped open; eyes stretched wide, directed to the sky. Gracie's body levitated and hovered above, her hair blowing, dancing in the swift wind. The blood from her forehead ran down and dripped from her chin.

She held her hands palms up with blood dripping through her fingers.

"Come on, help!" Julie shouted again. "Cody," Julie called out. Come help me."

Cody, being 6'4" and the tallest one of the group, scurried through the crowd and reached up. He touched the bottom of Gracie's feet, but he couldn't get a grip.

"Jump up," Julie shouted. "Jump up and grab her!"

Cody did as he was asked and jumped up and got a tight hold on Gracie's feet, and inch by inch, he tugged, wrenching her back toward the ground. Her body's position never changed; her legs were still crossed. He slowly pulled until her body reached arm's length and Julie could help. She grabbed hold of Gracen's legs while her arms stayed stationary in space.

The crowd backed away as Gracen's body glowed in the dark. Cody quickly released his grip as his face turned gray. Julie shouted at him to help her, but he backed away. Gracie's face was streaked with blood from her forehead carried by the hair that was still flying wildly in the wind.

Julie wrapped her arms tightly and fell to her knees, hauling Gracie back to earth. Gracie stood erect but limp. She pulled Gracen's arms to her side, shook her flaccid body and called her name over and over again.

The wind blew wildly through the crowd. Gracie's eyes rolled back to normal and she turned her head and stared at her fearful friends. With a smile, she slowly moved her hands and reached out to the group.

"EVILA SI DOG, EVILA SI DOG," she moaned. As the last syllable slurred from her lips, her body fell limp and dropped to the ground. She lay unconscious, not moving a muscle.

Julie knelt down beside her. She cried out for someone to call 911. Paula yelled to the crowd to help get Gracie back to the house. They all looked at each other, hoping someone else would be willing to help. No one wanted to touch her.

"I'm not touching that crazy thing!" Billy shouted.

"If it weren't for you, she wouldn't be in this condition, you no good bastard." Paula drew her hand back to slap him. Cody seized her hand. "He's not worth it, Paula. Don't waste your time. Come on, let's get Gracie up to the house."

"I don't think you should move her," someone called out from the crowd.

"Yeah, don't move her," a voice demanded from the beach.

Everyone turned to look. A short, muscular man descended from the top of the dune and faced the group.

"I'm a paramedic. My name is Daniel. I live right down the beach," he said, pointing to the left. "I was listening to the scanner when I heard someone was hurt down here. What's the problem?"

"It's my friend Gracie."

The paramedic hurried over to Gracen and knelt down beside her. He shined his flashlight down on her face. "What happened to her? Who did this?"

"Billy," Paula shouted, pointing to him.

"I didn't touch her. You're as crazy as she is."

"Boy, don't you go anywhere," the paramedic said firmly.

"I'm not. I didn't do it. Everyone here knows I did not touch her. She did this to herself."

The paramedic looked at Julie, hoping for an answer. She had none. She didn't know what had happened that night, and she didn't know what had happened when she and Gracen were children. Thankfully, before she could say anything, more paramedics came. All of them had the same question: "What happened here?" There was grave concern over Gracen's blood loss. Gently, they examined her, searching for her wounds.

"The only wounds are on her forehead and the palms of her hands. That's where all this blood came from," Julie said.

"What's her name?" Daniel asked.

"Her name is Gracie, Gracen Hudson. She's my best friend."

"Do you know what happened to her?"

Julie looked away, avoiding the question.

"Look, if you know what happened here, you need to speak up," Daniel repeated in a stern voice.

Julie sucked in a deep breath. "I really don't know. Last time this happened, I was too young and no one would tell me anything."

"Last time? Something like this has happened before?"

"It was years ago. It wasn't quite this bad. We were only six years old. It was on Gracie's sixth birthday. She's sixteen and it happened again."

"What happened again?"

"I told you I don't know."

The three other paramedics steadily working on Gracen hesitated for a brief moment and gawked at Julie. With all ears tuned for her answer, they continued to lift Gracie to a gurney and strap her down.

"Look, Daniel, we need to get her to the hospital. We can't wait for answers.

"Y'all go ahead. I'll stay until the police get here."

The paramedics climbed to the top of the dune and faded away into the dark. Daniel continued his interrogation of the teenagers.

"Well, did she just cut herself? What did she use?" the paramedic inquired.

"No, she didn't cut herself. It just happened."

"What's your name, kid?"

"Julie."

"Well, Julie, you look like a smart girl. You should know that there's no way stuff like this just happens. Either someone did it to her or she did it to herself. Is that it—are you covering for someone? Was it one of your friends here?"

A police officer lurched down the hill. "What in the hell happened out here? Somebody better start talking. I wanna know who did this to that girl."

"No one did it to her," Cody shouted. "We were all here. We all saw it. She did it to herself. She started screaming and yelling something in a foreign language."

"What language?" the officer asked.

"I don't know, some other kind of language. I've never heard anything like it. Her voice got really deep. Then, her hands started bleeding. Her eyes rolled back in her head. We thought she was dying. The freakiest thing was when she floated in the air."

"What?" the policeman shouted.

"She floated up in the air," Cody said again.

"You gotta be kidding me. Do I look stupid to you, son?"

"Do I look stupid to you?" Cody replied. "I'm telling you, we all saw it. She was floating in midair, just hanging there, with her legs crossed and her arms straight out. It was weird as shit. It was like she was on a cross."

"Next, I guess you're gonna tell me she looked like Jesus."

"I wasn't going to, but since you mentioned it, I guess she did kind of look like Jesus."

"How much have you had to drink tonight, kid? I think you might need to be tested for your alcohol content." The officer grabbed Cody's arm.

"Hey," a young girl yelled from the crowd. Everyone turned to see who it was. The girl with the piercings was holding up her cell phone.

"Look at this; I got it. I had the camera on my phone the whole time."

"Let me see that."

The police officer and Daniel played the video. The young people stood silently, waiting for their reaction, hoping someone could put what they had seen in perspective.

"I'm going to have to take this phone with me," the officer said, masking his shock.

"Like hell you are," the strange girl shouted, reaching out to retrieve her phone.

The policeman jerked the phone in close to his chest. "This is evidence now. I'm going to need this. No one will ever believe me without it."

"But that's mine."

"You'll get it back. Give me your name, address, and home phone number, and we'll be in touch as soon as we've processed the evidence."

She shook her head and walked away.

"Look officer, I'd like to go to the hospital to be with my friend. May I please leave?" Julie requested.

"I might need you later. Leave all your information here.

Did you say this party was for her?"

"No, she only came to this party to be with friends. Gracie is a good person. She just wanted to be part of the gang. You know, hang with everybody."

"Yeah, whatever you say."

30

Julie arrived at the hospital and ran to the emergency entrance. There were people everywhere. She could barely get through the doors. She pushed her way through the crowd to the nurses' station.

"What happened? Has there been a bus wreck or something?"

"No dear, quite the contrary."

"Well, what is it? An epidemic?"

"No. A young woman was brought in here earlier. People are saying she's been touched by Jesus," a female medical student whispered.

Julie looked around the room, and then she retorted, "It wouldn't be Gracen Hudson, would it?"

"Yes, it was. Do you know her?"

"She's my best friend."

"Your best friend? Hey guys, this is the Hudson girl's best friend," the nurse called out.

A camera flashed in the corner of the room. People were rushing to Julie like they were in a race, pushing and shoving each other, trying to ask questions.

"How long have you known her? Has she always done weird stuff? Can she heal people?"

Julie's eyes darted from person to person. Before she could consider answering any of their questions, the officer from the beach showed up.

"Hey, let's break it up in here. This is a hospital, not a newsroom. I want everyone outside. Now!" he shouted.

"But we want to see the miracle child. My daughter has

leukemia, and I want to see if she can heal her."

And my mother has emphysema," another person shouted. "She's not going to live without a miracle."

The police officer looked around the crowd. Everyone was begging for help. They just wanted to see for themselves, just a touch—a mere glimpse would be enough. They needed to see the miracle that everyone was talking about, the angel that God had sent to save them.

Who was she? Where did she come from? What did she look like? Could this be the second coming of Christ?

A bright light flooded the waiting room. Everyone turned to see what it was. "Where is she?" a man asked. They all shielded their eyes, still trying to determine the source of the glow.

Oh wow, it's Mr. Pepper from Channel 5 news," someone shouted.

The reporter turned to the crowd and smiled. He gave a slight wave and turned back for his answer.

"She's in the back. The doctors are with her," the nurse answered. "You need to turn those camera lights off. This is a hospital."

"Just trying to get a story, ma'am. I'd like to see the girl. This is one of the best stories that I've covered in a long time. Does anyone know exactly what happened out there on the beach?"

"She does," a girl stood up in the crowd and pointed to Julie. "She's her best friend."

Jim Pepper spun around. Julie was being swallowed by the crowd. He saw her duck behind an overweight man and hustled over to her. "Is that true, honey? Were you there? Are you her best friend?"

"Yes it's true," Julie softly answered. "We were just partying. She just returned to the states."

"Partying? So is all this a hoax? Cut the tape," he yelled to the cameraman. "I thought someone said that another girl had been attacked. I was told she beat the hell out of the perpetrator."

"She did," Julie softly replied.

"So, tell me what happened. Who cut this girl up?"

"No one did it. It just happened."

"There is no way, from what I was told, that something like this could just happen. There is no way someone is going to cut herself up like that. Come on, tell us really what happened out there."

"She wasn't cut. She was upset. She just got really mad at this boy who was there. He was hurting our friend. She tried to make him stop, and it just happened."

"What happened? How did it happen? Just take your time. Don't leave anything out." He turned to his cameraman and snapped his fingers for the lights to be turned on.

"I don't know what happened."

"I know. I was there," came a voice from within the crowd.

All bodies suddenly turned to look. Jim leaned to one side and looked around Julie. The crowd started to separate, one by one, until the person who had spoken was in plain view. There, in the back of the room, stood the girl who had waited outside the bathroom door, the girl who had recorded everything.

"I got it all on my cell phone."

"What!" Jim pushed Julie aside and made his was to the girl. "What's your name, kid?"

"Well, it's not *kid*, so don't call me that. My name is Rhonda. Rhonda Zulander."

"Rhonda, you said that you got this on your camera. Can we see it? Where is it?"

"Sure, if I had it. The police have it. They won't give it back to me."

"The police. What police?"

"I don't know. A cop's a cop. The one who was just yelling at you guys took it, but he gave it to another guy. I guess they took it back to the station."

"Well, tell us what you saw. What do you think it was? Did you see what happened?"

"Yeah, I saw. Man, it was some wild shit. Can I say that on TV?"

"No, but go ahead. What happened?"

"We were all in the house partying when we heard somebody scream. A few of us ran out on the beach to see who it was. We heard someone screaming these weird words, over and over. We looked out on the sand dune, and there she was. We saw Gracie."

"What was she doing?"

Rhonda gave a little chuckle. "We thought she was raping Billy. He was screaming for her to stop." Rhonda laughed again. "She was ripping his clothes off. Then, she started screaming some kind of weird stuff."

"We heard she was bloody. Did he hurt her?"

"No, but she was covered in blood."

"Where did it come from?"

Rhonda glanced over at Julie; she gave a small grin and then continued. "The blood came from her hands first. Then her forehead started bleeding. Her hair was plastered against her forehead and tied around her head. No one did it. Oh yeah, and there was a smell—like flowers. She smelled like a rose garden. You smelled it, didn't you, Julie?"

Julie didn't reply; she just shot daggers at her with her expression.

"Well anyway, this chick, you're not going to believe this."

"Try me."

"She just floated up. She levitated up in midair and was hanging up there, way up over our heads. She looked like Jesus."

"Wait a minute, kid, you want us to believe that she floated up into the air?"

"I don't want you to believe anything. I don't give a damn what you believe. You ask me what happened, and I'm telling you. And don't call me *kid*."

"I'm sorry about the kid part. But come on. People just don't float in midair."

"I didn't say people did. I said Gracie did. There must have been fifteen or twenty of us out there. We all saw it. When the cops give me back my phone, I'll prove it."

31

"Knock, knock," the hospital door opened. "Hello, I'm Jim Pepper with the Channel 5 news. I was wondering if you were up to answering some questions. You have the whole town on hold."

Gracie sat up in the bed. "What kind of questions?" a voice asked from the corner.

"Excuse me sir, I didn't see you. Are you her father?"

Gracie leered at Jerry. "That's a good question. Something that I would like to know too. Are you my dad?"

Jerry stood up straight. He was so astonished by her question, he didn't know what to say. He tried to open his mouth, but he had lockjaw. He looked over at the newsman, "I think you need to leave."

"But I just have a couple of questions." Jerry was shoving Jim and his cameraman toward the door. "Are you the second coming of Christ?" Jim shouted as Jerry pushed him through the door. "What were the words you kept shouting?"

Jerry slammed the door closed behind them. "Now what kind of question is that?"

Gracie gazed up. "It's one that needs an answer."

"Of course I'm your dad. Why would you ask me something like that?"

"I don't mean to be disrespectful, Dad, but I need to know."

"Know what?"

She pleaded with him with her desperate eyes. They puddled with tears, which began to spill down her cheeks.

"Dad, please. Please tell me who my real father is."

"I am. I am your father."

"No, you are not. And Mom is not my mother. You are my dad, but you are not my father. I don't know who I am. What kind of a freak am I? What kind of sick person did I come from?"

Jerry began to fidget. The secret that he was going to take to his grave was coming out; he could feel it. What was he going to do? How could he tell his wife? How did Gracie find out? The anxiety fevered his brain. His daughter would be devastated, and his wife's health might be destroyed again. His world and his lies were coming apart.

"Don't you have anything to say, Dad?"

Jerry looked at the floor. "Your mom doesn't know."

"Is that all you have to say, Mom doesn't know? Well I don't know either," she shouted. "What about me? Why don't you quit your damn lying and answer me honestly for a change? What part does Mom not know?"

"Please don't curse, Gracie."

"Don't curse!" she sat up and screamed. "I'll say whatever I want to say. You and Mom always try to act all holy. Well, part of being holy is honesty. Or did you forget that?"

"I was hoping you would never know. I thought I could take it to my grave." His voice cracked as tears filled his eyes. I'm not sure how to tell you."

"Just tell me the truth."

Jerry got a chair from the corner and sat down. "Your mom knows none of this. I paid an attorney to take care of it. Remember when we told you before about your mom having cancer and how she almost died giving birth?"

"Yes, I remember. I saw pictures of Mom pregnant. I've watched the video of both of you bringing me home from the hospital. You said Mom didn't know. She had to have known."

"No, she didn't. She always thought you were the baby she had in the hospital." Jerry cleared his throat and proceeded. "Our baby didn't make it. She died during the birth. Your mom would have been devastated. I had to do something. I never thought she would live. The doctors said she wouldn't. I begged the nurse to find me a baby for her to hold before she passed on. They found you. At first, we were just going to borrow you, but your mother began to get better. Every time she held you, she improved."

Tears rolled down Gracie's face and dropped onto the sheets. "She couldn't tell I wasn't hers? What about my real mother? Did she just not want me?"

"Your mom was very, very sick. At first she couldn't even hold you by herself. But like I said, every time she held you, she got better. It was a strange situation. Then, your birth mom got sick. She got cancer, had an aneurysm, and went blind."

"Oh my God," Gracie said placing her hand over her mouth.

"She loved you very much. She didn't want to give you up, but after she went blind, she felt she had no choice."

Gracie looked up at her dad, tears clouding her vision. "Did she die?"

"I don't know," he responded, lowering his head.

"You don't know?"

"After all the paperwork was signed and we left the hospital, I never heard from her again."

"You mean you never even checked on her? You took her baby and that was it?"

"No, that was not it. I bought her a house. She wanted a house on the beach, so I bought her a house."

"So you bought me from her? You paid her off?" Gracie cried harder.

"No, I did not. She made a point of telling me that there was not enough money in the world to buy you. But she had nowhere to go. She had no family, no money, and nowhere to go."

"So, what's her name?"

Jerry stared into Gracie's desperate eyes.

"Gracie, your mother was a very special woman."

"Am I like her?"

"No, absolutely not!" he snapped.

Gracie raised her eyebrows. "Why did you snap like that? Was she a bad person?"

Before he could answer her, someone else spoke up. Jerry spun around in the chair.

"She is a wonderful person, and her name is Susan."

Jerry jumped to his feet. He could not believe his eyes. There, holding the door half open, was his wife. She had been listening to Jerry tell his story.

She walked into the room, patted Jerry on his back, and sat down.

"How did . . . When did . . . I didn't know . . . "

"You didn't know I knew? Of course I knew."

"But how? Who told you?"

"No one told me, Jerry. As much as I love Gracie and have always loved Gracie, I knew my baby died when it was born. A mother knows." She looked over at Gracie. Gracie's hands and head were bandaged. "A mother always knows. Just as your mother knew we would love and take care of you. When I held you that first time, I knew there was something so special about you. The warmth that you gave me was unbelievable. You instantly filled the void that was so deep inside of me. I knew even though I did not give birth to you, you were supposed to be mine."

"I'm sorry, honey," Jerry muttered, glancing at both Mary and Gracie. "I'm sorry for lying to both of you."

Mary reached out and picked up Gracie's hand. "I spoke with your mother before I left the hospital. Your father is right. She would have never given you up if she had not gone blind."

"I began to listen closely to everyone talk about the poor woman down the hall who had given birth to this beautiful little girl: you. I put two and two together, and one day, I knew

I had to go meet her."

"When?" Jerry asked.

"It was one day when you were out. Anyway, one of the nurses wheeled me down to her room for a visit. I told her who I was and how sorry I was for her loss."

"Loss, what loss?" Gracie asked.

"Her sight, she had an aneurysm which caused a blood vessel to rupture, leaving her blind. She was very scared, and I wanted to do whatever I could to comfort her. I had battled cancer, and I thought maybe I could give a little support. She wanted you to have a wonderful life, and she believed you were someone who would change the world. She made me promise not to reveal that I knew the secret. She wanted you to believe in us completely. In her mind, if you found out that you were not our birth baby, you might come looking for her, and she didn't want that. She wanted you to fulfill your destiny— whatever that may be."

"But she was my mother."

"No, she gave birth to you, Gracen."

"There is a difference," Jerry kindly added.

"So, are you saying she never wants to meet me?"

"That is what the agreement was."

"Well, I didn't agree to that. Do you know if she's still alive?"

"I'm sorry, honey, I don't know. I never heard from her after I was released from the hospital."

Gracie looked up at Jerry. "Do you know? Did you keep in touch with her?"

"No, I did not."

"How could you both just take a baby away from a woman and never look back? How could you not wonder how she was? Did she not matter to you at all?" Gracie shouted at her parents.

"Gracie, you need to lower your voice. This hospital is full of news people."

"And why is that, Dad?"

Jerry began to mumble. His response was muddled. He struggled to communicate clearly. "Because of your accident. No one is sure what went on out there."

"What did happen, Gracie?" Mary asked.

"Dad, why don't you answer Mom?"

"I don't know what happened to you. I wasn't there. I can only tell you what I was told, which is that you've been hurt."

"Liar!" she shouted.

"Gracie!" Mary called out. "Don't talk to your father like that. And he's right; you need to lower your voice.

"He's not my father!" she shouted again. "Tell her who my father is, Dad—or do you know that secret too, Mom?"

"No, I don't know. I never asked her because it never had any bearing on my wanting you. I don't think your father knows either."

"Oh, he knows. Don't you Dad?"

"No, I don't know."

"Liar!" she shouted again. "Tell her the truth, or at least tell me the truth."

"Susan did not speak to me about the father," Mary replied, looking up at Jerry.

Gracen's lips began to quiver as she strained to speak. Her voice cracked, and she was gasping for air between words.

"Why," she sniffled, "do you continue to lie? I know who he is," she shuddered. "I just want you to say it. I want to hear it from someone else. I want you to tell me, please." Tears poured down her face as she begged her dad. "Remember when I was little and you would come into my room in the middle of night and talk to me? You always thought that I was asleep," she hesitated. "I wasn't. I heard you say you wished I could be normal. I heard you pray to God to make me like all the other kids. I heard the disappointment in your voice, and I tried to become the daughter that you wanted, but I couldn't. No matter how hard I tried, you always looked at me with discontent, because you knew who I really was. So now, please, tell me who I am, and who my father is."

"I don't know. I swear, I really don't know," he cried, trying to convince them both.

Mary turned toward Jerry. "I swear, honey, I don't know who her father is."

"Jerry, if you know, please be honest with her."

"I don't. I swear." He looked down at Gracie. "I swear. I don't know who he is."

"Yes, you do," a familiar voice came from the door.

Everyone turned to look. Standing in the doorway, as bold and cocky as ever, was Donna. She looked as if she hadn't aged a bit when she walked into the room.

"Miss Donna," Gracie shouted.

"What are you doing here?" Jerry snapped.

"I heard about the incident on the beach on the news. I knew it had to be my little Gracie," Donna smiled and winked at Gracie. She walked over to the far side of the bed. "What happened this time, Little Bit? You look like hell."

"So, you're the one who told. I should have known it was you. I should have known you couldn't keep your big mouth shut. Get out of here," he bellowed.

"Put a sock in it. I ain't going anywhere. I shouldn't have left last time. Look at this child. She's a mess. And I didn't tell anyone. She figured it out."

"She knew what?" Mary asked.

"She knew she was different. She tried to talk to you both, but you acted like it was a curse. You dismissed her like she had a disease. You thought she had an imaginary friend. You didn't want to believe the truth."

Donna looked down at Gracie, "Tell 'em baby. Tell 'em who your friend is. Tell 'em who your real father is. You can say it. Go ahead, Little Bit."

Both Jerry and Mary stared at Gracen, waiting for an answer, but Gracie said nothing. Jerry inhaled a big gulp of air, expanding his chest. He glared as his cheeks turned crimson. The guilt and anger that had been fermenting for years erupted.

He seized Donna by the arm. "I have had enough of your nonsense; I want you out of here now. You keep your big mouth shut and just get out!"

Donna tilted her head back, jerked her arm free, and did everything but chew Jerry up and spit him out.

"What's the matter Jerry, old boy, still can't handle the truth? But then again, truth was never one of your strong points. It's never been a very good feature of yours, has it? You have never been able to handle the reality about your daughter. That's why you fired me so many years ago. You always hid behind all that damn money, but it couldn't buy you a backbone, huh?"

"Fired," Mary cried, completely surprised, "I thought you quit. I thought that you . . . never mind what I thought."

"Nope, that's just another one of your husband's lies. He couldn't handle the truth about who his daughter is; he didn't want to accept it. He tried to hide the special qualities this little girl has, to mold her to be what he wanted, not what she is. He said I was crazy. After the incident on her sixth birthday, I thought she should know. I wanted to tell her, but Jerry rejected the idea. I knew she would wonder what was wrong with her and start believing the worst. He overheard me talking to her that night and thought I was revealing what I knew. He was livid and refused to believe that I hadn't. He became a scared little man. So, to make sure I didn't say anything, to make sure I would not tell you or Gracie, he had to fire me."

"So that's why you left me in the middle of the night. I was devastated when I woke up and you weren't there. I checked the mailbox every day. I thought you would at least write me. But you didn't. You never called or anything. Why?" Gracen asked.

"I couldn't. I signed an agreement when he hired me. I could not say anything to you or your mother, or I would go to prison for robbery."

"Robbery?" Mary asked, bewildered.

"Yep." Donna glared to Jerry. "You see, to secure my secrecy, we created a bogus crime report about my stealing jewelry from your home . . . signed and sealed by me. If I ever revealed anything to either one of you, Jerry would present this document and send me to jail. I was naive and very stupid. I just wanted to be a part of your life, and I would have done anything to do so."

"Why?" Gracie asked.

"Yeah, why? And what did you want to tell her? What was so important?" Mary asked.

"Why?" Donna turned to Jerry. "Would you like to answer? Would you like to tell them? It's your secret. I'm sworn to secrecy, remember?"

All eyes focused on Jerry, waiting for a response, an answer, any answer, but he said nothing.

"Can't think of any lies, Jerry?" Donna snarled aggressively. "The time has come for the secret to be told."

"What secret?" Mary asked again with concern.

"My secret?" Gracie answered. "Dad doesn't want anyone to know who I am, what I am."

"What do you mean? You're our daughter. That's all that matters to us. Right, Jerry?" Mary replied with assurance.

Gracie looked at her mom and squeezed her hand. Her lips parted with a comforting smile, and then she reached for Donna's hand.

"Donna always told me that I was special, and she always told me that I was different. I never understood how or why. It just always gave me great comfort to believe someone thought I was special. After she left—or was fired," she took a quick glance up at her father, "I did a lot of soul searching trying to find out who I was. I kept having a dream about this woman looking for me. She had long blond hair and blue eyes. At first, I began to think it was me all grown up. The dreams were recurring. They were never alike, except for the woman. She always appeared the same. She was always painting pictures, pictures of me. Every painting always had the image of God in the background, and I never could understand it. I wondered what He could want with me. The paintings gave the impression that God was always watching over me or helping me with something."

Donna looked over at Jerry and Jerry at her as they listened to Gracie describing the mother she had never known. A mother she had never seen. A mother she didn't know had ever existed. How could this be possible?

"The dreams started after Donna left and continued for years. One night, after one of the dreams, I woke up angry. *Why do I keep having these damn dreams? What do they mean?* I shouted out loud; I was afraid I had woken up both of you. When I didn't hear you getting up, I got out of bed and paced around my room. I couldn't go back to sleep. Something drew me over to the mirror. I stood there staring, examining . . . questioning who I was. Staring into my own eyes, I saw someone looking back at me."

Gracie took a deep breath and looked around the room.

"In the mirror, standing behind me, was . . . " she sucked in another breath, "was my mother."

"Oh my God," Mary cried out slumping back into the chair. "You must have been dreaming. That's not possible."

"No, Mom, I wasn't dreaming. She's come to me several times since then. I asked her who she was and why she was coming to me. She answered by saying that she had a message for me. She wanted me to know my father, and she told me who my father is," Gracen looked up at Jerry.

"Who is your father?" Mary asked. Have you contacted him?

Where does he live?"

A stony silence came across the room. They were all looking around, waiting for someone to answer, waiting for someone to say the magic word. But no one could seem to mouth that sacred word. Mary, the only one unaware of the truth, was waiting patiently to hear it.

Jerry finally broke the silence. "God," he whispered. "God is her father."

"Do what?" Mary shouted.

"He said God," Donna declared boastfully, with a smile that stretched across her face. She was happy to see after all these years that Jerry could finally say the words. He finally had acknowledged the truth.

"Have you all lost your minds? Why would you say God is her father? He's everyone's father, but you all say it like you believe that He is really her biological father."

"Because it's true, Mom, God is my father. I am the daughter of God."

Mary stared down at Gracie. "What kind of sick game is this? I can't believe you all would kid about nonsense like that—that you would deceive this child."

"It's not a game, and we are not kidding, Mom. Look at my hands. Look at my head." Gracie ripped her bandages off. "Look at this. These are the same wounds Jesus had. I have the wounds for proof. I have to make people believe who I am. You heard the Archbishop in Rome. He knew too. I'm more than a healer, more than someone with stigmata. I have to help people believe."

"Believe what?"

"Believe that God exists. I am the messenger, the chosen one. I am the daughter of God," she proudly blurted. "I was sent here to carry on the message of Jesus. The same message He was killed for delivering. I am the new faith, hope, and salvation. I am the daughter of God."

Suddenly, a camera snapped. "I got it!" someone shouted. "I got it on tape. She said she's the daughter of God," the man yelled to the crowd. "I got it all on tape."

Jerry jumped up and ran out into the hall; Mary and Donna hurried behind him. "Hey you," Jerry called to the man. "I want that camera," he shouted as he scurried toward him, making his way through the multitude of people who had gathered in the hallway. He knew that if this man took this tape to the media, everyone would know who his daughter was—or they would know who his daughter thought she was.

Was this really a bad thing? Could it be time for a miracle like this to happen to the world? Would his daughter have powers like Jesus did? All these things flashed through his mind as he continued running after the reporter.

The photographer ran faster as Jerry closed in. Jerry continued to rush after him, pushing, swerving, and jumping around people as he went, but the young man, being half his age, lost Jerry in the crowd.

Jerry looked all around at the different faces but could not see the man anywhere. He jumped up on a bench and looked around. He studied the crowd and could not believe all the people who had gathered to see his daughter. And he realized when the pictures were released to the media, people from all over the world would be flocking to see his child.

Jerry stepped off the wooden bench and somberly returned to the hospital room. Mary and Donna were waiting in the lobby, hoping that he had caught the cameraman. When Jerry told how he had lost him in the crowd, everyone was troubled. What was in store for Gracie now? What should they do? Should they move her to another hospital? Should they try to sneak her out in the middle of the night and disappear?

The three got on the elevator and went up to the second floor where Gracie's room was. When they stepped from the elevator, the crowd outside her room had gotten out of control.

The nurses were struggling to keep them away.

Jerry ran up and started yelling at people. "This is the hospital, for God's sake. You people need to get out of here and leave my daughter alone.

Gracie called out to the officer in the hallway. "Can you come in here for a minute?"

"Sorry, but I'm not supposed to leave my post."

"I won't tell. Anyway you're here to watch me, right?"

"Right."

"Well, come on in here and watch. I need someone to talk to. I'm lonely. They won't let any of my friends in here. Please come in and sit with me."

The officer stepped through the doorway and looked around. His nose wrinkled as he began to sniff the air. "This room smells like flowers."

Gracie gave a gracious smile and then softly replied, "Yes, it does."

"But there aren't any flowers in here," he said looking around the room again.

"No there aren't," Gracie said with a little chuckle.

The officer was leery of entering, but couldn't resist her pleas. He leaned against the door and sighed.

"What's wrong?" Gracie asked.

"Nothing's wrong. Why do you ask?"

"Why do you not come into my room?"

"I just need to stay next to the door so no one can . . . " he looked about, then continued his sentence, "get in here to you."

"Why do people want to get in here?"

The officer took off his hat and began to fidget. He glanced up at Gracie then back at his hat.

"Are you one of the officers who came to the beach?"

"Yes, I was there. How did you know?"

"I didn't, but you seem so nervous, I thought you might have seen what I did."

"No, I didn't. I heard some stories, but I didn't see anything." The kids out there, your friends, they seemed to be pretty torn up. They must have got hold of some good drugs. They told the reporters they saw you float up into the sky and hang there like Jesus," he laughed a little as he finished his sentence.

He glanced up at Gracie and saw that she had a straight face.

"What's so funny about that?"

"What's so funny about that? Are you kidding me? They said you were floating in midair. That's not possible."

"Isn't it?"

"No, it's not."

"What would it take to make you a believer? Would you have to see it with your own eyes?"

"Yes, I would, but you and I both know that's not gonna happen."

Gracie stared at the young officer. Her expression was blank. Without blinking her eyes, she said, "Thanks for coming in. You may leave now."

The officer was bewildered. He gazed at Gracie for a few seconds and slowly backed away until he was completely out of her room. He sat down in a chair that had been pushed against the wall by the surging crowd. He sat there, flabbergasted by the conversation. He wasn't sure what Gracie was trying to tell him, if anything. She had made him so uncomfortable, he really wasn't interested in anything she had to say.

The noise continued in the hallway. People were trying to sneak past the officer to get a peek at Gracie. Gracie could hear the officer ordering people to be escorted from her door. She heard the officer call for assistance to help hold them back. The hospital staff was doing everything they could to help, but it was not enough.

Gracie was concerned about so many people wanting to see

her. She started to wonder if it could be true. Could she be the daughter of God, and if so, why was she chosen?

Gracie slid out of her bed and walked over to the window and opened the blinds just wide enough to peep at the parking lot. People of all ages and sizes were standing around, waiting for her to come out. When they saw her at the window, they shouted and screamed. They called her name and many sat on the ground and bowed to her as though she were royalty. At first, she smiled and waved, but then she felt uneasy. She felt that it was not right. Why was this happening? She let go of the blind and turned away from the window.

Gracie scanned the room and walked over to the mirror that was situated above the sink. She stared at her own image. "Please, God," she prayed, "give me some answers. Please let me know who I am. Am I your daughter? You must help me. I feel so lost."

She closed her eyes for a brief moment then walked over to her hospital room door. She eased it opened and peered out into the hallway. Her father was only a few feet away, arguing with the police officer about the protection he wanted for her. He wanted to know what they were going do about all the people trying to get into her room. He demanded that someone sit outside her door twenty-four hours a day. The officer said they had it covered.

Gracie saw all the anger and frustration on her father's face. She saw how worried her mother was and how Donna was trying to comfort them both.

Gracie peered beyond them, a little further down the hallway. There were people in their pajamas, coming from the rooms, thinking that Gracie might heal them, begging for just a glimpse. The media was still there with cameras, saying this was news and the public had the right to know.

She eased the door shut and leaned against it. Her big blue eyes filled with tears that slid down her cheeks and splashed down onto her hands. The voices outside deepened and became muffled. Something was happening. Gracie tried to remove herself from the door but was frozen in place. Her heartbeat accelerated with anxiety.

A small light danced around her room. Gracie's eyes searched the perimeter to see where it had come from. It was the size of a small flashlight beam, a perfect round circle, no bigger than a quarter. It bobbled around the ceiling then slid down the wall above her head and hovered above her.

"What are you?" she asked as she watched the small light circling her body.

The light flew across the room and abruptly stopped at a far corner and began to get larger. It definitely appeared to be growing.

Gracie was speechless. Her heart pounded out of control. Her chest cavity felt as if it would erupt at any moment.

"Gracie, are you all right?" her dad asked, pushing his way into the room.

Gracie stumbled away from the door and jerked her head toward the corner. The light was gone.

Mary and Donna had quickly followed behind Jerry. Donna pushed the door closed behind her and stood against it. "Those people out there are crazy as hell," she said. "I've never seen so many maniacs in all my life."

Mary walked Gracie over to the bed. "You don't have to worry, honey, your father is going to protect you. He won't let anything happen to you. He's having security doubled outside your room."

"I'm not worried, Mom, and I'm not scared either. I know my father will look out for me. I'm in good hands," Gracie looked over at Donna and smiled. "You know, sometimes we have to applaud the goodness in people. This might be one of those times. People believe I'm something good, and they've come to see me. So far, the people are kind; they don't mean any harm. I am the messenger of God, and we all must accept that. I guess I've really always known it. But now, there's no turning back."

Mary turned her head and started to cry. Gracie rested her hand on her mother's shoulder to comfort her. "This is not a bad thing; this is a good thing. Don't shed tears of sadness for me; this is a blessing. I am here to bring joy, not sadness. I am here to spread God's name, and that is what I'm going to do."

Gracie's face glowed as she looked at her mother, "It's ironic that your name is Mary, the same as the mother of Jesus." Jerry rolled his eyes as Gracie spoke. Maybe that's why my birth mother was not chosen to be my mother, and you were chosen because you bear the same name. Maybe there is something about your name that God likes. Who knows? Maybe God has a sense of humor. I know none of you wants to tell me what I want to hear, but I'd like all three of you to sit down and discuss my mother, my birth mother. I would like to know who she is and if I can see her. I want to go see her, and Mom, please don't take offense at this, but I need to know more about her and why I am the chosen one. Maybe she can give me some answers."

Jerry quickly stepped up to the bed. "The chances of seeing your birth mother are very remote. I really detest the idea of you even looking for her. Nothing good can come from that. None of us knows what kind of life she's living now, and you might be surprised by what kind of woman she is. I do not like the idea. I don't like it at all."

"You know, Dad, you've always worried about what I might find out about my birth mother. Every time a stranger spoke to me when I was young, you were always right there by my side to pull me away. I never understood why until now. There's no need for you to worry, because I'm going to find out with or without your help. You need to let it go. I told you I'm going to spread the word. And I would like to know all about my past before I do.

"What word Gracie? What are trying to say? Do you even know what word you're supposed to be spreading? And as far as your past goes, your past is with us. Your birth mother has nothing to do with your past."

Gracie tilted her head up to her father and smiled, "Dad, don't be so angry. It will come to me. I know it will. When the time comes, I will know what to say. I know I have to let people know that God is still relevant; He is alive. God is here with us."

Donna cheered Gracie on, "You go girl. You tell the world. Praise the Lord, God is alive!"

"Donna, that is enough. She doesn't need any help from you. Why are you even here? You need to leave."

"You know what, Jerry? I have wanted to say this for a long time: kiss my royal ass. I'm not going anywhere. I am here to stay. I am right beside Gracie. Consider me a follower." Donna turned to Gracie, "Gracie, honey, anything you need, you just let me know." She placed a small piece of paper with her phone number on it on the side table.

"Thanks, Donna. Dad, please don't be angry with any of us. I just need some answers. I'm very tired now, so could you all just leave me for while? I'd like to be alone."

"Honey, I am not mad at you . . . just worried that's all. Your mom and I will let you rest, but if you need us, all you have to do is call," Jerry tried to reassure her as he kissed her forehead.

"I'll call, Dad, I promise."

32

A slender nurse knocked at the door and entered the room. Everything was obscured by darkness. She reached for the light switch.

"Gracen?"

"I'm here."

"Why are you sitting in the dark?"

"I was just thinking," Gracie softly replied.

"I imagine there's a lot on your mind, but don't worry, these things have a way of working themselves out. I'm sure God will help you find your way."

"God," Gracie laughed. "He seems to be coming up a lot lately. Do you believe what people are saying?"

"You mean about your being the daughter of God?"

"Yes, do you believe that?"

"I'm not sure what to believe, dear. I know there are a lot of people who have seen you do things that normal people can't do. So far, no one has been able to explain it."

"Look at me. I'm just a teenager."

"Well, that may be so, but I don't believe you're an ordinary teenager. You appear to have cared a lot for your friend whom you saved from that boy."

"Anyone would have done the same thing. He was hurting her. I had to make him stop. I wanted him to know how it felt to be taken advantage of. He needed to know how it felt to be helpless against someone like him. If we could turn the tables and make people feel how they make other people feel, everything could change."

The nurse stood smiling at Gracie, "Maybe that's what you're here for. They say God works in mysterious ways. This is definitely mysterious. You could be salvation for a lot of people."

"So, that's the word that I'll be spreading. I'm here to lead you bad people to salvation. I can hear it now. I'll be the most popular girl in town."

"Come on, Gracie, don't be so hard on yourself. I'm sure you'll find a way to deliver any message God truly intends for you to deliver. Don't dwell so much on what you're supposed to be doing. Just take some deep breaths and let it come to you."

The nurse began to remove the gauze from Gracie's hands and check her wounds. She snipped the edge with some scissors and slowly unwound the gauze; the first layer was clean. One layer after another was without stains. As she got to the last layer and pulled it away from her hand, she was amazed to see her flesh had healed. She flipped her hand from palm to back; nothing was there, not even a scratch. Quickly, she trotted around to the other side and began to unwrap that hand a little faster. Again, there was no sign of blood. There was nothing there: no wounds, no scratches, and no blood.

"Amazing, huh?" Gracie quickly asked. "That's the way it always is. The marks never stay."

"What about your head? Let me check your head."

"I'm not sure about my head. This is the first time anything has ever happened to my head, but if it's anything like the others, the marks will be gone."

Gracie lifted her head and the nurse carefully began to unwrap the bandage. It was the same process as before. She unrolled the dressing from her head and carried her own thoughts about the rumor that this was God's child. She had God's child in her hand. How wonderful that was. Then she thought all children are God's children. How could this one be different? She lifted the last bandage from her head. Again, there was nothing there. With a shake of her head and a deep breath, she stared at Gracie.

"So what's up? Does this mean I get to go home now? I'm healed, right?"

"I'm not sure what this means, Gracie."

"Well, I'm not sure either, but I am sure that I don't want to be here. I want to go home."

"I'll see if I can get in touch your doctor. I guess I'll say that your wounds . . . " she shrugged and rolled her shoulders, "disappeared. I'm sure the doctor will think I'm crazy. I imagine you will be here another night."

"Swell," Gracie said with a sigh, then quickly sat up straight. "If I'm going to be here another night, I need to know something. There was a little boy down the hall. I noticed him when I was brought in. He appeared to be really sick. Is he still here? And do you know what was wrong with him?"

"You must be talking about the little boy in 215. He's not doing very well at all. I can't discuss what's wrong with him, but I will say I don't think he will live the rest of the week. He has an incurable disease. That's all I can say."

"Do you think I can help him?"

"I don't think so. What is it that you think you can do?"

"I'm not sure, but if I have a gift, I need to use it somewhere. I need to try it out and see if it works, so to speak," Gracie laughed.

"Now, I don't think this is something to laugh about, and I'm not sure what kind of gift you may have. There's no way you're going to be able to go into that room. His parents stay with him around the clock."

"Would you ask them?"

"No, Gracie, I won't. Whether you do or don't have some kind of power is not up to me to say, but I'm not going to give these wonderful people false hope. They're having a hard time."

"Okay, you're right. I don't blame you. It was a dumb thing to suggest. Would you turn the light off when you leave so I can get some rest?"

"It wasn't a dumb thing to suggest. It was very sweet, but it's not appropriate this time. And you're right, you need some rest."

The nurse walked over to the door, turned off the light, and left the room. Gracie lay in the darkness wondering what to do. She was just a teenager. Why was she chosen? Or was she chosen at all? Maybe this was just some kind of paranormal occurrence; maybe it wasn't a gift from God. It felt more like a curse than a gift.

Gracie was overcome by the desire to test her powers to the limit. She jumped from the chair and plopped onto the bed with her phone in hand. She called Julie and relayed an idea. Julie was hesitant, but she agreed and said she would come straight over.

Gracie paced the floor to the window and back to the bed and over to the door. She pulled the door slightly open and peered down the hallway. All of the bystanders had been removed, but the police officer still sat at his post outside her door.

Through the crack of the door, Gracen saw Julie standing at the end of the corridor. She watched the police officer carefully, hoping he would turn his back and give her a chance to slip into the room. She waited anxiously, but he sat still, reading a book and looking up only when someone approached the room. Julie could come in if there were a diversion.

Julie tapped her foot nervously. Her lips were drawn together tightly. Her head suddenly jerked up and she stood frozen in time and space. The distraction came.

A large man, a patient, was making a scene in the hallway. He was unreasonable with the nurses and his loud cursing was disturbing the other patients. Nothing was calming him, and he refused to return to his room.

The police officer stood up and observed the disorderly man. He was a man of the law; he had to do something.

Dropping his book onto the chair, he hurried to the scene of the disturbance. This was Julie's only chance, and she took it.

With every step he took away from the room, Julie took one forward. She was like a slithering snake sliding down the wall to Gracie's room.

When she reached the door, she eased it open and slipped in like a ghost—unnoticed by anyone.

"Hey, Gracie," she whispered. "I didn't think he was going to ever leave. Thank God for the crazy man in the hallway, huh?"

"I'm so glad you came. I have to find a way to sneak down the hall. You need to think of something to get the officer's attention. He has to stay away from my door, so I can get out of here."

"What do you want to do?"

"I'm not sure."

"Hey, Gracie, I need to tell you something."

"What's that?"

"Do you have any idea what the words mean—the words you say when you're in a trance?"

"I can barely remember anything. Why?"

"I taped the words and listened to them over and over again."

"And?"

"And you say, 'Dog si evila' or 'evila si dog.'"

"Is that some kind of foreign language?"

"No, you're talking backwards."

"What?"

"I wrote it down and studied it, and this is what it says: *Dog*, which is backwards for *God* . . . *si* backwards is *is*, and *evila* is *alive*. God is alive! That's what I think you're saying."

"That would make sense!" Gracie said.

Gracie and Julie sat on the bed trying to come up with some way to distract the policeman. They knew they had to make sure that he was not looking toward Gracie's door. The two of them came up with a plan, and Julie sneaked away from the room unseen by the guard.

Gracie could hear commotion and peered into the hallway to see where everyone was. Julie was doubled over as if she were in pain. So far, her plan was working. Gracie slipped into the hall as Julie lay on the floor screaming and kicking. The nurses came running to her aid.

Quietly passing the other rooms, Gracen confidently strode down the drab hallway to Room 215.

For some reason, she was drawn to this little boy and had an unsettling feeling that there was work for her to do in that room. Pressing her hand against the door, she slowly pushed it open wide enough for her to peer inside. All was quiet, so she stepped in.

She glided around the end of the bed and observed the child. His flesh was chalky. He was close to death. His coal black hair looked dry and brittle in the dim light. His left arm had an IV needle in it, and machines were humming as he slept peacefully. He never knew she was there. His parents were nowhere around.

Gracie looked at all of the get-well cards and baseball memorabilia from friends and family. A cap with a Braves logo was hanging on the safety bar of his bed.

She tiptoed over to the little boy and stroked his forehead not knowing what else to do. Reaching for the boy's hand, she held it loosely in hers. She reflected on happy memories. Slowly, she rocked back and forth and softly hummed a soothing tune. She wasn't sure what the tune was; it just seemed to come to her as she hummed.

She placed the child's hand back at his side. Rubbing both

of her palms together, creating the warmth of friction, she held her hands over his body. With her eyes closed, she continued to wave her hands back and forth and kept on humming.

Back and forth her body swayed, and her hair blew as if a gentle breeze had filled the room. As Gracie continued, her body rose from the floor and levitated over the boy. With her arms stretched out from her sides, her hair flowing down, she hovered.

The warmth from Gracen's body transfixed the little boy, rejuvenating his cells. His back arched as he lifted himself to receive his gift. It was an immediate transaction.

A bright light flashed in the room. Gracie was pulled from her trance and fell to the floor. Startled and disoriented, she sat with crossed legs on the floor, her head settled in the cup of her hands. A lady hurried over, knelt down beside her, and asked if she was all right. She rubbed her head in confusion.

The woman grasped her arm and helped her to her feet.

"Is the boy all right?" she whispered.

"Yes, he's the fine, what were you doing with him?"

"What do you mean? I was just seeing if he was okay."

"Are you related to him?

"Mommy," a hoarse voice called out.

Gracie turned back to the little boy. His eyes were open. His tongue darted out and slowly dragged along his dry lips.

A nurse entered from the hall. "What are you two doing in here?" she shouted.

The unknown woman stepped out of the way. The nurse was furious at them both and demanded that they leave immediately.

Gracie was trying to explain about the boy, but the nurse wasn't hearing it. She shoved them both to the door and closed it tightly behind them. Without a word, the woman disappeared. Gracie waited for a report, for anything, but the report never came. The door remained shut.

With disappointment, Gracie lowered her head and slowly started back toward her room.

A young woman with short black hair hurried behind her. She reached out and put her hand on Gracie's shoulder. Gracie cocked her head and looked at her from the corner of her eye.

"What is it that you want from me?" Gracie asked. "And who are you?"

"My name is Belinda. I work for the *Charleston Evening Post*. There have been a lot of rumors going around about you. We're all in a race; someone has to get the story."

"And you thought you would be that lucky one?"

"No disrespect, honey, but so far I am. I have enough from the camera at the beach to make my own decisions about how I want to go with the story."

Gracie stopped in the hall and stared at this tall, dark-haired reporter. With her head lowered she replied, "There is no story." Gracie stopped in the hall and glared at her. She studied her for a moment and examined her from top to bottom. She had huge brown eyes to go with her raven tresses. She was fashion model slim and wore expensive clothes and shoes that synchronized perfectly. Her lips were ruby red and matched her fingernails.

"I'm sorry you've wasted your time because I don't have any inkling about what is happening, and I can't clarify any of it for you."

"Do you think you're a saint?"

Gracen chuckled, "I am far from being a saint. And the camera is blank. There will be nothing of any importance on it."

Gracen solemnly sauntered toward her room leaving the reporter speechless at her smug response.

The officer glanced up from his book as Gracen came into sight. He did a double take when he recognized her. Leaping from his chair, he hurried to her side.

"How did you get out without me seeing you?"

"I just want to go home."

"But how did you get out here?"

"I just want to go home," she repeated in response to his question.

As the door clicked shut, she heard him call out, "Don't you do that again! I could lose my job."

Gracen sat on the edge of her bed exhausted and unaware that she had helped the boy. Then she saw Donna's phone number on the bedside table. Leaning over, she slid the piece of paper to her hand with her fingertips. Her thumb traced each number with deep concentration. She picked up the phone and dialed Donna's number.

With the fourth ring, Donna answered in a sleepy voice.

"It's almost midnight, and I was asleep. This had better be an emergency," she answered crossly.

"I'm sorry, Donna, I didn't know what time it was. I'll call back in the morning."

"Little Bit, is that you?"

A sniffle echoed through the phone. "It's me."

"What's wrong?" she asked.

"I can't heal anyone; you were wrong."

"What are you talking about?"

"I tried to heal the boy in 215, and it didn't work. I'm not special. I'm not the daughter of God."

"You hold tight. I'm coming up."

"Coming up from where?"

"I stayed in the nurses' quarters on the first floor. I was sleeping on the couch. I'll be right there."

A tear dripped from the corner of Gracie's eye as she hung up. She drew her legs to her chest and wrapped her arms around her shins, resting her chin on her knees. Her large blue eyes were lost. She felt she had disappointed everyone who believed in her. The biggest disappointment was to God; He was the one who had the most faith in her, and she had let Him down.

It had taken Donna almost thirty minutes to arrive at Gracen's room. She stepped into the dimly lit room and saw Gracen on the bed, still hugging her knees.

"Little Bit, don't be saddened by defeat. You can't win them all."

With dismay she replied, "I thought I could heal him, Donna. I thought that was what I was supposed to do."

"And it probably was."

She countered with cynicism, "If it was, I would have healed him."

With a burst of joy, Donna chuckled and sat at her feet. "You did heal him. You did it."

"What! What are you talking about?"

"Whatever you did worked. That's what took me so long getting up here to you. I stopped in and checked on the boy. He's well. He's still weak, but all his vital signs have returned to normal. The entire staff is saying it was a miracle."

Gracen threw her feet from the bed and grabbed Donna's hands. Are you sure?"

Donna replied with a shake of her head and a smile that stretched from ear to ear. "They said he just woke up and was asking for his mommy."

"That is so wonderful, and I'm not even sure what I did." She glanced down at her hands. "I healed him with my hands, Donna, but I don't even know how."

33

After hours of celebrating and planning, Gracen lay quietly, overjoyed by her success. Donna had drifted to sleep in the recliner next to the bed.

"A modern day saint," she whispered with elation. "Who will believe in me, an ordinary teenager? Should I change my wardrobe? No, I am me, and that is the person and image God has chosen. He did not say I had to look different, and He did not choose a different looking person."

Her mind wandered and eventually migrated to a state of deep concentration about her origins. *Where did I come from? I must find out who my birth mother is. Was she spiritual? Do I get this gift from her?*

Gracen pushed the covers down with her feet and slid from the side of her bed. She scurried to the chair and tapped Donna's shoulder. "Donna, Donna, wake up."

Dumbfounded, Donna raised her head. "What? What's wrong?"

"Nothing is wrong, but we need to go."

"Go, go where?"

"California."

"California! Why?"

"You said that is where my birth mother is and I have to meet her." Gracen retrieved clothes from the small hospital closet and scampered to the bathroom.

Donna squirmed from the chair and stood outside the door. "Oh, wait a minute here, Little Bit. We have to talk to your parents."

"I know, so let's go," she said, pushing the door with her

foot as she pulled her blue shirt over her head.

"The doctor hasn't released you yet."

"Doesn't matter. You and I both know there is nothing wrong with me. I'm calling my dad and letting him know you're bringing me home.

"Sounds good to me, I think."

Although Jerry was not pleased with Gracen's decision, he agreed. Within the hour, they had arrived. Donna relayed the particulars of the miracle at the hospital. As far as she knew, no one had any idea that it was Gracie who healed the boy.

Jerry was adamant about keeping this a secret. He did not want people flocking to his door. Mary, Donna, and Gracen agreed for the time being. In Rome, the Archbishop had also explained how trying all the attention could be.

"Dad, Mom, for now, I agree to keep this a secret. I still have questions that I have to know the answers to. I don't want you to be disappointed with me, but I have to know who my birth mother is."

"No, you don't," Jerry replied angrily.

"Yes, she does." With a sweet voice, Mary corrected him. "Gracie does have that right. She deserves to know. If you and Donna still have any information on her whereabouts, I implore you to let us know." Mary continued to speak as she walked toward the stairwell. "I am going to pack, so please don't dilly-dally around too long."

Gracen quickened her step toward her. "No, Mom, Donna is taking me."

Stopping abruptly, she turned and faced Donna. "Donna? Why should Donna take you? You are our daughter," Mary replied with defeat in her voice.

"I'm sorry, Mom, but I want my birth mother to feel comfortable with me, and I believe she'll be more at ease with Donna there, not you or Dad."

"Oh, of course dear, can we at least drive you to the airport?"

"Wait a minute here, I never said that I was okay with this."

"Dad, no disrespect to you, but it doesn't matter whether you are or not, because I am going, with or without your blessing."

"But you don't even know if she is alive. You have no idea what lifestyle she is living now. At least let me have her checked out before you go."

"No, I do not want her to know."

Jerry stood scratching his head. He waved his hand in the air and responded, "Whatever you want."

34

It wasn't long until Donna and Gracen were in the air, California bound. Gracen was dressed in jeans, black low-heeled sandals, and a royal blue shirt that reflected the blue of her stunning eyes.

"Do you think she'll like me?"

"Everyone likes you, Little Bit."

"No, I mean, do you think she will like who I am?"

"Your birth mother's name is Susan, and she already knows who you are."

"What do you mean? Sure about what?"

"She knows, my dear, that you are the daughter of God. She always said that you were the modern version of the true child of God."

"Was my mother insane?"

"No," Donna laughed, "To the contrary. She was the only one who never gave up hope. She said you would become a famous healer for the world to be proud of."

Gracen pondered the idea for a brief moment and asked, "Do you believe her?"

"With all my heart, I do."

"So when will I let the world know?"

"I'm sure God holds that knowledge and will share it in due time."

Grace rested her head on Donna's shoulder and disappeared into her own little world. Her thoughts rolled like the raging sea. The world was full of sickness and pain. How would she help everyone she needed to help? God had led her to the boy in the hospital, but there were thousands of others. Why him?

Would God always lead her or would she venture on her own? It was a lot for a sixteen-year-old to understand.

After five hours of flight, the plane descended for a perfect landing. The car they had rented from Hertz was a red Mercedes with all the bells and whistles. After signing the necessary papers and receiving the keys, they hopped in, buckled up, set the GPS, and took the shortest route to Santa Cruz.

"Are you sure she still lives at the same address?"

"I see no reason she would have moved."

"What do I say to her?"

"Don't be so nervous. The words will come."

"Easy for you to say. She knows you."

The route was beautiful. The winding roads were lined with large trees and gorgeous homes.

As the GPS reported that they were only two miles from their destination, Gracen began to twist her hair around her fingers, pulling at the long strands a little faster with the passing of each house.

"The homes here are incredible! I'm used to the ocean, but here, people can see that view from mountainside."

"That is why your mother chose this place, because of the view."

"I thought you said she was blind."

"I did, but she felt if she could hear the roar of the waves, she would see the beauty in her mind's eye."

"She sounds smart."

"Arriving at destination," the GPS reported.

"What do I say, Donna?"

"Unbuckle your seat belt, open your door, and take a deep breath. I'll be by your side the entire way. Just calm down and breathe."

Gracen stepped from the car, took a gulp of air, and exhaled several times before reaching the front door.

Donna laughed at her apprehension and awkwardness as the doorbell sounded.

"Do I just say, 'Hey, I'm your daughter'"?

Before Donna could answer, the door open slightly and German Shepherd's nose poked through the crack. As the opening widened, a hand appeared on the dog's harness.

"Sit, Skipper. May I help you?" a voice sounded from behind the door.

"I'm sorry to bother you, Susan, and I hope you remember me."

"I could never forget you, Donna," she said stepping from the shadow of the door.

"It's been sixteen years. I can't believe you recognize my voice."

"I'm blind, Donna. The voice is all we have to remember people."

"It's you."

"Excuse me, Donna, is someone with you?"

"You are the lady I've seen most of my life. You were always there in the shadows, watching me. Why didn't you ever talk to me?"

"Gracen? Is that you, Gracen?"

"Yes, Susan, it's Gracen. She wanted to meet you. I hope we're not imposing."

Susan let go of her dog, closed her eyes, and smiled. She held her hands out toward Gracen and asked permission to touch her face.

"May I?"

Gracen glanced at Donna, "Sure."

Donna guided Susan's hands to Gracen's face. Susan took her time and traced over every curve. With her eyes still closed, the tears slid down Susan's face and dripped to her arms.

"Where are my manners? Please come in."

Susan reached down and retrieved the dog's harness and

turned around.

"Please follow me."

Closing the door behind them, Donna and Gracen did as they were asked.

"You have a beautiful home," Gracen said, gazing into the darkness.

"I have something for you to see. If the lights are not on, please let me know."

She led them to French doors that were draped with white silk sheers. It was situated on the ocean side of the home. Without hesitation, she turned the glass knob and shoved the doors open, exposing the beauty beyond. The sunshine flickered through the room with bright rays revealing a majestic pictorial history of Gracen's life.

Gracen stepped past Susan and walked in with disbelief. Every inch of the room was replete with images of her from childhood to the present day. Gracie and Donna walked around and examined each one.

"Oh my God, Donna, I feel like I've walked back in time—into my past. Can you believe your eyes?"

"I know what you mean, Little Bit. This is unbelievable."

"Look at this picture. I believe it was my first day at school," Gracen said lifting a large print.

"Well, it has a school bus there, so probably you're right."

"No, I mean really—my first day. The same clothes, hair, shoes, everything. I had this same outfit on. I remember because I got to pick it out and I was so excited. If you're blind, how could this be possible?"

"I rode the waves of the ocean and landed at your door. The travel in one's mind's eye can be faster than light."

Gracen raised her brows. She and Donna stared at one another, knowing what the other was thinking: Susan did sound crazy.

"Everyone has to give up something," Susan said. "You

know God took my eyes, and that was just one of my sacrifices. The other one was you. But He gave me vision. He gave me insight. I see more clearly now than I had ever seen before. He has let me see you every day of your life. I have laughed with you and held you in my dreams. I cried with you and loved you in my paintings. I know it wasn't the same as being your mother, comforting you when you were scared or just being there to answer simple questions."

Susan turned away for a brief moment, and then, she lowered her head and spoke very softly. "I have been there every minute of every day and every step that you have taken. You have been in my heart from the first breath of air that you took in this cruel world. And you will continue to be there until the last breath of air that I take. You are my child and always have been. Even though it broke my heart to let you go, I did it so you could have a better life than mine. I hope you do not hate me for that. I trusted God, and He has given me the pleasure of seeing you grow, even if it was only in the mind's eye."

Gracen's eyes glazed over with tears. She ran to Susan's side and seized her hands. She knelt down, kissed them, and bowed her head.

"You have watched me through the darkness and I have seen you in the shadows. God made you my guardian angel to keep me safe, and you did. And I worship you for that."

"Please stand and do not worship me. I did what any mother would have done."

"You were unselfish and thought only about my well being. I've had a wonderful life of pure love from my parents. I've come here to ask some questions, if I may."

"Okay, but let's go sit outside and feel the breeze from the sea."

With one hand out in front and the other on the dog's harness, she continued to lead them to the grassy knoll in the backyard.

"The view is spectacular, huh?" she asked with her eyes closed and her head tilted to the sun.

"Yes, Susan, the view is breathtaking. This setting appears to have been made specifically for you."

"Well, Gracen, come sit down by me and ask away," she patted the chair next to her.

"I would like to know who my father was."

Donna shook her head knowing that was not the right question to start off with.

Sucking at the air, Susan replied. "God is your father, Gracen."

"God is the father of us all. Who is my biological father?"

"God."

Gracie sighed, "Can you explain how that could be?"

"No I can't. I can only tell you that I had not had sex, and I became pregnant. It all happened in the church."

"Yes, Donna told me the story. Isn't it possible that you may have forgotten?"

Susan turned in the direction of Gracen. Isn't the real question that you want to ask, *Could I have been too messed up on drugs?*"

"Well, isn't that possible?"

"Gracen, you have a gift. It is a gift from God, just as Jesus was given the gift. You have it only because you belong to Him."

"If I am gifted, as you say, let me heal you."

"The gift is not for me, and I am not sick."

"But you're blind."

"I see clearly with my heart and you should too. There is nothing more I would ever want to see unless it were your face. What I see is myself as a child, but it is really you. Do we look that much alike?"

"Yes, you do, Susan. The resemblance is amazing. Gracie is a little you."

"I would give anything to see you, just once. To hold you and feel your heart beat with the rhythm of mine, to see me duplicated in the depths of your eyes and let you enter my soul and feel my love."

Gracen stood up and knelt at her feet once more. She began to hum and Susan joined in on the tune. Their tone was synchronized as one. Gracen placed her hands on the crown of Susan's head and prayed.

Donna witnessed the blood drain from the palms of Gracen's hands. Their heads wavered together as their monotone chant rose to a faster tempo. With the sweet purity of her voice, Gracen whispered, "God is alive, God is alive, and He wants you to open your eyes and see me."

With the fluttering of her lids, and two tight squints, Susan opened her eyes. She cried with laughter and jubilation as she viewed her sixteen-year-old for the first time.

Donna stood in the background weeping like a baby as she witnessed the miracle taking place before her.

Gracen stood and walked to the edge of the yard and thanked God for her gift.

She looked to the heavens and shouted, "Our God is alive and watching over us, so have faith! Ride the waves of the sea to freedom and your sins are washed to the depths of the ocean floor. God, cleanse our world of evil, sickness, and pain. Applaud the goodness and kindness in mankind. At the end of our lives, we are all laid to rest, and may peace be laid with us!"

***

"I am a child of God as all of you. Does the blood of God travel through my veins? Does God have blood? No one really can answer these questions, not even I . . . but what I can tell you is I have been given a gift, and I have been chosen for a

purpose that I do not yet fully understand.

"*I have learned to accept my precious gift to comfort, heal, and guide those in need. I will continue to follow the path that has been laid before me.*

"*I did not choose the people I have helped; they were chosen for me through our God, our Father and through the body of Christ. I am criticized and laughed at by many. I have been bullied, spat on, and called unmentionable names. The punishment of evil lies in God's hands, and the consequences of their malicious behavior will be bestowed upon them come Judgment Day.*

"*None of this shall make me falter because now I know who I am. I am the daughter of God.*"

ABOUT THE AUTHOR

Excitement, mysteries, and the unknown are captivating to me. Solving a mystery, makes my blood boil. I love it.

As a child, I grew up in a rural area in South Carolina. Reminiscing about my childhood made me want to become a writer. My cousin and I made up many stories to act out as children. We would pretend to be whatever or whomever we wanted to be. As an adult, life is not that simple, we are who we are, but as a writer, I can become that child again and create my own fantasy.

Some people read a story to escape their everyday lives and some people write to break free from the captivity of realism. I break free and go all over the world in just a matter of days.

I have been with my husband for thirty-three years; we have two wonderful sons, four great stepchildren and twenty-three grandchildren. I have a wonderful mother and four siblings. I love and enjoy all my family very much.

I love all animals, horseback riding, boating, and the beach; if I am outdoors, I am happy.

Life is too short to take for granted and not enjoy. I am not a person to let it slip away; I am carefree and loving every minute.

Sandra LaBruce is also the author of Haunted Secrets.